"Murder in the Tea Leaves"

Le Doux Mysteries #5

By Abigail Lynn Thornton

MURDER IN THE TEA LEAVES

First edition. March 29, 2022.

Written by Abigail Lynn Thornton.

DEDICATION

To my Heavenly Father,
who knew putting writing into my life
would be one of my greatest joys.
Thank you.

ACKNOWLEDGEMENTS

No author works alone. Thank you, Cathy.
Your cover work is beautiful!
And to Laura, for your timely and thorough editing!

CHAPTER 1

Because I'm the one who cursed you...

Wynona's hand shook slightly as she set down the teacup in front of Jubilee, one of Wynona's most loyal patrons. "Here you go," she told the pixie. "Rosehip with a hint of vanilla." Wynona forced a smile and clasped her trembling fingers in front of her. "Your knee should be feeling better in no time."

Jubilee smiled, the wrinkles at the edge of her eyes a testament to her age as well as her excitement. "Thank you, dearie. I always feel so much better after one of your brews."

Wynona nodded, keeping the smile in place, then walked away. She kept her calm, peaceful facade up as she surveyed the room, making sure her patrons were happy and content, until she walked into the kitchen.

As had happened many times since the moment her Granny Saffron had been the one to curse Wynona at birth, Wynona felt as if the very air in her lungs had been stolen.

She paused on the other side of the door, a sharp pain hitting her sternum. Leaning her hands onto her knees, Wynona tried to catch her breath. Tried to calm her racing heart. Tried to force herself to believe that her grandmother's act hadn't been the ultimate betrayal. Unfortunately, just like all the other times...her body and mind wouldn't listen.

Tears pricked her eyes and Wynona squeezed them tight, willing the moisture to go back to where it came from. Her day was only half over. She couldn't break down. Not now. Not *again.*

It had been a month since the life altering confession and Wynona knew she needed to get a handle on herself and her emo-

"

tions, but she wasn't sure how. When Granny had admitted to the heinous act, Wynona had fainted. *Fainted!*

Rascal had forced everyone to leave, promising only that when Wynona was ready, they would talk.

Four weeks and Wynona still wasn't sure she was ready. After waking up from her...moment of weakness...Wynona had spent the next few days pretending the incident never happened.

She couldn't wrap her mind around it. Granny had cursed her. Granny had been the reason Wynona had spent the first thirty years of her life being treated like dirt. Good for nothing but to be trod on by her powerful family. She was the reason Wynona had felt worthless and spent so many days hiding and crying as a child. She was the reason Wynona was hated by her mother, sister and eventually disowned by her father.

She put a hand over her aching heart. "How could she do that to me?" Wynona whispered, still gasping for air.

A grunt caught her attention. "Don't know a good thing when you see it."

Wynona kept her eyes down. She knew Lusgu had spoken, but she was too hurt to listen. Before the revelation, she would have tried to interpret his words, since he often knew more than anyone else. But right now she didn't have the strength. Was he saying she should be grateful for the curse? Was he saying Granny was doing something good?

It didn't matter. It hurt too much and Wynona hadn't forgiven Lusgu for his part in keeping it all a secret. She wasn't sure how deeply he was involved, but the fact of the matter was...he knew Granny Saffron and had taken some part in the whole farce that was Wynona's life.

With another grunt, Lusgu moved on and Wynona blew out a breath of relief. She had been working around him for the last several weeks, but just didn't know what to say.

A scratching sound caught her attention and Violet squeezed her way under the kitchen door. *Mrs. Maganti needs more eclairs.*

Wynona nodded and waited while her familiar climbed up to her usual spot on Wynona's shoulder before gathering a plate of refills. Fortifying herself with a deep breath, she used her back to push open the door and walk back into the dining area. "Hello, Mrs. Maganti," Wynona said pleasantly. She cleared her throat. "I heard you might need a refill."

"Oh yes," the witch gushed, clasping her hands together. "I can never get enough of those sweets." She gave a sheepish grin, her white bun of hair trembling from side to side. "I really shouldn't indulge so, but..." She shrugged in answer to her quandary.

"Tea time is made for indulgence," Wynona assured her, feeling a slight amount of tension leave her body. She adored her customers, and creatures like Mrs. Maganti and Jubilee were a reminder of why. They were simply sweet and kind, exactly the type of people Wynona enjoyed associating with.

Using her tea skills to help them feel better or to add a little luxury to their lives was everything Wynona wanted out of life.

After seeing the witch was taken care of, Wynona started to walk away, only to stop when a warm sensation ran through her chest. She blinked. Where had that come from?

A burst of giggles and chatter had her spinning, only to smile when she noticed the tall, handsome man standing in the room entry. She rubbed at her chest a little as she realized the emotion was actually Rascal's, her boyfriend and soulmate.

Yet another crazy revelation to add to Wynona's growing pile. The bond between them had become complete when Wynona had burst the last bits of her curse to smithereens while trying to thwart a spell from a particularly nasty witch in an effort to save Rascal's life.

Now she could sense his emotions when they were particularly strong or when he was close. That warm feeling? Wynona now recognized it as the one she got every time Rascal walked into the room. He loved her, and she loved him. There was no way to deny it, even if she had wanted to. Of the two bombs that had landed in her lap, this one had been much easier to swallow. Although shocking, it hadn't turned her world upside down the way the knowledge about the curse had.

Rascal stalked across the room, his golden eyes intent on her, and Wynona felt a delicate shiver race down her spine.

"Hey," he said softly, once he closed the distance between them.

Wynona could hear her patrons whispering and laughing at her expense, but she didn't care. "Hey."

One side of his mouth quirked up and he tucked a piece of her black hair behind her ear. "Are you free for dinner tonight?"

Wynona nodded. "When does your shift end?" She took in the uniform he was sporting, judging that he had simply stopped by for a small break.

"I get off at five." He made a face. "I should probably shower the precinct off of me. Is six okay?"

Wynona grinned and nodded again. "I'll have something ready."

"I can pick up take out."

She shook her head. "No. I've got some vegetables that need to be used. I'll make a stir fry or something."

Rascal rolled his eyes good naturedly and kissed her cheek. Then rubbed the top of Violet's head. "Not too many vegetables," he whispered before straightening and grinning at her.

Wynona laughed softly, watching him walk away. His wink just before disappearing was all she hoped it would be.

"Whew!" Jubilee fanned her face as soon as the front door closed. "Hold onto that one, honey. They don't make 'em like that anymore."

Wynona's pale cheeks flushed bright red as heat traveled up her chest and neck and landed in her face. She laughed, slightly uncomfortable, but agreeing nonetheless. "I plan to," she said, to the amusement of her patrons, most of whom were older women.

"If I was twenty years younger," Mrs. Maganti hedged, leaving the sentence to interpretation.

"Twenty years ago, you were still old enough to be his mother, Moira," Jubilee said with a smirk.

Mrs. Maganti glared. "Maybe he likes older women." She preened. "With age comes wisdom, you know."

"In most cases," Jubilee muttered as she took a drink.

"Ladies!" Wynona held her hands in the air, calling for peace as the rest of the room erupted in laughter at Jubilee's dig. Wynona, herself, was having a hard time holding back her amusement. "Let's all get along, huh?"

Mrs. Maganti straightened, but continued glaring, though Wynona knew it was for show. The two women saw each other far too often to be at odds. It was simply a game they played, and obviously enjoyed.

"As much competition as Mrs. Maganti would offer, no matter her age," Wynona offered, "I'm afraid I know a good thing when I see it." She pointed toward the front entryway. "And that, my dear friends...is definitely a good thing."

Violet snickered while the women laughed again before settling into a tone more common in a tea room.

The afternoon stretched on and Wynona found herself exhausted when it was finally time to go home. Swallowing down the mixed feelings of hurt, Wynona pushed a tight smile onto her face. "Thank you, Lusgu," she said, knowing she sounded anything but sincere.

Lusgu eyed her, then grunted and went on his way, disappearing into the portal he had created in the corner of her kitchen.

Wynona's shoulders sagged when he was gone. She wanted to forgive him, she really did, but right now the feelings were far too new. Hopefully, someday she would understand better.

Debating whether or not to text Rascal and ask him to pick up that take out, Wynona hurried to her office to grab her phone and the keys to her mint green Vespa before speeding into the chilly evening air.

She knew the flush on her cheeks had to be bright as she and Violet arrived home, the air helping shake some of the fatigue from Wynona's shoulders. Her little cottage next to the Grove of Secrets was small, but homey, and Wynona loved it.

Once inside, she quickly grabbed everything she needed for dinner and began chopping and mixing. Rascal would be there soon and she knew he was always ravenous after a shift.

When her front door opened fifteen minutes later, the tingling sensation running through her limbs kept her from being alarmed. "You made it!" she called out, knowing he would follow her voice to the kitchen.

Heavy footsteps made their way through the house and came up right behind Wynona. She glanced over her shoulder just as he stepped up to her back and wrapped his arms around her waist.

"Smells good," he whispered, leaving a kiss against her cheek.

"Think you can keep your wolf at bay long enough for it to finish cooking?" she asked with a grin. "There's even veggies to help," she teased, knowing his wolf side preferred the meat only.

Rascal chuckled.

Oh, how she loved that sound. She couldn't have made it through this last month without him. But as much as she wished she could stay in her little bubble of all things Rascal...Wynona had been thinking this afternoon.

"I think it's time," she said softly.

He stiffened behind her, a low growl rumbling through his chest and his protective instincts coming to the surface. "Are you sure?"

Wynona shrugged and shook her head. "No. But if I don't do it now, then when?" She sighed, and stirred the contents of the pan.

"I honestly don't know if I'll ever be ready. I think it might be like pulling off a Band-Aid. The quicker it's done, the less it will hurt in the long run."

"And if it isn't?"

Wynona kept her eyes on the food, unable to look up. "Then I guess we'll find out."

Rascal walked away from her back and she could hear him shuffling through the cupboards. A glance back told her he was setting the table, but the furrow in his brow said he was also thinking over everything she said.

She left off speaking, knowing he would respond when ready. Turning off the stove, she brought the rice and stir fry, along with some tortillas, to the table. They began to eat in silence, Wynona waiting out Rascal's response.

The food was nearly gone before he sighed and scrubbed his face with his hands. "I get off at seven tomorrow. Want me to set it up for seven-thirty?"

Wynona smiled gratefully at him. How spoiled was she? She knew Rascal didn't like the situation. He had hated the fact that she'd been hurt, yet he not only was willing to let her find out more, he refused to let her do it alone.

She reached across the table and squeezed his hand. "That's perfect." She gave him a secret smile. "And just for you, I brought home Gnuq's leftover lemon bars today."

His eyebrows shot up and a genuine smile spread across his face. "There were leftovers?"

Wynona laughed as she stood, taking her plate to the sink. "Only because I set them aside."

This time, Rascal's growling was playful as he jumped up and pulled her into his arms. He kissed her until she couldn't breathe, then whispered, "And that's why I love you so much."

Wynona just shook her head, laughing a little before letting her forehead rest against his chest. Tomorrow was going to come far too soon and it was moments like this that were going to be the thing to save her. No matter what happened with her grandmother, Wynona was grateful she would always have this.

CHAPTER 2

Wynona was going to throw up. She knew it. Her stomach churned and she pressed a hand to it as if that would calm her anxiety. She rubbed Violet's head, as it was curled up on her shoulder.

It's going to be fine, Violet assured her. *I'm sure Granny has an explanation for everything.*

"I sure hope so," Wynona murmured. With her powers fully awakened, Wynona knew she could have just spoken to Violet in her mind, but some habits were hard to break. "I guess I just can't come up with any logical explanation as to why she would curse me," Wynona whispered hoarsely.

Violet murmured more assurances, but they were lost on Wynona as the clock chimed seven. Gathering her courage, she picked her keys up off the dresser and headed to the garage. They were meeting at the tea house, since Wynona didn't want to have the conversation in her sanctuary.

It was dark as she rode down the streets to reach her tea shop and Wynona found herself driving slower than normal. Apparently, her courage wasn't as prevalent as she would have wished.

She unlocked the shop from the back entrance with shaking fingers and flipped on the lights in the kitchen. She knew Lusgu would see it and arrive in time for the seven-thirty meeting. She wasn't exactly sure how his portal worked, but somehow he always knew when she was in the shop.

She worked her way into the dining room and forced her legs to arrive at the front door and unlock it. She had barely walked away when the door opened, startling her and causing her heart to skip a beat. But the peace that hit her calmed her immediately. "Rascal," she breathed.

Rascal was still in uniform, obviously having come straight from work. "Hey, sweetheart," he said in a grumbly tone. Closing the short distance, he kissed her cheek. "You ready for this?"

Wynona shrugged. "Nope. But it needs to happen. I can't keep..." She shook her head. "I just can't keep pushing it off."

Rascal nodded and reached up to take Violet from Wynona's shoulder. The purple rodent purred her satisfaction, then climbed down to snuggle in his breast pocket. Her twitching nose came out and Wynona could have sworn her familiar was smirking in delight.

Glad someone's having a good time, she thought wryly.

"I want to get some tea brewing," Wynona said, turning back to the kitchen. "And I might need sugar for fortification."

"Sounds good to me," Rascal replied, walking behind her. "I'll help."

The sound of boiling water hit Wynona's ears as she and Rascal entered the kitchen. *Lusgu.* Wynona paused and gave the brownie a shaky smile. "Thank you," she said with a polite nod.

Lusgu grunted and went back to directing the dishes into forming a tray.

"I'll get the pastries and cups," Wynona offered. Within a few minutes she had everything she needed from the kitchen and Rascal carried the food out to the dining room.

The door chimed and Wynona felt her heart skip another beat. She jerked her head toward Rascal, who growled softly.

"I'll go see them in," he said softly.

Wynona felt grateful relief flow through her. "Thank you." Turning to the large display of antique cups, she took a calming breath and let it fill her chest until she had calmed enough to let the cups speak to her. Tilting her head, she focused on the cups and waited until they spoke to her. It was a skill she hadn't realized involved magic until Daemon, her friend and black hole, pointed it out. The antique cups she was attracted to often had residual magic in them and it pulled at Wynona. She took the time to pick one out for each person, sans her grandmother, and set them on the table.

Mrs. Reyna watched her with narrowed eyes. "You have more of her inside of you than you know."

Wynona kept a placid facade and sat down gingerly at the table. She folded her hands on top to keep them from shaking. "Thank you for coming tonight." She let her vision go purple for a moment, but no specter appeared in her vision. Wynona blinked the sight away. "Is Granny coming?"

Mrs. Reyna sighed and nodded. "I saw her earlier today and she was planning on it."

Wynona nodded and the table grew awkwardly quiet as they waited for the rest of the guests to arrive.

Lusgu came out of the kitchen two minutes later, the tray with the hot water floating behind him.

Once it was on the table, Wynona began to create teas for each person. Her magical instincts were easier to hear than ever now that the curse was fully dissipated.

"Thank you," Mrs. Reyna murmured as she accepted the cup from Wynona.

Lusgu didn't show similar gratitude, but his face softened a little and Wynona took that as a good sign.

When the hairs on the back of her neck began to rise, Wynona knew their last guest had arrived. "Hello, Granny," Wynona said clearly, letting the room know the witch was there.

"Oh, do make yourself corporeal," Mrs. Reyna snapped. "This isn't a time for games, Saffy."

Saffron cackled as she became visible to the whole room. "You never were any fun, Mazelina."

Mrs. Reyna huffed and took a sip of tea, her eyes closing for a moment, as if savoring the brew. "You know, I think the young one is better at this than you were."

Saffron glared. "She better be. A lot went into her future."

"Speaking of..." Wynona interrupted. The last thing her nerves could handle right now was a fight among the elderly women. "I asked you to come tonight because you promised me an explanation." Wynona straightened and stuck her chin in the air slightly. "I'd like to get straight to business."

Rascal patted her knee under the table, offering his support.

Saffron sighed and sank into a chair. "I always knew I'd have to explain myself someday, but..." She shrugged. "I'm not any more prepared now than I was when you were born."

Wynona bit her tongue. Snarky responses, no matter how well deserved, weren't going to help right now.

Granny's dark brown eyes met Wynona's in an intense glare. "Before you were born, your mother begged me to read the tea leaves on your behalf."

Wynona blinked. "You could read the future in the tea leaves? I thought it was about answering questions?"

Saffron shook her head. "The tea leaves will always offer advice and warnings, but when the skills are developed, you can see things that have yet to be." She shrugged. "Or glimpses anyway."

Wynona was barely breathing. "And what did you see?" Saffron's face shifted and she went from looking resigned, to weary. Whatever had happened had taken a great toll on the older woman.

"I saw a witch so powerful that her skills had never been seen before."

The words were a bomb that landed in an utterly quiet room.

It took Rascal squeezing Wynona's knee in order to force her lungs into moving again. "What?" She gasped.

Saffron nodded slowly. "You were the exact child your parents had wanted when they brought the two witch lines together. Powerful enough that no one would ever be able to touch you."

"But..." Wynona stammered. She snapped her mouth shut. She had no idea what to say to that.

No wonder you had such trouble controlling it, Violet muttered.

"Then..why?" Wynona couldn't even say a complete sentence in her shock.

Saffron's lips pressed into a tight, white line before she spoke. "Because I also saw the person you would become, not just the witch."

"In other words," Mrs. Reyna piped up "you were a word that my mama would have washed my mouth out for saying."

Saffron glared at her friend, who shrugged behind her teacup.

"Someone had to say it," Mrs. Reyna snipped. "You're too emotionally involved and beating around the bush. Just tell the girl the truth."

Saffron took a deep breath and nodded. She turned back to Wynona. "It's true. You were untouchable in magic, but also in personality. Your parents would have raised you to be strong, elite and an all-around horrible person."

Wynona blinked rapidly. Tears were pricking the back of her eyes, but she didn't want to let them fall. "I've spent my entire adulthood trying to be a good person," she said hoarsely. "I help those who are struggling. I offer a hand to anyone and have never placed one person above another."

"Exactly," Saffron said, leaning forward in eagerness. "You are *that* person, because you *didn't* have everything. If I had left you alone, your parents would have raised a monster. By taking away your magic, you became the exact opposite." Her smile was wide. "You fought for the underdog and justice before your magic was whole. Now it will only be easier."

"So you're saying you cursed me for my own good!" Wynona's voice was higher than normal and when Rascal's finger squeezed her knee again, she gripped his fingers, nearly crippling them in her grip.

Rascal growled. "Do you have any idea what all she endured because of your act?" he asked.

Saffron nodded. "Only too well," she said without remorse. She tucked a piece of hair into her bun. "But believe me when I say Hex Haven is a better place for it."

Wynona shook her head. "I have spent thirty years feeling worthless and being treated like it was a crime I existed at all. And that was better than just trying to offset my parents' influence?"

Saffron's eyes hardened. "The tea leaves are never wrong, Wynona. If I saw you as a monster, it was because my influence wouldn't have made a difference." She hissed. "Do you really think your parents would have let me get close to you if they had any idea of what you were capable of? They'd have cut me off!"

"You were stronger than them!" Wynona shouted. "They couldn't have cut you off without your consent!"

Saffron just shook her head some more and settled back into her seat. "The fact remains...anything I did wouldn't have been enough. You'd have been a source of destruction for everyone and your life would have been miserable."

Wynona looked away. On a logical level, she understood what Granny was saying, but on a personal level, her hurt had only gotten worse. She'd been a sacrifice, plain and simple. Granny had sacrificed Wynona and her powers in order to protect everyone else.

What was so wrong with her that she wouldn't have been able to resist being horrible? How could someone who spent their life trying to be kind have been a monster in another life? And why did the person, whom she'd thought had loved her the most, have to be the one to hurt her the most?

Rascal scooted his chair closer. "Do you want me to send them home?" he whispered.

Wynona shook her head. "No. I want this over and done with." She took in a shuddering breath. "So...what?" she pressed. "You lied to my mom? Cursed me in the womb and then tried to make up for it by teaching me tricks with herbs?"

"You don't understand," Saffron pleaded. "Everything I've done, I've done for you." She shook her head in disappointment. "You have to look at the whole picture."

"I'm trying," Wynona argued. "But what I'm seeing is that you only spent time with me in order to keep me from becoming the monster you saw in the tea leaves." Wynona's nostrils flared as her frustration rose to the surface. "I thought you loved me. I thought you saw how my family treated me and wanted to help alleviate the pain." She shook her head. "But it was all a lie. Everything has been a lie. My powers, your cursing, my relationships..."

Saffron's eyes widened. "You really think my love for you was a lie?" she whispered.

"What else could it be?" Wynona continued. "You just said you saw how horrible I was going to be. That the only way to stop me was to take away my very essence. If I'd had my powers, my parents would have kept us apart, so you took it upon yourself to rectify that." Her eyes flooded. "Are you telling me that you loved a monster?"

"Get over yourself," Mrs. Reyna growled, ignoring Rascal's warning sounds. "Your grandmother spent her life putting together a plan that would save not only Hex Haven, but you as well. Your magic could kill us all if not harnessed correctly, and she gave you the skills to do so the only way she knew how. Your parents are the most selfish, power-hungry couple we've had in the palace in a long time, and if you think we would have let you make it worse without putting up a fight, well..." She pointed a gnarled finger at Wynona. "Think again."

Lusgu cleared his throat before Wynona could respond to the angry diatribe. "Pain is personal." He grunted. "But fades in time."

His words made Wynona pause before responding. "How were you two involved?" she finally asked, keeping her eyes on Lusgu.

Mrs. Reyna huffed. "She couldn't exactly help you when she was dead, now could she?"

"Hush now," Saffron said to Mrs. Reyna. "You're only making things worse. Wynona isn't our enemy. She's trying to absorb a lot of information and redirect a lot of memories. Give her a chance."

Mrs. Reyna sighed. "I suppose you're right," she admitted to Saffron. "But anyone with a lick of sense should see this was done for her good."

Saffron shook her head and turned back to Wynona. "Lusgu and Mazelina were friends of mine that helped with some of my...more discretionary work."

Wynona frowned.

"We helped her when she needed to do things under the table," Mrs. Reyna explained. "No one in the palace knew we were acquainted, which allowed us to go undetected to the political world."

Wynona wasn't sure she could handle more revelations at this point, so she let it go.

"As you grew, I continued reading the leaves," Saffron continued. "I saw your mate." She nodded to Rascal. "And I put Mazelina in a position to keep track of him." Saffron pointed to Lusgu. "And Lusgu was sent to help you control the spurts that would happen as the curse dissolved. He has a gift for stopping others' magic." She smirked. "Along with an obsession with cleanliness."

"So you knew I would open the tea shop," Wynona said weakly.

Saffron nodded.

"Have you seen everything?"

Saffron shook her head. "No. I don't want to see it all, but I tried to keep my eyes on the most important." She started to reach across the table, but halted, unsure if she would be welcome.

Wynona didn't respond. She wasn't sure how she was feeling at that moment.

"Your thoughts are saying otherwise, but Wynona, I love you. I've loved you since before you were born and it has nothing to do with your powers. The time spent raising you in my herb house were some of the greatest years of my life." She smiled hopefully. "I know I hurt you, but I wouldn't change what I did for anything. You've turned out better than I could have ever hoped for, and I know now that your powers will only be used for good. You can make this world a better place...if you're willing."

Wynona's mind spun. There was too much information and too many emotions for her to think straight right now. "I...I think I need some time," she said softly.

Saffron nodded, looking disappointed, but understanding. "I know. I'll always be here when you're ready." Without another word, she disappeared.

When the hairs on Wynona's neck calmed down, Wynona knew her grandmother had left the building entirely.

Mrs. Reyna groaned as she stood. "You know where to find me," she grumbled before shuffling to the door and out into the night.

Lusgu studied Wynona for a moment before climbing down from his chair. He glared at Rascal. "Someone had to make you work for it." He grunted, then marched into the kitchen.

Wynona rubbed her aching forehead. "I don't even want to know what that meant."

Rascal snorted. "Don't worry. Message received."

"I think I need to sleep," Wynona said. "I'm going to leave all this for the morning."

Rascal helped her stand and left a lingering kiss on her forehead. "I'll see you home," he said softly.

Wynona nodded, too tired to argue. Right now her heart was in a fight with her head and truthfully, she wasn't sure whom she wanted to win. There were obviously two sides to every story and Wynona had come into this meeting feeling like hers was the one that mattered most. After hearing everything else...now she wasn't so sure.

CHAPTER 3

"The party is here!" Prim shouted as she waltzed into the tea shop, flowers bursting from her arms.

Wynona smiled at her friend's enthusiasm. "Oh my gosh, Prim. They're gorgeous." She hurried over to relieve Prim's burden. The fairy was in her human sized form, but still, the flowers had to weigh a ton. "What are these for?" Wynona asked as she set one of the vases down on a dining table.

"You," Prim said breezily. "After your cryptic phone message, I felt like maybe you needed a pick me up."

Wynona spun and grabbed Prim in a tight hug. "Thank you," she whispered thickly. "You're the best friend ever."

Prim squeezed back. "I know, she said cheekily.

Wynona laughed and let go, wiping at her damp eyes. "Sorry about the message, but I didn't want to say anything somebody else might hear."

"I figured." Prim perched on a chair. "The vases are filled with masterwort and beardtongue for courage. Gerbera and alstroemeria for friendship. Lavender and calendula for healing, plus some amethyst for clarity." She folded her hands in her lap. "Now...spill it." A bright pink eyebrow rose high. "I'm guessing you finally spoke to dear old Grandmama."

Wynona nodded and sank into the chair next to Prim. "Yes. And it was a doozy of a conversation." Taking a deep breath, she spent the next twenty minutes spilling everything Granny had shared. The visions, the set up for her life, the keeping track of her to make sure Wynona grew up differently than what the tea leaves had predicted and finally, how Mrs. Reyna and Lusgu fit into the whole situation.

Prim's eyes were so wide when Wynona was done that she looked like a deer caught in the headlights of an approaching vehicle. "Leaky cauldrons..." Prim shook her head slowly. "That's...a lot."

Wynona nodded. "Yep."

"Your grandma is crazy."

"Yep."

"But it also sort of makes a twisted type of sense."

Wynona sighed. "Yep," she said for the third time. "In fact, I'm not quite sure how I feel about it. The story makes my time with Granny feel...dirty, somehow. Like it wasn't real."

"Like a woman trying to prevent a catastrophe rather than a grandmother loving a granddaughter?" Prim asked.

"Exactly," Wynona said with a nod. She shrugged. "Granny says that's not the case, but..." Another shrug filled in what she couldn't say.

"Yeah." Prim pinched her lips together. "It does seem suspect, but honestly, if she didn't love you, she could have handled your growing up much differently. She didn't have to spend time with you personally. She could have simply had you killed, instead of magic bound." Prim gave Wynona a look when the witch jumped at the callous words. "I know that sounds harsh, but you live in a paranormal world, Nona," Prim defended herself. "Creatures kill each other all the time. Only some of them get caught by your insane sleuthing skills."

Wynona rolled her eyes, but didn't respond. Prim was right. Granny didn't have to take the situation so personally. Once her magic was bound, Granny could have left Wynona to her own devices and that of her parents, since the foretelling wouldn't have come true anymore.

Until you got your powers back later, Violet muttered as she scurried into the room.

"Awesome, thanks," Wynona said wryly. "Because I didn't have enough trouble believing her."

Violet climbed the table leg, but didn't say anything else. She had been fairly quiet on the subject of Granny Saffron and Wynona didn't have the mental capacity to ask her familiar's opinion. Once on top, Violet began grooming herself, completely ignoring the two women.

"I suppose the real question here is, what are you going to do now?" Prim asked, fingering one of the petals in the vase at her elbow.

"I don't know," Wynona said softly. "I'm not sure what to believe, I'm not sure what to feel..." She threw her hands in the air. "I'm not even sure what do with my magic. I supposedly have more magic than anyone else in Hex Haven, but I can barely control it, and I have this horrible feeling that my family is going to be showing up on my doorstep at any moment, demanding to know what's going on."

Prim scowled at the mention of the presidential family. Ever since meeting Wynona, the fairy had had no love for the arrogant group of witches who ruled their town. "If you have more power than anyone else, then you're stronger than your parents," Prim murmured. Her eyes widened and she straightened. "Which means they can't do anything to you because you outrank them! Ha!" Prim looked at Wynona triumphantly. "Maybe we should call for another election! You can take over the presidency because you're more powerful!"

"Whoa, whoa, whoa!" Wynona said quickly, shaking her head so fast she felt slightly dizzy. "I don't want anything to do with ruling Hex Haven. I don't like my family and I don't agree with how they rule, but I absolutely, definitely and without any sort of doubt at all...don't want to do it myself."

"Thank goodness for that," a deep voice growled from the doorway.

"Rascal!" Wynona panted for a second as her heart calmed down. "I didn't hear you come in."

He stalked over and kissed her temple before slipping into the empty seat on her other side. "You two were too busy planning to take over the world," he teased.

"Only Prim," Wynona retorted, giving her friend a mock glare. "She apparently has a thing for being in charge."

Prim pointed a polished purple nail at Wynona. "I'd be better at it than your dad."

"On that, we can agree," Wynona said, then sighed. She pushed both hands through her hair, holding it back from her face. "It's all so messed up. What am I going to do? Should I simply forgive Granny and move on? I hate feeling like this." She bit her lip. "It's not normal for me to be so angry and I've noticed that my magic still reacts to my emotions."

She held up her hands, purple sparks dancing between the digits. "It's no wonder Granny was worried about me becoming a monster," she whispered. "If my parents had spoiled me, then every time I didn't get my way, I probably would have blown something up."

Rascal grabbed her hand, essentially stopping the flow of sparks, and brought it to his lips. "Wynona Le Doux," he said in a deep, harsh tone. "You are one of the best people I have ever met and I won't let anyone, not even you, disparage my soulmate when I know her heart."

He raised a knowing eyebrow at her and Wynona felt her cheeks flush with heat.

"I don't like it either," he continued. "I don't like what she did, I don't like that you were hurt as a child, I don't like that you're hurting now, and I definitely don't like that your trust in your memories has been shattered." He kissed her palm again. "But I know you. I can *feel* you in a way that no one else can and I know that you are far more capable than you know. If you want to forgive your grandmother, you have it in you to do it and follow through with her plans." He growled. "But if you want to hold back and fight against what she seems to have planned for your life, then I'm right here beside you to help." He glared at Prim. "Even if it means taking down the president."

Prim pumped a fist in the air. "Yes!"

"No," Wynona said firmly. "I'm glad I'm not the only one who thought Granny was hinting toward something more." She met Rascal's glowing gaze. "She certainly sounded like she was hoping I would do something about our rotten political system with the way she set up my life, but I have no interest."

Prim groaned, then grinned good naturedly. "I suppose it's too much to ask you to be bloodthirsty."

Violet snorted, but didn't offer anything more.

The bell on the door chimed as someone else slipped into the shop and Wynona stiffened.

"That must be Skymaw," Rascal muttered. "I thought maybe he should know what's going on."

Daemon looked warily around the corner, his eyes immediately going to Prim. The tips of his ears turned pink and he cleared his throat. "Deputy Chief invited me," he said, raising an eyebrow. "Is it okay that I'm here?"

Wynona nodded, keeping an eye on Prim, who had suddenly gone silent. "Of course, Daemon. Please. Have a seat." She pushed against the table and stood up. "Let me grab some cups and a few pastries."

Rascal followed her to the kitchen and helped make the job a little easier as he carried a full tray to the front.

"I'm starving," Daemon breathed before grabbing a croissant.

Prim sniffed and the black hole slowed his face-stuffing. Swallowing what appeared to be a big bite, he sat back. "Sorry," he muttered.

Wynona glared at Prim before smiling at Daemon. "I'm glad you like them. I'll pass it along to Gnuq and Kyox."

Daemon nodded and polished off the rest of the pastry.

Glancing over, Wynona realized Rascal had finished two in the same amount of time and she shook her head playfully. "Well, one thing is for certain. I can't go out of the tea business or you two officers would fade away from lack of food."

Rascal chuckled and kissed her cheek. "Thank you for feeding me."

Prim played with a lemon bar. "But back to our topic at hand…" she pressed.

Wynona nodded. "Right." She took a few minutes to catch Daemon up, though from the lack of surprise on his face, she was positive Rascal had already given him several clues as to what was going on. "So, I guess I'm just trying to figure out where to go from here," she said lamely.

Daemon nodded. "Yeah…that's…rough. Sorry." He shrugged his massive shoulders. "I wish I knew what to say, but…" He scrunched up his nose, making his masculine looks a little more boyish. "Your family is crazy."

"That's what I said!" Prim cried before catching herself and going back to being calm. "I mean…yes. Her family is a problem. For sure."

Daemon eyed the fairy before turning to Wynona. "What do you *want* to do?" He wiped his mouth on a napkin. "You said you're not sure what you *should* feel or what you *should* think. But maybe we should start with what you actually *do* think and feel."

Wynona blinked. She opened her mouth, shut it and then opened it again. "That's actually very insightful. Thank you, Daemon."

Rascal groaned. "I should have known he'd be better at girl talk than me."

Daemon blushed again and Wynona whacked Rascal's shoulder. "Knock it off," she scolded. "He's being a good friend."

Rascal leaned into her face, his eyes flashing. "Then what am I supposed to be?"

Wynona found herself losing her concentration as she stared into his handsome face. Goodness...this soulmate thing was no joke. "You're supposed to be a good boyfriend," she whispered.

A slow smile crept across the shifter's face, but before he could lean in, Prim slapped a hand on the table.

"Before we set the shop on fire," she said, pointedly glaring at Rascal, "perhaps we need to figure out how to help Wynona."

Daemon's face was still red and he rubbed the back of his neck, letting Wynona know he was uncomfortable with the situation.

There'll be time for kissy face later, Violet snickered.

Wynona rolled her eyes. "Right. Well. Honestly, if I'm answering Daemon's questions, I feel hurt and confused. And I think I need more time to process it all before I make any decisions." She looked around at her group. "Which basically means this meeting was all for nothing because it doesn't help me move forward or address the issues at all."

Prim spun a flower in her fingers. "No. It means you're being calm enough to think rationally, and I think time will be your ally. No matter what your grandmother has planned for you, a few more days won't make or break it." She stood and stepped forward to hug Wynona. "Keep the flowers close. They can help." Straightening, she waved to the men. "I need to feed my carnivorous crew before bed. I'll see you all later." At the doorway, she looked back one more time, her eyes flashing from Daemon to Wynona. "You know how to reach me," she said, making a phone with her fingers.

Wynona smiled. "Thanks, Prim. You're the best."

Prim gave a little curtsy and disappeared.

Wynona turned to Daemon and studied him. If she wasn't mistaken, there was something simmering between her two friends, but Wynona wasn't quite sure what it was.

"Don't. Say. A. Word," Daemon snapped before grabbing a muffin. He stuffed the whole thing in his mouth.

Wynona held up her hands while Rascal snorted. "Wasn't going to."

Daemon glared as if not believing her. Standing, he opened a napkin and filled it with goodies, then began to walk away. "When there's something else I can help with, let me know."

"Bye!" Wynona watched him go, already feeling lighter just from saying everything out loud.

With Rascal's arm around her shoulders and Violet munching on a cookie, the world seemed rather quiet at the moment. Unfortunately, Wynona knew from experience it more than likely wouldn't stay that way. But for this evening, she would soak it up and allow her thoughts and emotions to sort through themselves. She had no idea what direction she would go now...but Prim was right, Wynona didn't have to know it all tonight. Answers and solutions would come with time and Wynona would do her best to be open to them. At this point, that was all she could do.

CHAPTER 4

"Have you seen this!" Prim shouted, bursting through the front door of the tea shop.

Wynona gasped and put a hand to her chest. "Goodness, Prim. What in the world is going on with you?" She frowned. "I thought I locked the front door."

Prim smirked. "You did."

"Then how in the world did you get in?"

Prim couldn't have looked more satisfied if she'd been a cat with a canary. "Let's just say that vines can do amazing things."

Wynona put her hands on her hips. "Are you kidding? You *broke* into my shop with one of your plants? Why not just knock?"

Prim widened her bright pink eyes and shrugged. "Where's the fun in that? Besides..." She waved at the mess Wynona was cleaning up. "You just closed. I knew you'd be busy."

Wynona rubbed her forehead. "Oh, good grief."

Prim snickered. "Kind of makes you want to have me join your detective team, doesn't it?"

"I don't have a detective team," Wynona muttered. She held up a hand to stop anything Prim might say. "And I'm not planning on creating one either."

Prim marched forward and pushed Wynona's hand down. "You might change your mind after you read this." She thrust a tablet into Wynona's vision.

Wynona frowned, took the device and glanced at Prim in question.

Prim nodded toward the electronic screen. "Seriously, take a look."

Taking a deep breath, Wynona looked down, ignoring Violet climbing up her leg to get a better view. "Heiress found..." She gasped. "Dead?"

Prim pointed to the screen. "Harmony Roseburg," she stated. "The only other witch richer than your family."

Wynona slowly shook her head. "I've met her," she whispered thickly. "Well..." Wynona tilted her head to the side. "Not quite. I've seen her at family functions and I've met her in passing, but..." She shrugged. "I wasn't exactly the witch my parents were showing off at the time."

Prim nodded. "We just need them to keep that type of thinking," she snapped.

Wynona shook her head. "It's already starting," she told her best friend. "Celia texted today, saying Mother would love to get together for a luncheon."

Prim's mouth dropped open. "What did you say?"

Wynona looked up sharply. "The only thing I could say. I said I was busy, but thank you for the invitation."

Prim laughed. "Only you would be polite while turning down someone who wants to chain you up and use you like a bargaining chip."

Wynona shrugged it off. She'd seen her parents schmooze creatures before. She knew exactly how this would go. Polite invitations, followed by random social visits that were difficult to avoid, and eventually threats if she didn't comply.

Let's just hope you master your powers before the threats part, Violet offered.

Agreed, Wynona sent the thought back. She went back to the tablet. "Does it say what happened to her?"

Prim took back the tablet, scrolling through the article. "They think she might have drowned in her pool."

"Seriously!" Wynona tucked a chunk of hair behind her ear. "That seems odd. A witch would just be able to use her magic to escape. Especially one as powerful as Mrs. Roseburg." Wynona shook her head. "There had to be more to it than that."

Prim frowned. "I don't know...it looks like an accident, they said."

"Huh." Wynona studied the picture of the older but beautiful witch. Magic could do wonders for wrinkles. "If it was an accident, I'm sure Chief Ligurio will have that figured out soon enough."

"And if not, you'll be getting a call for your help in solving a murder." Prim grinned. "And this time I can be your sidekick." She lowered her voice. "After all, you might have to break into the mansion."

Wynona rolled her eyes and Violet snorted. "Prim. Even if this ends up being murder, which I sincerely hope it doesn't, I won't be the one solving it. It's not my job, and my hands are full with trying to figure out things with Granny and avoiding the grasping hands of my family." Wynona huffed. "I think that's enough to keep anyone busy."

"Pity," Prim mused. "Your ability to capture criminals might make your family think twice about trying to be sneaky."

Wynona laughed softly. "Somehow I doubt that would put them off if they had it in their heads to do otherwise. They've had too much power for too long. Me solving a case or two isn't going to scare them off."

"Eh...we'll see." Prim sniffed the air. "I do believe you might have some leftover treats." She pumped her pink eyebrows.

Wynona laughed. "Of course. Help me clean up and I'll bring us out a decent dinner."

Prim grumbled good naturedly. "Always putting me to work. I don't think this is how friendships are supposed to go."

Wynona's smile helped relieve some of her tension. She had already been on edge with the message from Celia, but follow that up with news of Mrs. Roseburg's death and all of Wynona's fought-for peace was gone.

We need to find Prim a boyfriend, Violet grumbled when Prim began to sing as she worked.

Wynona nearly choked, then glanced at her familiar and gave her a look. *That wasn't nice.*

Her singing isn't nice!

Wynona rolled her eyes. *Leave her alone. It makes her happy.*

Doesn't make my ears happy, Violet continued.

Wynona threw up a mental barrier to drown out the mouse's voice. Her familiar and her best friend often bickered, though Prim didn't always know it. Violet thought the fairy was a little too "peppy" and "bright", but Wynona loved them both and had no intention of giving either up. They'd simply have to learn to get along.

Prim danced as she sang, picking up tablecloths and gathering a pile of laundry. If she had been born with wings, the fairy would have been several inches off the floor, but just as Wynona had been born with no magic and Violet was a purple mouse, Prim had a little quirk which made her different.

Wynona paused for a second as she realized how much her curse had influenced her life. Escaping her family had been an act of sheer desperation, but being raised with people who hated her had taught Wynona about how precious life was. Before ever opening her shop, Wynona had tried to stop Celia from killing Violet. Even a rodent deserved a chance, though the Le Doux family as a whole didn't see it that way.

It was Wynona's quick thinking and unknown magic that had turned the mouse purple and brought them together as the pair they were now. And Wynona's friendship with Prim had been built on the foundation that they were both outcasts. Even allowing Lusgu to stay on as janitor was Wynona's way of trying to help someone who didn't seem to fit in.

Careful, Violet warned since Wynona's wall had dropped during her daydreaming. *You're awfully close to admitting your granny was right.*

Wynona took in a deep breath through her nose and used her back to push open the kitchen door since her hands were full of a heavy tray. "I know," she whispered. "But perhaps I need to be willing to see her side."

Letting pain go in order to do that isn't easy.

Wynona nodded, but let the conversation drop. She wasn't ready to say Granny had done a good thing, but she would try and keep an open mind.

"Wy?"

Prim pushed the kitchen door open. "Lover boy is here." Prim smirked.

Wynona smiled. "He can hear you say that, you know."

"I never thought he couldn't." Prim scowled. "Now if he would just leave giant man back at the station."

"Giant man?" Wynona asked, walking toward the door. Rascal was coughing as if he had choked on something, but the curve of his lips said it was covering something that made him laugh.

"Oh. Hello, Daemon," Wynona said, realizing the men had arrived together. She walked over to Rascal and whacked him on the back a couple of times. "Do you need a drink?" she asked sweetly as she realized what Rascal had been laughing about. Luckily, Daemon didn't have the same sensitive hearing as the wolf.

Rascal shook his head and wrapped an arm around her waist. "No." He cleared his throat again. "I think I'm okay." Still grinning, he bent to kiss her temple. "How was your day?"

"Better than yours, I think," Wynona replied. "We saw the headline about Mrs. Roseburg's death."

Daemon groaned. "Yeah...that's a media circus in the making." He looked a little sheepish when Prim snorted.

Good grief. What is her problem with him? Wynona thought.

Can't you hear her heart rate pick up? Violet asked. *She's attracted to the big lug.*

Wynona's eyes widened. She had been guessing that Daemon was attracted to Prim since he blushed every time she was around, but Prim ignored him! In fact, she went out of her way to *not* acknowledge him.

I didn't say she handled it well, Violet snapped. *Maybe if she'd sing while he was around, she'd scare him off and it would be a moot point anyway.*

Rascal choked again. With his soulmate connection to Wynona completed, he could hear her familiar loud and clear, making him privy to the mouse's rude comments.

Enough, Wynona scolded. *They're adults. Let's let them figure it out themselves.*

Violet grumbled, but let it go.

Looking back at the group, Wynona realized Daemon and Prim were both looking at her and Rascal as if they were crazy.

Rascal got himself under control and straightened. "Speaking of," he said in an authoritative voice, "we have to get back to the station soon." He opened his eyes wide, giving Wynona fake puppy dog eyes. "We were hoping you had something we could eat really quick before going back to work."

Wynona pursed her lips. "First Prim and now you two? I feel like I run a cafeteria!"

Rascal pulled her closer before she could escape and kissed her cheek again, nuzzling his nose and whispering against her skin. "But you run the best cafeteria in Hex Haven," he said. "Plus, I needed to see you. It's going to be a late night."

Wynona softened, but still pulled away. She loved it when he teased her like that, but they had an audience. "Fine, fine," she teased, softening her words with a smile. "Have a seat and I'll be right out."

"Use your magic," Rascal told her.

Wynona paused, then sighed. "Shoot. I never remember to do that!"

He shrugged. "I know. But you need to practice using it in every day life in order to be more in control."

Daemon raised his hand. "Plus, I'm here and can help control it."

Wynona nodded and gave the black hole a tired smile. "Thank you. I appreciate that."

Prim sniffed, but didn't say anything, so Wynona ignored her.

"Okay...here we go." Wynona's nerves were instantly on edge. The truth of the matter was, her magic scared her. It was like a living, breathing force and she could understand why Granny Saffron had said she was the most powerful witch in existence. It felt like she had a power the size of the Atlantic Ocean at her beck and call and Wynona had no idea what to do with it.

She raised her hand, purple sparks immediately beginning to dance among her fingers.

Hang on. Violet scrambled down the table leg and rushed to Wynona, climbing until she was on Wynona's shoulder. She could better help Wynona control her magic if they were touching skin to skin.

Nodding firmly and with determination, Wynona walked to the kitchen door and opened it, holding it open so she was working from a small distance. Carefully, she aimed her magic at a clean tray, then the containers of pastries. With a flick of her fingers, the stove came to life and Wynona's eyes widened when the gas flame was a little higher than she was comfortable with.

"Facilis," came a gruff voice.

The flame grew smaller and Wynona threw a grateful look to her janitor. She had no idea how the brownie had such power, but it was useful nonetheless and Wynona understood why Granny Saffron had put him in her path.

Focus, Violet snapped.

Wynona went back to wiggling her fingers, purple ribbons dancing across the room as she brought a water-filled teapot to the heat and all the ingredients she needed to the tray.

It took another five minutes of work and Wynona was feeling overly warm by the time she was done, but when the tray settled on the table without anything breaking or spilling, Wynona absolutely counted it as a success.

"You're amazing," Rascal whispered, hugging her from behind and kissing her neck.

Wynona relaxed into his hold. "Thanks. I know there are more efficient ways to have done that, but I figured this required a bit more control." She could feel him nod behind her.

"Good idea. The ease and shortcuts can come later." He gave her one last squeeze. "But for now, let's eat."

Wynona huffed a laugh. Her shifter was always hungry. She joined the rest of her friends at the table, then stood up and went back to the kitchen. "Lusgu?"

It took a moment, but the brownie finally poked his head out from the portal he had created in the wall. He looked far from pleased with the interruption, but Wynona ignored his scowl.

She took a fortifying breath. "Would you like to join us?"

For just a split second, Lusgu's face softened, but the look was gone so fast that Wynona knew she would have missed it if she hadn't been paying attention. Finally, the brownie shook his head. "Too messy," he grumbled, his head disappearing into the wall.

Wynona sighed. She knew she wouldn't get him back out, but offering the olive branch had been the right thing to do. She forced a tight smile and turned back to the room. "Let's get you fed before you go back to work. I'd hate to have Chief Ligurio complain that you two weren't doing your fair share."

Chuckling ensued and Wynona sat down and let herself enjoy. She could certainly come back to all the chaos in her life after her friends were gone. It wasn't going anywhere.

CHAPTER 5

The shop was due to open in twenty minutes, but someone was already banging at the door. Frowning, Wynona walked over, a little frustrated that she had a patron unwilling to follow the rules.

"I'm coming, I'm coming," she murmured to herself.

"Wy?"

Wynona gasped and hurried to unlock and pull the door open. "Rascal! What are you doing here?" He often stopped by after his shift was over, but it was unusual for her to see him in the mornings. As soon as she opened the door and looked at him, a feeling of weariness slammed into her.

Put up your barriers, Violet shouted.

Wynona squeezed her eyes shut and shoved a steel wall around her brain. Immediately, the feeling receded.

"Sorry," Rascal said, his voice low and gravelly. He looked a mess. His hair was always slightly unkempt, but now it was standing on end. His eyes were bloodshot and shining a bright burnished gold, telling the world his wolf was close to the surface. His uniform shirt was untucked and his boots covered in dust. "Can I, uh...come in?"

"Oh my gosh, yes!" Wynona stepped back. She looked him over as he came in and her heart pinched. Something was definitely wrong. "What's going on? You feel exhausted."

Rascal nodded and pushed a hand through his hair. "We've been up all night at the crime scene."

"Crime scene?"

Rascal blew out a breath. "The one with Mrs. Roseburg."

Wynona's eyes bulged and Violet scampered across the room, climbing Rascal's pants until she settled in his pocket. "All night? Why in the world were you there so long?"

"You know how I mentioned the media had gotten a hold of the story too early?"

She nodded.

"Well, we couldn't get them off the grounds. The daughter wanted to talk to everybody, milking the story for all it's worth." He walked the rest of the way into the dining room and plopped onto a wingback chair in the corner, leaning his head back and closing his eyes. "We put up a tape line, but with the family giving the journalists permission to be there, our work was slowed down."

Wynona stood next to the chair and ran her fingers through his hair.

Rascal moaned and relaxed into her touch. "I needed some of your famous tea to keep me awake last night."

"From the bloodshot eyes you're sporting, I think your wolf helped you."

Rascal nodded, his eyes still closed. "I had to shift a few times in order to keep the perimeter clear."

Wynona snorted. "You're telling me you turned wolf in order to get the media to back off?"

A half smirk tugged at his lips. "If it works, it works."

Wynona smiled and shook her head. "Would you like some tea now? Or are you headed home to nap?"

Rascal sighed and opened his eyes, looking up at her. "I don't have a lot of time before I have to be back at the office. This case is a doozy. Can I grab twenty minutes on the couch in your office?"

"Of course. You know I'm always happy to help." She took his hand and guided him down the hall. "When you're up, I'll have something ready for you to help." She pushed open her office door. "What's making this one so difficult?"

Rascal teetered to the side before righting himself, then opened his mouth to answer, but Wynona covered it with her fingers.

"Forget I asked. You need rest." She pulled him farther in and helped him lay down. Grabbing an afghan off the back of the couch, she covered him all the way up to his chin. "Sleep. I'll see you later."

Rascal grabbed her hand before she could escape too far. "Thank you," he muttered, pulling her fingers in and kissing them.

Wynona smiled down, though his eyes were closed. "Always."

"Love you," he grumbled as she walked out the door.

"Love you too." Wynona carefully shut the door and briskly walked to the dining room. She needed to get his brew together before her regular patrons showed up. The first hour after opening was always busy.

Use your magic, Violet called out, running behind her. She must have crawled out of Rascal's pocket when he laid down.

"Right," Wynona answered. Taking a deep breath, she began moving her fingers, letting the teacup that was speaking to her float through the air and land on a side table. Heading to the kitchen, she once again forced herself to stand in the doorway, but this time she closed her eyes, picturing Rascal. She did best when she could see a person to know what their needs were.

Keep your hand down, Violet encouraged. *Let your thoughts do the actions.*

Pushing a long breath out and dropping her shoulders into a relaxed state, Wynona went through the whole process only in her mind. She heard a few clinks and shifting of objects and she hoped that she wasn't making a mess. Lusgu had been up and about this morning, so she trusted he would stop her if she got out of hand.

Look!

Wynona opened her eyes and her jaw dropped. She'd done it. She'd done it! A tray sat on the table with a kettle of water. An infuser filled with herbs waited on a small plate and another plate with three croissants sat in the other corner, creating room in the middle for the teacup she had already picked out.

Wynona turned slightly, beckoning the cup forward, and carefully landed it right in the middle.

Lusgu walked by at that exact moment and with a careless flick of his finger, the kettle began to boil.

All of Wynona's pride crashed like the fragile china she had been handling the moment before. She had forgotten to heat the water. Or had she imagined it and it hadn't worked? Now she couldn't remember.

Violet patted Wynona just under her ear. *Almost there.*

Wynona rolled her eyes. "Thank you, Lusgu," she said. She really was grateful for the brownie, but sometimes his help made her feel like an idiot. She made tea for a living and she had forgotten to boil the water. Wouldn't her customers be impressed?

Concentrating again, Wynona lifted the tray and brought it out of the kitchen, settling it on the side table that had held the teacup only a moment before. She would wait a few more moments before immersing the infuser.

Glancing at the clock, she realized it was time to open and there would undoubtedly be ladies on her doorstep. Straightening her hair and blouse, Wynona went to the door and ushered everyone in.

It took her almost exactly an hour to get everyone settled, and then a moment of peace before she realized Rascal hadn't come out of her office yet. With a discreet jerk of her finger, she had the water reboiling, and set the infuser inside the cup, adding the hot water before walking down the hall.

"Rascal?" She poked her head in the door, then smiled. The poor man was still knocked out cold. He really must have had a rough night. She bit her lip, debating whether or not to wake him. He had said he only had twenty minutes, but it had been an hour. She sighed. She probably needed to get him moving, but she hated to do it.

Walking over, she perched her hip on the edge of the couch and cupped his cheek. "Rascal," she said softly. "Come on, handsome. Time to get up."

He groaned and rolled over. "Ten more minutes."

Wynona laughed softly. He apparently liked his sleep as much as he liked his food. "You've been sleeping over an hour."

Rascal's eyes widened and he sat up so far he nearly bonked heads with her. "Whoa." Rascal grabbed her upper arms, keeping them from hitting foreheads. He blinked rapidly. "I don't think the room is supposed to spin."

Wynona stood and backed up so he could follow. "No, it's not. Which is why I have tea and a couple of rolls for you. Hold on." She went to open the door, but Rascal took her arm.

"You're the best." He kissed her temple. "Thanks." Without another word, he slid out the door and turned toward the restroom.

Wynona let the heat of his touch settle in her chest and tried to keep her smiling to a minimum as she walked out to get his food. She checked all her customers, then met Rascal back in the office. "So..." she began as he dug in. "Tell me about the case."

Rascal grinned. "Are you thinking about getting yourself hired again?"

Wynona smiled back, but shook her head. "No. And I don't think Chief Ligurio would appreciate it if I did."

Rascal shrugged. "I don't know. We're kind of stumped on this one."

Wynona leaned back, folding her arms over her chest. "How so?"

Rascal wiped his mouth and sighed. "Hang on." He grabbed his phone and punched out a text before settling in at the table. "Needed to tell Chief why I was late." He blew out a breath.

The rough stubble on his chin was drawing Wynona's eye and she found herself wanting to run her fingers over it. She blinked away the thought when he began speaking, forcing herself to pay attention.

"We're gonna have to work fast on this one, with the media breathing down our necks," he began. "But the suspect situation is a mess. She had two kids and an ex-husband. The ex claims to have a solid alibi, though we've only spoken to him on the phone at this point." Rascal twisted his lips to the side. "The daughter was cut off a year ago and has been living with a friend. She claims she was there. The son is the only one living at home and is as spoiled as spoiled gets." He shook his head. "Both kids were eating up the attention, thriving on the media's noise."

Wynona nodded. "I remember. I haven't seen them in years, but even as children they were difficult to handle. After Ms. Roseburg's divorce, I didn't see her as much." Wynona shrugged. "Not that I ever got close to her, mind you. But she spent less time with my mom after that."

Rascal rolled his eyes. "Right."

Wynona mock glared. "I can't help who they are."

He leaned over and kissed her cheek. "They aren't you and that's all that matters."

His words brought to mind Granny's explanation and Wynona found herself reaching for one of his croissants before pulling back. She still felt completely unsettled over the whole situation, but her hips did *not* need her eating her worries in carbs.

"Anyway...there were also twenty-three cats living in the mansion—"

Wynona choked. "Twenty-three! Why did she need so many? Was she using them like Ms. Soulton did? Were they for enhancing her magic?"

Rascal shrugged. "I don't know. They weren't locked in a lab, if that helps. But they're definitely roaming around the place and the son claims there are twenty-three of them."

"Huh." Wynona frowned. "That just seems like an odd amount. Why twenty-three? Why not an even two dozen?"

"No idea." Rascal jammed the last of the bread in his mouth and cleaned his hands. "I hate to eat and run, but I need to get back. We're actually pulling people in to interview today and I'd like to listen in on them."

"Can I fix you dinner tonight?" Wynona asked, standing as he did.

"I'd love that." Rascal gave her another kiss, this one on her waiting lips and much softer and longer than his earlier ones, before winking and ducking out the door.

Wynona put a hand to her heated cheeks and sighed. She loved that shifter and was so grateful he was in her life. He had become her anchor in the storm and she was better for it.

Cleaning up the tray, she carried it to the kitchen, checking in with her customers along the way. Her pace picked up when she noticed a few needing food or tea and Wynona threw herself back into work.

The rest of the afternoon flew by with a steady stream of customers, but even doing her favorite job in the world wasn't enough to keep her mind from wandering back to the case Rascal was working on. He was right, it would be high profile for sure, especially once the will had been read. If the daughter had been cut off, it would be interesting to see if she inherited anything, or if the favored, but spoiled son got it all.

And why in the world did she have so many cats? She was plenty powerful by herself. In the witch community, needing an outside influence was sometimes construed as a sign of weakness, and Ms. Roseburg was anything but weak. She had money, looks and magic, second only to the Le Douxs. Were the cats there for magic? Or simply because she liked animals?

Wynona shook her head. It really didn't matter. She wasn't going to help on the case and it really wasn't any of her business. Her life was complicated enough as it was.

Agreed, Violet offered from her spot under the china cabinet. *No way are we working another case with an insane number of feline predators.*

Wynona could hear the disdain in the mouse's voice. *Don't worry,* Wynona thought with a grin. *Even if we got involved, you've got a wolf protector. Those cats wouldn't stand a chance.*

Still... Violet sniffed. *Dirty little buggers. We're better off without them.*

Wynona smiled and went to get another kettle. Her reasons might be different, but Violet was right. They were better off staying away from this one.

CHAPTER 6

S teady...steady... Violet encouraged.

Wynona allowed a small smile to cross her face as she watched the dishes and trays move throughout the room. The shop had closed twenty minutes ago and instead of her usual habit of walking around to pick up, Wynona was using her magic. It was so much easier now that the curse was fully gone, though she still worried about using a sledgehammer for a job that required a toothpick, at times.

Her ability to hold back the mass of magic, however, had greatly strengthened since her magical burst had burned through the last threads of the curse. While Wynona wouldn't describe things as easy yet, she had great hope they would become so.

Not to mention, it'll make your life a lot easier, Violet responded wryly.

"Now if only blocking my thoughts was as easy," Wynona muttered. She threw up her barrier in her mind. She really needed to be careful about that. Her barrier needed to be instinctual, yet like using magic for everyday life, Wynona still forgot about it. She didn't mind being able to communicate with Violet, but she didn't appreciate having every thought in her brain broadcast through her familiar and subsequently, her soulmate.

Still...she had obviously improved in her control over easy things, she knew with a little extra practice she could get her mental situation set up as well.

The last teapot rattled on the tray as the front door opened. "Prim!" Wynona scolded, putting her hands on her hips. She glared at the doorway, waiting for her friend to come through. "You really need to knock instead of—" Her words trailed off as she realized it wasn't Prim. "Rascal! How did you get in? The door was locked!"

Rascal frowned. He looked even worse for wear than he had this morning. "Uh...no it wasn't."

Wynona wracked her brain. She was positive she had locked that door.

I don't remember you locking it, Violet offered.

"Wow." Wynona rubbed her forehead. "I guess I'm not doing as well as I thought." Her forgetfulness was a testament to how full her brain was. She was still struggling with Granny and now worried about Rascal and the murder, it was a wonder the door had even been closed.

"Can I sit down?" Rascal asked. One side of his lips twitched. "Or will I get another scolding?"

Wynona mock glared. "Prim broke in the other day and I haven't forgiven her for it yet." Rushing over, Wynona tugged on his arm. "But sit down, or you might fall down." Once he was seated in the cushioned recliner, Wynona really studied him. Her initial perusal had been correct. He was done. There was no way he could go back to the precinct tonight. "You didn't get a break, did you?" she murmured, brushing his unruly hair away from his forehead.

Rascal closed his eyes and shook his head back and forth. "We're fighting time, since the media are all so close. Usually, we can work for a bit without their interference, but the ghost reporters are worse than normal, plus all the social media sites." He groaned. "If we could just get the kids to stop talking to people, we might be able to make some headway."

"Let me get you something to drink and then I'll take care of dinner," Wynona said softly. Her heart pinched. Rascal was such a good officer. It was no wonder he was the deputy chief at his age. When they first met, Rascal had teased it was because of his nose, but Wynona now knew better. Rascal cared and he went the extra mile.

He wasn't willing to just send his men out, he was going to be among them.

Lusgu was already heating water when Wynona stepped into the kitchen. "Thank you," she offered.

The brownie grunted, not looking at her, but his grunt seemed a little less disdainful than normal. Could he be softening toward her?

Violet snorted and Wynona shook her head. As interesting as that might be, it wasn't a priority right now. She began walking to the cupboards, but her familiar stopped her.

Powers, the mouse stated firmly.

"Right." Wynona huffed. She closed her eyes and worked her way through everything she needed, only this time working slightly faster. Lusgu had already taken care of the heat, so Wynona only needed to gather ingredients.

A proud smile lit her face as she walked back out, the tray floating behind her. It seemed when she had a mission, her magic was all too happy to cooperate. She mentally set the tray down and held up her hand before Rascal could reach for anything. He needed something to brighten his day and this wasn't perfect, but it would do.

Narrowing her gaze in concentration, she poured the water, stirred the infuser and sent the cup and saucer into Rascal's waiting hand.

"You're amazing," Rascal said with a smile.

Wynona couldn't help but return it. "I'm learning," she admitted, then plopped herself in the chair next to his. "Tell me what's going on."

Rascal smelled the tea and sighed. "I don't even know what that is, but it smells good." He chuckled. "My brothers would have a heyday with the fact that I'm a regular tea drinker now."

"Comes with the territory of a tea healing witch being your soulmate, I suppose," Wynona said lightly. "Oh. Hang on." She grabbed her phone and punched in a few buttons on an app. "Okay. Pizza will be here in twenty." Tucking the phone back in her pocket, she focused on him again. "I know you can't share all of it, but maybe talking about what you can will put it in perspective."

His twinkle came back to those golden eyes. "You're curious, aren't you? You just can't help yourself."

Wynona rolled her own black ones. "I was trying to help."

He took a long sip. "I'll pretend that's the real reason...for now." He smirked.

Wynona tilted her head and waited him out. She would never admit he was right, he already knew.

Rascal sighed and slumped in the seat. "The family still believes it was an accident, and everyone conveniently had an alibi."

"Still just the ex-husband and the two kids? No one else?"

Rascal shrugged. "We're looking into the possibility that Ms. Roseburg was having an...interlude...with the pool boy."

Wynona pinched her lips. "You're kidding, right? Why does that feel so cliche?"

Rascal returned her smile. "Because it is. Wealthy heiress, handsome young pool boy? It's the oldest trick in the book."

"Is there any possibility he killed her for her money?" Wynona pursed her lips. "Why not just marry her?"

Rascal scratched behind his ear. "Marriage does seem simpler, but creatures have killed for far less reasons than the millions she had in the bank."

"Is there going to be a will reading?" Wynona asked.

Rascal nodded and drained his cup. "Yeah. Though the son is positive it'll all go to him." He scrunched his nose. "I'm surprised you haven't been following it all online. The media have been having a heyday with the siblings fighting about the money."

Wynona blew out a breath. "I hate that money separates families so easily."

Rascal shrugged. "I think I've gotten used to it. It's almost always a factor in a case."

"Which is incredibly sad."

He nodded. "I won't argue that. But when creatures feel they're owed something, they'll go to great lengths to get it."

"And the ex? What was his name?" Wynona rubbed Violet's head while she searched her brain. "Mr...Killoran? Is that right?"

Rascal beamed. "Good memory. Yes. Ms. Roseburg never took on his name. It allowed her to keep her family fortune for herself only."

"Who's the family lawyer?"

"Mr. Romulus Melion." Rascal yawned. "He's a leopard shifter and has a reading planned for after the funeral in a few days."

"Do *you* think it's an accident?" Wynona pressed.

Rascal shrugged. "I'm not sure. All signs point to her slipping and falling in the pool, but I think some pieces are missing. And with this much money involved..." He didn't need to finish his thought, Wynona knew exactly what he meant.

"Tell me what seems suspicious."

Rascal took a deep breath, then leaned over and pulled her out of her seat and onto his lap. "There. I can think better this way."

Wynona smiled as she reached one arm around his shoulders. "You might be able to, but my brain gets all muddled."

He tapped her nose. "I'll take that as a compliment."

Violet snorted. *You would.*

Rascal laughed, the sound glorious and free, which helped lighten Wynona's worry for him. They'd get through this, one day at a time. She'd just have to make sure he was fed and got good sleep in the meantime.

"Your suspicions?" she pressed.

"Right." Rascal settled his arms around her waist. "The poolboy is a merman. The fact that she drowned is hard to overlook in that case."

Wynona raised her eyebrows. "You think he murdered her?"

"I think it could have been murder or simply play time in the pool gone wrong, but it seems a little odd that she died in his domain."

Wynona nodded, encouraging him to continue.

"And the kids. No one is upset by their mother's death. Again, no real proof, just...suspicious. People who are disliked by those closest to them seem to have shorter life spans."

Wynona shivered. This just made her glad all over again that she had escaped her family. "Did you look for signs of magic? Did Daemon check things over?"

Rascal nodded. "Yeah. The pool was clear of magic." Rascal grinned. "We remembered to have him check this time. Aren't you proud of us?"

Daemon's ability to see residual magic was something Wynona had brought to light and pointed out how it could help investigations. It had taken a little time, however, before the team began using it on a regular basis.

"And the body?"

Rascal shrugged. "The body was fine. No signs of trauma. She wasn't in a swimsuit though. Which is just another point toward the suspicious category."

"Was there any magic on the body?"

Rascal stiffened.

Wynona gave him a look. "You didn't look, did you?"

He growled low. "I thought of the crime scene, but didn't think of the body. You'd think after watching Daemon work with that breaking curse, it would be the first thing we thought of."

He reached into his pocket and pulled out a cell phone. "Chief," Rascal said in a strong tone. Gone was the weary, broken shifter who had entered her door a while before. He was in full police mode now. "We need Skymaw to check the body for magic."

Rascal nodded slowly and Wynona could hear the rumblings of Chief Ligurio, though she didn't know what he was saying.

"The body's still down in the morgue. The autopsy hasn't come through yet, though I expect it any time. Now would be ideal to send him down there." Rascal paused again. "Right. I'm at the tea shop. I'll wait to hear."

Wynona ran her fingers through his hair. "Where's Daemon?"

Rascal looked up at her. "He'd already gone home. Chief's going to call him back and send him to the morgue. The body should still be out since we don't have the autopsy yet." He pushed a hand through his hair. "I can't believe I missed that."

"You've been so tired since this all started, it's a wonder you can remember your name," she teased. A knock came on the door and Wynona pulled out of his hold. "That's got to be dinner. Hang on."

"I can get it," Rascal said, starting to rise, but Wynona pushed him back down.

"Let me take care of my shifter," she said, kissing his lips lightly.

Rascal's eyes began to glow and he sat back down. "I think I can handle that."

She grinned and walked away, letting a little of her feelings flow through their connection. Rascal responded with another growl, but this one was anything but angry. This soulmate thing was going to be fun.

She was back in minutes, two boxes of pizza in her hands. She paused at the look on Rascal's face. "What did I miss?"

"Skymaw was already at the station, picking up something he'd forgotten." Rascal's eyes hardened. "He ran downstairs and looked her over."

Wynona knew she wasn't going to like what he said next.

"There was a spot of magic on the back of her head."

"The back of her head?" Wynona's eyebrows shot up as she realized what that meant. "It was a healing spell, wasn't it?"

Rascal nodded. "That's Skymaw's best guess."

"So she was hurt and someone healed her." Wynona shook her head, her heart plummeting to her stomach. "This wasn't an accident."

"Nope." Rascal's glowing eyes had nothing to do with their flirting now. Instead, his face had gone hard and his demeanor stiff. "As of right now, we're looking for a murderer."

CHAPTER 7

Wynona pulled her helmet off her head with a sigh and shook out her hair. She wondered how Rascal was. After a quick bite of dinner, he had rushed back to the station. It looked like Wynona was spending her evening alone.

Violet snorted and Wynona amended her thought.

Sorry. It'll be just the two of us.

Violet sniffed and washed her face. *I have a date.*

"What?" Wynona shouted. She glared down at her shoulder. "What do you mean, you have a date?"

Violet scrambled down Wynona's shoulder and scurried away. *Sorry! Gotta hurry.*

Wynona blew out a breath, causing her hair to shift with the wind she created. "Sheesh, even my mouse has company tonight." Trudging inside, she dropped her supplies on the counter and didn't bother to put them away. Lusgu would have a fit if she'd been at the shop, but this was her home and Wynona didn't have the energy to deal with it at the moment.

She immediately went for the kettle, then stopped herself. "Use it for everyday things," she scolded, then sighed. Goodness, was she worn out.

Imagine how Rascal feels!

Violet's mental shout made Wynona jerk, but she couldn't see the purple mouse, so she chose to let it go. Stepping back, she used her magic to fill the kettle and then imagined it boiling, attempting to forgo using the stove.

The water sputtered a little, but ultimately the heat worked well. With a smile, Wynona finished making her tea and walked to the couch. Maybe she would simply read a good book tonight and let her mind rest from all the decisions that were resting on her shoulders.

Granny was probably waiting impatiently to talk to Wynona again, but Wynona just wasn't ready. When she spoke to Granny again, Wynona not only wanted to be able to forgive, but she also wanted to know exactly how to address Granny's desire for Wynona to try and take over Hex Haven.

Just as she was taking a soothing sip of chamomile and mint, there was a knock from the front entryway.

"Who in the world?" Wynona opened her senses and realized that Rascal was there. Jumping to her feet, she rushed to unlock the door. "Rascal! I didn't..." Wynona trailed off. Rascal wasn't alone. "Hello, Chief Ligurio." Wynona nodded to Daemon, who stood behind his commanding officers.

"Ms. Le Doux," Chief Ligurio said sharply. "May we come in?"

Wynona nodded. "Of course." She stepped aside and pulled the door farther open to allow the three men inside. "Have a seat, please." She waved to the sitting room and closed the door behind Rascal.

"Sorry," he whispered, touching her low back and kissing her cheek. "But he insisted."

"Insisted on what?" Wynona whispered back.

Rascal tilted his head toward his chief and shook the answer *no*.

Wynona pinched her lips. Darn that vampire hearing.

"Ms. Le Doux?"

"Coming." Wynona gave Rascal one last look before walking to a chair. She folded her hands in her lap. "What can I do for you, Chief?"

Chief Lugurio cleared his throat. "I'd like to talk to you about your powers."

Wynona blinked.

"After your...explosion at the witch's home, I told you I would want a full accounting." He raised a black eyebrow. "Strongclaw told me you've been dealing with family issues, so I let it go, but now I need to know. Just what is it you can do?"

Wynona's eyes darted to Rascal, who looked sympathetic, but also resolved. Apparently, he wasn't going to run interference for her this time. It was just as well. She had dodged the bullet long enough. Wynona had kept a secret from him and after all they had been through together, he deserved to know the truth.

"The explosion you were referring to," she began, "was the rest of my curse being broken."

He nodded. "I had guessed that. I'm also guessing that means the person who cursed you died."

Wynona nodded. "Yes. It was my grandmother."

The vampire went very still, which made him appear much more like the corpse he was. "Your grandmother?" he asked carefully.

Wynona nodded.

"I remember working the case when you were born," Chief Ligurio said softly. "Your grandmother, Saffron Le Doux, was one of the biggest supporters of us finding the culprit."

Wynona looked away. "So I heard."

He leaned forward, his red eyes flaring. "I think you need to tell me everything."

So Wynona did. It took a full thirty minutes, but she told him everything. *Well...*she amended in her mind, *everything except my situation with Rascal.* They didn't need to announce their soulmate status to the world. It was a gift and Wynona was going to keep it safe.

By now the chief had leaned back in his seat and was studying her hard. "Show me." It wasn't a demand, but it was awfully close.

Wynona considered refusing, but what good would it do? Once again, she felt as if she owed him something for lying for so long. Wiggling her fingers, she showed him the purple sparks, then brought her teacup over from its spot on the side table.

That eyebrow went up again. "Anything else?"

Wynona gave him a look. "I'm not a trained monkey," she replied.

"I understand that," he snapped. "But I need to know what you can do so I know if I can use you."

"Chief Ligurio, I don't plan to make a habit of helping solve your cases."

"I know *you* think that, Ms. Le Doux," he said with a smirk. "But both of us know you're too curious for your own good, not to mention you seem to have a deep sense of justice. The idea of someone being falsely accused or someone suffering needlessly bothers you." He paused, the smirk still on his face, as if he understood exactly how those words made Wynona squirm. "Your soulmate is the lead on my detective team and I'd be a fool not to think about how your connection and your skills could help us keep the streets a little safe in Hex Haven."

Wynona considered his words, noting that he already knew about the soulmate bond. While she might have owed him an explanation, they were crossing into other territory here. She didn't owe him help and she didn't owe him a demonstration. At least not more than she already had given him. "What are you wanting me to do?" she asked. She could at least hear him out, even if she ultimately turned him down.

"Can you read the leaves in the bottom of your cup?"

Wynona frowned and stared at her tea. "I'm not sure. I haven't tried a deliberate one since the curse-breaking."

"You don't have to," Rascal said quickly. His brows were furrowed, showing his concern, and Wynona couldn't blame him. He had seen her magic since the beginning, when she'd nearly maimed her friends and hurt herself. It made complete sense that he would worry for her.

Chief Ligurio glared. "Ms. Le Doux. I'm not going to beg, but this isn't just about you. It's about helping others and using your powers for good." He leaned in. "In fact, this is about the exact reason your grandmother saw fit to bind your powers. Helping us would be fulfilling the very destiny she set you up for."

Anger was starting to build in Wynona. "I decide my destiny, Chief Ligurio," she said in a soft but firm voice. "My grandmother made decisions before I was able to myself and I'm still trying to come to grips with what she did to my life. While I'm grateful for some aspects, I find that others deciding who and what I should be isn't how I want to live my life."

The vampire nodded. "I can understand that."

"Yet you're still trying to manipulate me into helping you."

Chief Ligurio snorted. "I suppose that's true." He rubbed the back of his neck in a rare show of emotion. "Ms. Le Doux." He paused. "You once gave me leave to call you Wynona. May I still do that?"

Wynona nodded. She liked the chief and didn't want to fight with him, but she was also learning she wanted to like herself. At first that had simply meant not being like her family's legacy. Now she was beginning to understand that it meant choosing her own path no matter what others thought, even those who claimed to love her the most.

"Wynona, I'm asking...not ordering...I'm *asking* if you would please consider showing me your powers so we can determine whether or not they will help us in the case."

"I'm here, Wynona," Daemon inserted for the first time since the men had arrived. "If you're worried about things getting out of control, I can help."

"Do you still blow things up?" Chief Ligurio asked, not seeming worried in the least.

Wynona shrugged. "It's better now, but I'm still a novice." She turned toward the kitchen and took a few seconds to bring a tea tray with cups and the few leftover cookies she had into the room. "Manipulating objects is my main concern right now. I haven't pushed to harder skills because I'm trying to build the foundational skills."

"Understood." Chief Ligurio took his floating cup. "Thank you," he said politely. His demeanor was much more relaxed than usual, and especially since he had arrived.

Wynona wasn't sure what exactly had brought it on, but she wasn't upset about it. She had wanted the chief to treat her as an asset since she'd met him. Now that he wanted it, however, she was unsure. "I just don't see how I can be of help." She waved at Daemon. "Daemon can see the residual magic and with witches involved, that should be all you need. The merman, if he was actually involved, doesn't have any regular magic, and I haven't heard anything through the grapevine to make me believe my powers are going to make or break this case for you."

Chief Ligurio opened his mouth to respond, but a knock caught them all off guard.

Rascal immediately began to growl and Wynona turned to him with surprised eyes. "Who is it?" she asked.

Rascal stood and marched toward the door. "Your sister."

Wynona jumped to her feet, her tea sloshing over her hand. "Celia?"

"Wynona!" Celia yelled from the doorway. "Call off the puppy."

Chief Ligurio pushed past Wynona and stood behind his deputy chief, who was blocking Celia from entering. "If he's such a puppy, why don't you give him a good scratch and walk in yourself?"

Celia sneered before turning her dark gaze to Wynona. "Mom and Dad won't be pleased with the company you're keeping."

"Your parents have no say in Wynona's life," Rascal said in his low tone.

Celia rolled her eyes. "Neither do you. Perhaps you should let the little witch speak for herself."

Wynona pushed her way past the large vampire and stood at Rascal's shoulder. "Rascal can speak for me anytime," she said softly. "Why are you here, Celia?"

Celia smiled widely, showing off her straight white teeth. "Why, to issue an invitation to my dear sister. Aren't you going to let me in?"

"I don't think that's a good idea," Wynona said. Inviting her volatile sister inside with three police officers, one of which Celia had dated under false pretenses, was asking for something horrible to happen. "I'm not interested in going to tea or lunch with you and Mom. Please tell her that you delivered your message and it was turned down." Wynona turned to go, but Celia grabbed her arm.

Wynona spun, jerking her arm away

Celia pulled back, hissing. She looked at her fingers. "That wasn't very nice," she said tightly.

Wynona tried not to react when she realized she had a purple haze covering her body. It must have repelled Celia when she had been too grabby. "Don't touch me without permission," Wynona said weakly, still trying to process the new skill she'd discovered. It would be a miracle if she managed to survive the arrival of every part of her magic.

Celia glared, ignoring Rascal's growl. "I guess it's true then. Mom said your magic was worth coming after..." She trailed off, almost sounding sorry, but not enough to soften her stand. Celia threw her hair back and straightened her shoulders. "If you don't come nicely, you know they'll take you by force."

Rascal growled out a curse and his upper body began to shake.

Wynona could see the fur forming on the back of his hands as he fought his urge to protect her. His wolf wasn't going to stay back for much longer. She grabbed his arm, forgetting about the purple haze.

Rascal yelped and jerked away from her, but his shaking stopped. "Geez, Wy."

She covered her mouth. "I'm so sorry! I forgot it was there!"

Celia snickered. "Having a little trouble with control, dear sister? We can help with that."

Rascal went right back to his protective stance. "She's not going anywhere with you."

Celia gave him an unimpressed look. "You're no match for me, dog."

"And you're no match for the law," Chief Ligurio said from behind Wynona. "Go home, Celia. Or I'll tell your parents where, or better yet, *who* you were with last Friday."

"How did you—?" Celia snapped her mouth shut. "Fine," she forced out. "But this isn't over." Her eyes bore into Wynona. "Mom and Dad won't send messengers much longer. They want your magic and they'll do anything to get it."

"Goodnight, Celia," Wynona said. Careful not to touch Rascal, she stepped back and closed the door. Turning, she watched the three men who had had her back during that little confrontation. Wynona might have been born in privilege and wealth, but her group of friends were worth far more than her family would ever be.

She held up her still glowing hands. "Daemon? A little help?"

CHAPTER 8

Wynona sat down on the couch, leaving quite a bit of space between her and Rascal. She hadn't meant to shock him, but she wasn't quite sure how he was feeling about her at the moment and she didn't want to hash things out with the other guests still in the room. Daemon had sucked the magic out of her, which had helped the protective bubble leave, but Wynona still felt uneasy.

As soon as she sat down, Rascal scooted over and put his arm around her shoulders.

Tears pricked the back of her eyes, but Wynona blinked them back. How was it that she got the sweetest soulmate in the history of soulmates?

He leaned into her ear. "If you'd open your mind, you'd know exactly how I'm feeling and it's not the least bit upset...at you." His voice was so low it was barely audible, but it was the only way to keep their conversation private with supernatural ears in the room.

Wynona looked at him, letting her guard down just enough to realize he was telling the truth. He was absolutely livid at Celia and her family. Toward herself, personally, however, there was nothing but warmth and love. She sighed and leaned into his side. "Thank you."

He nodded and turned back to the chief.

"As you can see, Chief Ligurio," Wynona offered, "I'm not always in control." She held up her hands. "I don't even know what all my powers are yet, and those I do have aren't always easy. I have no idea what that purple...covering was. Obviously, it was protective, but I don't know how I did it, I don't have a name for it and I don't know how to do it again."

The chief studied her, his red eyes narrowed. "I'd like to offer you a deal."

Wynona raised her eyebrows. "I can promise to listen, I can't promise I'll comply."

One side of the vampire's mouth twitched. "Fair enough." He straightened. "It looks like your family is on the move."

Wynona nodded and she felt Rascal stiffen next to her.

"But you're still trying to get control of your magic, which is your best asset against them, correct?"

Again, Wynona nodded.

He leaned forward, resting his elbows on his knees and staring her down. "I can help."

Wynona paused. He had helped at the door, scaring Celia with some kind of secret, but Wynona hadn't paid attention. She'd been too worried about the magic bubbling along her skin that she didn't know what to do with.

Rascal held up a hand. "Hold up. Where's Violet?"

Wynona rolled her eyes. "The little she-devil had a date."

Rascal choked on a laugh. "Really?"

Wynona nodded. "Yeah. Took off without saying goodbye. Must have been someone special."

He grinned. "Good for her."

Wynona shook her head, then turned back to the chief when he cleared his throat. "How do you propose to help, Chief Ligurio?" Wynona asked, coming back to the topic at hand. "I'm grateful for what you said a few minutes ago to Celia, but surely you can't always know what she was doing on a Friday night."

The vampire smirked, looking a little too triumphant. "I have no idea what she was doing last Friday. I just made an educated guess."

Wynona's jaw dropped while Rascal chuckled. "Do you have any idea what she would do if she knew you were lying?"

Chief Ligurio shrugged. "I'm not afraid of your sister."

Wynona snapped her mouth shut. Chief Ligurio and her sister had dated a while back, before Wynona had ever left the castle. She had gathered that the feelings had been real, but Celia had been pushed by their father to manipulate the situation and when Chief Ligurio found out, it ruined everything. Though Wynona was sure there were still some lingering feelings between the two, the bitterness was going to be hard to overcome if they ever gave it another try. "No...I suppose you're not." Wynona couldn't help but laugh under her breath. "Though that would make you one of an elite few."

The chief shrugged. "You mentioned before that you weren't interested in money. If I promised to help use my influence to hold your family off as long as possible, would you promise to help us?"

Wynona had been sure she would automatically say no to his proposal, but he was definitely offering her something useful, and now she wasn't quite so sure.

Rascal squeezed her shoulders. "You can work with me again," he teased, his golden eyes flashing.

"I can't say I didn't enjoy it," Wynona said carefully to the chief. "But I want to have a regular life. I love my tea shop and I want to spend time with friends and...others." She darted a glance toward Rascal, who was still smiling. "I feel like the last month has been one big revelation after another and that everyone around me is wanting not only my time, but wants to control my future."

Chief Ligurio pushed his lips to the side. "I can understand that, though I don't necessarily agree with it. I don't want to control you, Ms. Le Doux. I want your help. I'm asking for it voluntarily, but offering something of value in return."

"And after this? Are you going to continue coming to me each time a case gets difficult?"

"Are you saying you *never* want to help again?" Chief Ligurio snorted. "You forget, I've seen your face when the last piece of the puzzle clicks into place. I know you enjoy it."

"I didn't enjoy being trapped by a witch and almost watching Rascal die," Wynona blurted out before she could think better of it. She had mostly kept those feelings hidden. So much had been happening when she'd woken up from the hospital that her fear over losing Rascal had been shoved to the side.

Talking about another case, however, was bringing them all to the forefront. Especially now that she had acknowledged how much she loved him and understood that their bond was something special, Wynona was terrified of losing him. One moment with their guard down had almost cost her the other half of her soul and she wasn't sure she could do it. She had barely gotten Rascal. She couldn't let go yet.

"Ah..." Chief Ligurio nodded his head slowly. "Now we come to the crux of the matter." He leaned forward again, his face deadly serious. "Wynona, there's no way for me to convince you that your soulmate's job isn't dangerous."

Those dang tears pricked her eyes again and Rascal pressed her in closer to his side.

"And we both know that I can't promise he'll never have his life threatened again." The vampire took a deep breath. "But I can say that he's gotten the position he has for a reason. Strongclaw is a good detective and he cares deeply about justice. That witch caught you all off guard, but his track record is excellent when it comes to dealing with criminals. He lives for it and is better than anyone I know at containing them."

Wynona glanced over at Rascal, who gave her a soft smile.

"And yet he's better with you at his side."

Her head whipped around, her eyes wide. "Excuse me?"

Chief Ligurio put his hands in the air. "You see things outside the box. You have a book education that most of us will never achieve and now you're developing powers that only make you stronger. The two of you are a nearly unstoppable team. You've had a close call, but instances like that only make officers better, because they're determined not to let it happen again. Next time you won't be caught off guard because you've learned that lesson."

Wynona scrunched her nose as she felt her heart softening toward the chief's pleading. "You don't play fair. You know that, right?"

He straightened, a rare, wide smile on his face. "Yeah, well, you didn't either when you first stepped into my office. Do you have any idea how long I've spent keeping the Le Douxs as far away from me as possible?"

Wynona folded her arms over her chest. "Are you really sure you need my powers?"

The chief nodded solemnly.

Daemon raised his hand and Wynona looked his way. "We're not in school," she teased.

The large man shrugged. "I didn't want to get zapped for insubordination."

Wynona rolled her eyes while Rascal snorted.

"I just wanted to say that the deputy chief has promoted me to being his personal assistant, though my officer title hasn't really changed. I'll be around to help in case you're having trouble..." He grinned. "Like a few minutes ago."

Wynona threw up her hands. "You all have an answer for everything."

"Then I guess all that's left is for you to say yes," Rascal added.

Wynona took a deep breath and nodded. "Okay. I'll do what I can to help." She looked at the chief. "But I might need that protection. I won't have as much time to practice if I'm investigating."

He nodded. "You know I will."

And she did. The chief might have been difficult to get to know, but Wynona was one-hundred-percent confident he was a man of his word. "So what now?"

Chief Ligurio stood up, grabbed his tea cup from the side table and walked over. "Can you read this?"

"You still want a demonstration, huh?" Wynona took the cup.

Chief shook his head. "No. I'm hoping it'll give us a little insight since I've been involved in the case."

Wynona nodded. "Okay. I'll try." She closed her eyes and let her magic begin to swirl. "You might want to let go," she whispered to Rascal.

He huffed and stayed where he was.

Wynona pushed her worries out of her head. She wouldn't be able to concentrate on her reading if she was worried about him. Hopefully her magic didn't feel threatened during this. She'd hate to shock him again.

She felt the wind begin to pick up and her hair fluttered across her face.

COMING!

Wynona's eyebrows shot up, but she managed to keep her eyes shut. *I thought you had a date.*

It was a dud, Violet explained. *This is much more interesting.*

Wynona felt the tiny claws grip her legs as the mouse scrambled up to her usual spot on Wynona's shoulder. Once they were touching skin to skin, Wynona felt her worries dissipate.

The strength of her magic was always awe inspiring, but with her familiar at her side, Wynona felt much more in control. She focused her mind on understanding what the tea leaves had to say just as she felt a tug on her fingers. She opened her hand to let the mug rise, and when she opened her eyes, it was spinning in a very similar situation to what she had experienced before.

I think we can do this, Wynona thought in shock.

Violet snorted.

Feeling the flow begin to wind down, Wynona reached out and took the cup, bringing it to her eyes, which she guessed were glowing purple at this point. She studied the dregs, her mind immediately responding to the vague shapes contained therein.

"Knots...changes...anchor..." Wynona's eyes floated from one symbol to the next. She allowed her intuition to guide the order in which they were read. "Sum..." Wynona looked to the last one. "Heart." She blinked rapidly, bringing herself back to the present. Using her magic seemed to separate her from the outside world and Wynona always appreciated coming back to herself.

"And what do those mean?" the chief asked. He was several steps back from where he had started and Wynona realized she must have frightened him.

Her cheeks heated. "Sorry," she said. "I'm really not trying to be flashy."

He held up his hand. "I'll get used to it. Let's just worry about the clues."

Wynona nodded and swallowed hard. "Um...Knots mean you hold anxiety and stress." She glanced up as the chief nodded.

"Comes with the job."

She shrugged. "Easy enough. The changes mean you have challenges ahead." She tapped her fingers against her knee as she worked to remember what came next. "The anchor says you don't change easily."

Rascal coughed, hiding a grin behind his fist, which only grew wider when his boss glared.

Wynona bit her lips between her teeth. "I don't think a lot of the reading was about the case," she hedged.

Chief Ligurio put his hands on his hips. "Just spill it, Le Doux."

She hesitated, but finally gave in. "The sum means there will be a bringing together...and the heart refers to romance."

The vampire stiffened and Rascal's jaw dropped open. Daemon began choking so hard he headed to the kitchen for a glass of water.

"Are you telling me you just read a fortune of the chief's love life?" Rascal choked out.

"Shut it, Strongclaw, or I'll shut it for you," Chief Ligurio growled. He turned back to Wynona. "Next time tell me to shut up."

She nodded. "Sorry it wasn't what you wanted."

He waved his hand. "My fault. I'll take responsibility for this one." His eyes narrowed. "This time." With stiff legs, he began walking toward the door. "Strongclaw! Skymaw! Out!"

Rascal kissed Wynona's cheek and jumped to his feet. She followed and walked them all to the door. Chief Ligurio turned and handed her a card. "It's my cell. Call it if you need it."

Wynona studied the card, then nodded. "Thank you." She sighed. "And first thing tomorrow, I'll come in before opening to see what's been done on the case."

"Thank you," Chief Ligurio said, his voice back to being sharp, as if their evening had never happened.

Still chuckling, Rascal kissed her again before disappearing into the dark, Daemon on his heels. Wynona closed and locked the door, resting her head against it. "That was a disaster."

I don't know. I thought it was very eye opening.

Wynona shook her head. "He wanted clues about the case. I read him a love letter."

Ah...but the question is, whom will he be sharing hearts with? Violet rubbed her paws in glee. *I could fantasize about this for days.*

"And on that note, I'm headed to bed." Wynona walked toward her bedroom. She could feel her legs beginning to shake with each step, a testament to using so much magic. She would look forward to the day when her magical endurance was beyond that of a five year old, but for now...sleep was the only cure.

CHAPTER 9

Wynona arrived bright and early at the station. She took off her helmet, picked up Violet from her riding basket and headed inside. There was nothing for it, but to jump into this investigation with both feet. Wynona had to admit that they were right. She was curious and she liked to see justice prevail.

Doesn't mean you have to be the one to enact it, Violet grumbled, rubbing her eyes. She hadn't been happy about getting up earlier than normal, despite the fact that her date had ended in time for a decent bed time.

Wynona rubbed her familiar's head, but didn't bother trying to placate her. Violet was in the mood to be grumpy and there was nothing Wynona could do about it.

"Wynona!" Officer Amaris Nightshade grinned, her sharp white teeth on full display. "I heard you were coming by today."

Wynona walked up to the front desk. "Yep. Apparently, I've been pulled onto the case."

"So I heard." Amaris looked around and then leaned in. "Word is that Chief Ligurio had to ask you himself. Is that true?"

Wynona pinched her lips between her teeth. "Let's just say we came to an understanding." She didn't think the new leaf she had turned over with the chief was going to last if she gossiped about him behind his back.

Amaris' grin grew. "Loyal to a fault." She sighed dramatically. "Oh well, I suppose that's why we all like you so much." She pointed over her shoulder. "The three amigos beat you this morning. You'll find them in Chief's office."

"Perfect. Thank you!" Wynona waved and headed down the hall. She had been in this station enough times to know exactly where she was going and was soon knocking on the chief's door.

"Enter!" Chief Ligurio shouted.

Wynona pushed open the door and smiled at the men. "I almost feel like I should have brought muffins. It's like one of those study groups I heard about in college."

The flash of Rascal's wolf let her know that wasn't a good joke, having reminded all of them of her difficult home life while growing up.

Wynona cleared her throat. "Sorry." She stepped in fully and closed the door behind her. "Can I see the case file?" She took the offered folder and sat down in a vacant chair next to Rascal. Setting it in her lap, she looked around. "Did I interrupt something else? Should I wait in the hall?"

Rascal took her hand and kissed the back of it. "We were just going over theories. Why don't you look through the file and we'll get you caught up."

Wynona nodded and went back to the folder. She rifled through the pictures, pressing her lips together at the sight of Ms. Roseburg's body. That was one thing she knew she would never get used to, no matter how often she helped the police. Creatures, once they had passed on, were a sight Wynona just wasn't comfortable with. "Why don't you tell me about the scene again?" she asked, her eyes still on the folder.

"Her body was found in the pool," Chief Ligurio answered.

"By whom?" Wynona asked.

"Her son."

Wynona looked up. "Zander found the body? When?"

Rascal pushed aside a couple of papers. "In the morning. Said he was going for his morning swim and there she was."

Wynona frowned. "He was going to exercise?"

Chief Ligurio nodded. "Why do you sound skeptical?"

Wynona shrugged. "He's just never really been the athletic type, but then again...it wasn't like I knew him well." She looked up. "What did he do?"

"Called emergency services," Daemon offered. "When we got there, the body was on the tile and she had been declared dead."

"And when did the media show up?" Wynona pressed.

Rascal pushed a hand through his hair. "Almost immediately. Zander had already called his sister and his father. Both showed up within minutes of us and the media was on their heels."

Wynona slumped back in her seat, reaching up to pet Violet. "And the family welcomed them in?"

Chief Ligurio nodded. "Yes," he ground out. "We almost couldn't get the scene taped off before they were hounding us on all sides."

"And neither Zander nor Silvaria seemed upset about the death?"

The chief shook his head. "No. In fact, they mostly seem relieved."

Wynona tilted her head to the side. "I remember you mentioning that Silvaria had been cut off. Has she moved back into the mansion?"

The chief looked at Rascal, who shrugged, as well as Daemon.

"I think we should check into that," Wynona said.

"Agreed," Chief Ligurio said.

"What did the body look like?" Wynona asked. "In fact, can I see the autopsy?"

Rascal took the folder from her and thumbed through until he found the report she wanted.

Wynona read quickly before looking up at Daemon. "The magic was on the back of her head?"

Daemon nodded. He reached back and tapped his skull. "Right about there. It looked like it had knitted something back together, but the color was fairly faint by the time I saw it."

"What color was it?"

"Blue."

Wynona huffed. "Dang it."

"Ms. Le Doux?" Chief Ligurio inserted. "Did you have a thought?"

Wynona let the papers drop so she could focus on the chief. "Sometimes the color of magic is kind of a...signature, if you will. If the color of the magic had been unique, we could have used it to pin down possible suspects."

"But now we can't?"

Wynona shook her head in response. "No. Blue is a very common color. I know Ms. Roseburg had blue magic. It's possible one or either of her children do. And I can personally name you another half dozen witches with different shades of blue in their magic."

Chief Ligurio scrubbed his face. "Good information to have, but not useful right now."

"Sorry. Unusual colors can be helpful, but blue is far from unusual."

"So noted." He tilted his chin toward the file. "Anything else stand out to you?"

Wynona looked through the papers, but nothing caught her attention. "I really think I'd do better if I could see the pool house. Is that possible?"

"Strongclaw. You can take her."

"Chief," Daemon interrupted. "I should go."

Chief Ligurio glared, but Daemon didn't back down.

"I promised I'd be around to help."

The chief sighed and pinched the bridge of his nose. "Fine. But don't be gone all day. If we don't have news on this soon, the reporters are going to eat us alive."

Wynona stood. "Can I take this with me so I can study it later?" She held out the file.

The chief waved her away. "I don't have to tell you what will happen if you lose it."

"Nope," Wynona quickly responded. "I'll be careful." She gave Daemon a grateful smile, then followed Rascal to the door. "Oh, and Chief?"

"What?" he growled.

"A little willow bark in your blood will help." Before he could snap at her about minding her own business, Wynona ducked out into the hall and hurried after Rascal.

"We should take the truck," he said as they headed out to the parking lot.

"I need to take my Vespa," Wynona lamented. "I might need to go straight to work."

Rascal took her hand and pulled her away from the mint green scooter, toward his monster of a vehicle. "I'll drive you wherever you need to go. The truck is much faster and looks more official."

Violet snickered while Wynona gave him a look. One that Rascal didn't seem the least bit put off by.

"Thank you," she murmured as he helped her up into the passenger side. One of these days she wouldn't be wearing a skirt while trying to climb into his unusually high cab.

Daemon followed in his own squad car and it only took ten minutes for them to arrive at the Roseburg mansion.

Even though Wynona had seen it in pictures, the mansion was still breathtaking. She had grown up in a palace, which technically was far larger than this home, but after living in her tiny cottage for over six months, it made the mansion appear uncomfortably grand.

Rascal took her hand and Wynona found herself grateful not to be alone.

Violet sniffed. *You wouldn't be alone if the pup wasn't here.*

Rascal let out a playful growl. "Watch it, Vi. My wolf eats meat."

Violet squeaked and chittered with outrage.

Rascal chuckled and knocked on the front door they had reached.

"Play nice," Wynona hissed at them both. "We're supposed to be professionals."

Rascal picked up Violet and tucked her into his pocket. "We are. I don't know why you would ever think otherwise."

Before Wynona could argue, the door was pulled open.

"What do you want?"

Wynona blinked at the rudeness of the man in front of her. His long hair was half covering his face and hadn't been combed in a while. His clothes were all the right brands, but they were hanging off his frame, his arms showing that he was quite thin, especially for a man. While she watched, he pushed a hand through his hair, revealing his second, bright blue eye, which traveled up and down Wynona in a slow, lazy manner.

"You must be related to Marcella." The man's demeanor changed and a grin tugged at his lips. "Did the president send you? Does he want to talk to me?"

Wynona looked at Rascal, who was ready to tear the younger man apart.

"Umm..." She stepped slightly closer, trying to keep Rascal from doing anything he shouldn't. "I'm Wynona Le Doux. I'm working with the police and came to study the crime scene."

His blue eyes widened before getting a hold of himself and sneering. "A Le Doux working with the police? You've got to be kidding."

Who is this idiot? Violet snapped.

"I'm sorry, I didn't catch your name," Wynona said politely. She clasped her hands and stuck her chin in the air. When in doubt, she had learned early on to feign confidence. It usually worked wonders.

The man huffed. "Zander Killoran." he folded his arms over his chest. "Though if you were really working with the police, you should know that."

Wynona held back a wince. How did she not recognize him? Of course, she hadn't seen him since he was a teenager and it had been at a party at her parents' home. In other words, Zander had looked much more put together, with his hair done and his tux ironed, than he did right now in his grubbies.

"Who is it, Zan?" A woman, who could only be his sister, came up behind him. "Ugh," she groaned, tossing her hair over her shoulder. "You again? I thought this was all settled."

"Until we have your mother's killer, the case will continue to be ongoing," Rascal said tightly.

His wolf was still close to the surface, but Wynona could tell he was in control again and she stepped aside to let him lead.

"We need to access the pool house. Please let us in."

Zander smirked, but stepped back and waved an arm in a sarcastic manner. "Go ahead. I wouldn't want to upset both the police *and* the president's daughter." He winked at her as she walked inside.

Wynona ignored the dig and the flirting. Her father had declared her disowned a long time ago, though that might have changed now that they were interested in her magic. But if either of them were close with her parents...it wasn't Wynona.

She followed Rascal, grateful that Daemon had brought up the rear. She felt like a police sandwich, but also much safer than if she had been trailing in the back of the group.

Her senses were on high alert as they walked through the home. Wynona could feel eyes on her from every corner, but she was unable to find the culprits, until a loud hissing caught her attention and she realized the hidden stalkers were the cats Rascal had warned her about.

"They don't like my wolf," he whispered.

Violet snickered and Wynona had to hold back a grin. She wouldn't admit it out loud, but she kind of agreed with Violet. Those cats didn't feel friendly, so having a predator on her side was a definite plus.

Rascal pulled open the large glass door leading to the pool and Wynona jerked a little as the humidity smacked her in the face. The smell of chemicals assaulted her and she wrinkled her nose.

The sound of grunting broke the silence and Wynona stretched around Rascal to see what was going on. "Who's that?" she asked softly. From her vantage point she could see an arm, which she assumed was connected to a body, scrubbing down the side of the pool, which had been drained.

"That..." Zander said proudly. "Is Marsh Monroe."

By now they had reached the side and Wynona could clearly see the handsome man, who was working without a shirt on as he cleaned the entirety of the Olympic sized pool. Marsh turned to glare, his blue hair glinting in the lights. "Mr. Killoran," he said tightly. His light gray eyes turned to Wynona, Rascal and Daemon before nodding.

When Marsh took in a deep breath and the slits on the side of his neck rose and closed, Wynona had a sudden revelation. "You're a merman." She gasped.

"Yes," Zander answered for Marsh, Zander's blue eyes practically glowing with hatred. "And my mother's lover as well as her killer."

CHAPTER 10

Rascal spun faster than Wynona was able to keep track of and had Zander by the throat. "Think carefully before you accuse anyone of that," Rascal growled.

Despite Zander's wheezing, he grinned. "A little touchy, huh? Wonder what the president would think of his daughter slumming with a furball?"

"Rascal." Wynona stepped forward and tugged on his arm, which was starting to grow the very fur Zander had been poking fun at. "Let him go." Rascal didn't move, but he didn't continue to get worse either. "Rascal," she said more softly, turning his face toward hers. She smiled, though it trembled slightly. His eyes were glowing and wild, and she knew he'd gone into full protection mode. Zander would be no match for an extra large wolf if it came down to a fight. "I'm fine. You know who we are to each other. Let him go and let's hear what everyone has to say."

"He has no right to you," Rascal said in a low tone.

"I know," Wynona responded quickly. "None. Whatsoever. My heart is taken."

Rascal closed his eyes and breathed deeply through his nose. The fur slowly receded and his grip on Zander's neck lessened.

Zander stepped back, rubbing the red spot, his silvery blue magic quickly healed. "I think maybe I should file a complaint," he whined.

"I think maybe you should learn to shut your trap," his sister snapped.

Wynona turned, not having realized the woman had followed them into the pool room. Silvaria stood, holding a tabby cat in her arms and petting it slowly. Her blue eyes were glued to Rascal, looking a little too predatory for Wynona's liking.

"I think there might be something to this wolfy thing." Silvaria tilted her head and smirked. "Color me intrigued."

Wynona had to fight down her own jealousy at the not-so-hidden flirting and turned back to Zander. "Why do you think Mr. Monroe killed your mother?"

Zander huffed and folded his arms over his chest. Now that she was looking more at him, she could still see the same spoiled boy he had been when they were younger. Wynona was older than him by several years, but whenever possible, she had watched her parents' parties from the shadows. The Killoran children had been some of the loudest, most obnoxious guests ever allowed in the palace, and considering who the Le Doux's associated with, that was saying something.

Magic, power and money seemed to be a combination that ruined people.

Which is why Granny tried to save you.

Wynona gave a slight nod of acknowledgement to Violet's reminder. She really would have to forgive her grandmother at some point. But right now, she was busy. "Mr. Killoran?" she pressed.

Zander scowled. "Who else could it have been?" He waved his hand toward the merman, who was watching with a livid expression on his face, his nostrils and gills flaring. To his credit, however, he didn't speak. "Flipper, here, is a gold digger. He's been after my mother for years and when she finally relented, he killed her so he could access her money."

Wynona looked at Mr. Monroe. "Not to put too fine a point on it, Mr. Monroe, but I would like to ask where you were the night of the murder?"

The merman's face was red as his hands clenched and unclenched. "I thought it was innocent until proven guilty," he snarled.

"I will be asking everyone the same question," Wynona assured him. "You just happen to be the person we're talking about at the moment."

Marsh snorted, but nodded. "I was at home. I work on the pool in the mornings and the evenings. By six I'm back in my own pool for the night."

Wynona felt heat hit her cheeks before she asked her next question, but she knew it needed to be done. "Have you ever spent the night in this pool?"

There was a pause and another tightening of fists, but finally Marsh nodded.

"Ha! See! I told you!" Zander shouted, his face sharp with anger.

"And you, Mr. Killoran?"

Zander turned. "What?"

"Where were you the night your mother was killed?"

Zander's jaw dropped as his sister laughed. "You think I killed my mother?"

"I think anyone who knew her might have killed her," Wynona said easily. She was grateful when Rascal stepped a little closer. Daemon had stayed by the door, watching but not interfering...yet. From the pitch black of his eyes, he was watching for magic to spill and at the tension in the room, Wynona had a feeling it might happen before too long.

Zander pushed long hair out of his face again. "I was here. Sleeping." He made a face when she waited. "My room is on the other side of the mansion. I didn't hear a thing."

Wynona tucked that away. "And you, Ms. Killoran?"

Silvaria finally pulled her gaze away from Rascal, though it appeared to be difficult. "Ms. Killoran?" She tsked her tongue. "Surely, we know each other better than that, Wynona."

Wynona didn't respond. She was irked, but she also knew Silvaria was baiting her. Luckily, Celia had prepped Wynona for occasions just like this with lots of practice.

Silvaria shook her head. "Celia was right. Now that your magic is here, you think you're better than everyone else." Silvaria walked slowly forward, the cat still in her arms.

Wynona didn't move. She wasn't one to let bullies win.

The blonde witch leaned into Wynona's bubble. "Spoiler alert...you're not."

Wynona smiled. "Thank you. Now if you wouldn't mind telling me where you were?"

Zander snorted at Wynona's persistence. "Give up, Sil. She's not interested in being *your* friend." The look in his eyes said the emphasis was on purpose.

Since they're so interested in your magic, Violet muttered, *I've half a mind to give them a little demonstration.*

Wynona didn't move. She was afraid if she did, Violet's wish would come true. Her magic still responded to her emotions more times than not and Wynona had about had it with the spoiled adults in front of her. "Ms. Killoran, I'd like a straight answer please."

Silvaria shook her head, causing her long, silky hair to billow behind her. "So formal..." She sniffed. "I was at a friend's house. I've been staying with her ever since...*Mother*...forced me out."

"And how long ago was that?"

Silvaria dropped her eyes to the cat. "Six months ago." Her bitter tone said it all.

"Can your roommate corroborate your story?"

Silvaria's head jerked up. "Oh, now I'm the suspect? Why not accuse my father next?" She held up the cat, who immediately began to wiggle. "Or Duo. Maybe he did it."

Wynona held perfectly still. It was a wonder Ms. Roseburg had any children living with her at this point. Both of them were dramatic, spoiled and neither cared about their mother at all, except that she had the money. A sliver of pity ran down Wynona's spine. This was exactly how her family would eventually be. When one of her parents died, no one would truly mourn them.

Kind of makes you glad Granny got you out, huh?

Since when did you become such a big cheerleader of hers? Wynona asked.

Violet scrubbed her face. *I don't know. But the longer I think about it, the more I realize she was right. Your family is rotten and I'm glad we're not part of it.*

Wynona sighed. "While I will be talking to your father, unless scratches or bite marks were found on the body, I don't think I need to speak to Duo."

Silvaria bared her teeth and dropped the cat to the ground, who immediately darted away.

A prickling on the back of Wynona's neck had her on high alert. She recognized that sensation as one that told her there was a ghost in the area. *I need my ghost vision,* Wynona mentally sent the thought to Rascal, not wanting to advertise her skill.

He looked at her with a raised eyebrow, obviously having got the message. "Mr. and Ms. Killoran. I'd like you to please wait in another part of the house for now. When we have more questions, I'll send Officer Skymaw to fetch you."

"Fetch." Zander snorted, but complied. "I thought that was your territory."

Wynona could hear Rascal's wolf growl in her head and she realized, once again, just how open their connection was. It seemed every time she turned around, she had something new to get used to.

This isn't a magic thing, Violet said wryly. *It's a soulmate thing.*

"Really?" Wynona asked, forgetting to keep it in her head.

The departing group stopped and Wynona shook her head. "Sorry. Just talking to myself." She ignored Rascal's smirk and turned to

Mr. Monroe. "Can you explain to me what you're doing?" She needed to know if she could get rid of him so she could use her sight. While the world might know her magic existed, Wynona wanted to keep her exact skills as much of a secret as possible. Her parents didn't need that kind of leverage.

The merman grumbled and went back to scrubbing. "I'm still under contract for the next seven months. The Killorans want me to clean the pool so they don't have to swim in the same germs their mother died in." He looked over his shoulder, his face sour. "Really, it's just a way of punishing me. You heard what they thought."

Wynona nodded. "Is it alright if I look around a bit?"

Marsh shrugged. "Suit yourself. This isn't my place."

"Thank you." Wynona walked away from the edge of the pool so he couldn't see her and blinked a couple of times, until the world turned purple.

"What's going on?" Daemon whispered from her left.

"I feel a spirit," she whispered back. "But I didn't want everyone else to see my eyes."

Daemon nodded. "Right." He glanced toward the door as if keeping an eye out for others. "See anything?"

Wynona turned in a slow circle. The feeling was persisting, but she saw nothing. "That's odd." She turned another circle. "I can't see them. Last time I had this feeling, I could find kind of a purple...blob...for lack of a better word, when I turned this skill on. Now I don't see a thing, but the feeling is still there."

Daemon scratched under his chin. "I don't feel any magic except yours, so..."

Wynona blinked the vision away. "I'm not sure what to make of that." She looked up at the black hole. "Maybe I just don't know how to use it very well yet?"

"It's possible, but you said it worked last time, right?"

Wynona nodded. "Several times, in fact."

"Then I don't think you're the problem."

Rascal stormed back in. "Can we just find a reason to arrest those two and be done with it?"

A snort from the pool reminded all three of them that they weren't alone.

Wynona walked over and sat down on the edge. "Mr. Monroe, may I ask you a few more questions?"

"Not like I can avoid it," he said testily.

Oooh. Eye candy during the interrogation. We should do this more often.

Wynona glared down at Violet, while Rascal choked.

"I don't want to know," Daemon said, sauntering away. "I'll look for anything residual that I missed before." His eyes went black as his magic came to the surface again.

Wynona turned back to the merman, who was grinning at her. She frowned, until he winked.

"I'm part fish," he clarified. "I don't understand your familiar word for word, but us animals can usually get a grasp of things." His grin widened. "And your soulmate's wolf can stand down. I'm not as stupid as Zander thinks I am. I prefer my women a little more...experienced."

Wynona's cheeks heated to the point where she was sure she could have burned down the Grove of Secrets. A short growl from Rascal grew softer as he walked away, apparently taking the merman at his word. "Tell me about your relationship with Ms. Roseburg."

The smirk fell from the pool boy's face. "She was nothing like what the paper's portrayed." His brows furrowed. "And her children didn't deserve her."

"Were you with her because of her money?"

He shrugged. "Gifts and trinkets are nice. I'm a simple man." He waved his arms around. "Cleaning pools isn't exactly lucrative and when your only magic is creating fins when wet, I'm not high on the power food chain either."

"So...that's a yes."

"It's a bonus." His lips turned down. "I really did like her. We weren't headed toward marriage, but I was having a good time."

Wynona nodded. That might not have been her choice of relationship, but Wynona tried not to judge creatures too harshly. "Did you ever talk about her will?"

Marsh frowned. "Why?"

"Were you hoping she would change her will to leave her wealth to you?"

"I see. You're trying to find a motive." It wasn't a question.

Wynona tilted her head. "I'll be searching for motives until we find the right one, Mr. Monroe, whether I'm speaking to you or one of the children, or Mr. Killoran."

"And what does your father have to say about this hobby of yours?"

Wynona blinked. "Why should he have anything to say?"

Blue eyebrows shot up. "Celia's been telling everyone that you were going to be joining the family again soon. Your father confirmed it in a press conference just yesterday. Said you had mended your ways and would be welcomed back to the palace very soon."

The blood drained from Wynona's head and she swayed slightly, Violet squeaking in surprise.

Strong legs appeared next to her and Wynona wrapped her arms around Rascal, his hand landing on her head. "Wynona is her own person," the shifter said tightly. "Her father has no say in it."

Marsh studied them, then finally nodded. "It's not like I have room to talk. Most men my age aren't spending time with divorced witches old enough to be their mothers." He turned around and went back to scrubbing while Wynona climbed to her feet.

Rascal wrapped an arm around her waist. "Do you want to go?" he asked.

"How did we miss this?"

He shook his head. "I'm not sure. I'm usually pretty up to date on the news, especially when it concerns the president." He grabbed his cell. "Let me have someone find it and we can review it later, but I'll ask again. Do you want to leave?"

Wynona thought about it, but shook her head. "No. That's just letting them control me. I have another hour until I need to be at the tea house. I should look around."

Rascal nodded and let go of her slowly, making sure she was steady before putting distance between them.

"Incoming."

Daemon's words had Wynona watching the door and she groaned internally when she saw who was approaching.

"Hello, dear sister," Celia said through a smile that was anything but sincere. Silvaria was standing behind Celia with a triumphant look on her face. "Miss me?"

CHAPTER 11

Wynona was positive that she did a terrible job of hiding the shock on her face. Her sister was *not* the person she had expected to see today. Truthfully, Wynona had no desire to see her sister any day. "Hello, Celia," Wynona said as politely as possible. "What brings you here?"

Rascal was still growling low as he stepped to Wynona's side. Even Daemon had taken up a defensive position. His eyes were hard and solid black, just waiting for someone to make a move.

Celia studied her nails. "A little birdie told me I might find you here." Her sly glance toward Silvaria explained exactly who that tattletale was. "I didn't realize you were trying to make friends with other witches."

Wynona stuck her chin in the air just a little higher. "I'm here on official business," she said calmly. "Please step out. We're in the middle of an investigation."

Celia put her hands on her hips. "I don't think that's what Mother and Father would like you to waste your talents on, dear *sister*."

Wynona was really beginning to hate that word, but letting Celia know that her pushing was wearing on Wynona's nerves would only make things worse. "I've told you before that nothing I'm doing has anything to do with Mother and Father. I've been living on my own for a while now and have my own life."

Rascal stepped forward. "Ms. Le Doux is correct. This is a marked crime scene. Please leave or I'll have you removed."

Celia didn't budge, nor did she appear to hear Rascal's threat. "I've been curious," she said, walking slowly to the side as if to circle the pool. "These powers..." Celia's dark eyes darted to Mr. Monroe, then back to Wynona, dismissing him as unimportant. "I'd like to see what you're capable of."

"I'm not here to give you a show, Celia," Wynona said, turning to follow her sister. Even with Daemon in the room, Wynona didn't trust the other witch not to pull a fast one. "Again...please leave. I doubt Father would be happy seeing your name splayed across the papers because you were arrested for trespassing."

Celia paused and splayed her hands to the side. "But I'm not. I was invited." She nodded toward Silvaria, who was still smirking near the door. "By the owner of the home."

"This home isn't owned by anyone yet," Rascal snarled. "Not until the will has been read."

Celia finally acknowledged the officer. "Don't threaten me, dog. My father will neuter you so fast it'll make your head spin."

It took Wynona a second to realize that the crackle of magic in the air wasn't coming from her sister.

Easy, Wynona, Violet warned. *I might hate her even more than you—after all, she did try to kill me—but zapping her into oblivion won't help matters.*

Wynona took in a deep breath, willing her magic to relax.

Besides, there are witnesses.

Wynona snorted, then coughed, trying to cover it up. Even Rascal had to clear his throat. "Celia," Wynona said, forcing her voice to stay soft. "Why are you really here?"

Celia's posture slowly softened. For just a split moment she had looked afraid when the strength of Wynona's magic had filled the room, though after tossing her hair, Celia did her best to cover it up. "I told you. Mom and Dad sent me."

"But why are *you* here?" Wynona pressed. "Why doesn't Mom come herself? Or Dad, for that matter. Why are they sending you?" A burst of inspiration hit her and Wynona ran with her gut. "What do they have on you?"

Celia's eyes flashed silver, the color of her magic, and sparks began to drip from her fingertips. In only seconds, the sparks died and Celia looked down in shock.

"That's enough of that," Daemon said, his tone just as dark as his eyes.

Celia hissed when she saw him. "Are you so afraid of me that you'll pull my magic, but not my sister's? Maybe she's not as powerful as Mom thinks."

"Your sister is in control of herself," Daemon said slowly. "I trust her."

The words did far more to boost Wynona's confidence than she would have imagined. She knew that Daemon was simply saying that in order to put Celia in her place, but they were welcome nonetheless.

Celia snorted. "Right. I saw just how in control she is." She turned back to Wynona. "My life is none of your business." Stalking back around the pool, Celia headed toward the door. "Call me when you're ready to come home. I won't chase you down with sweet invitations anymore."

Wynona waited until Celia and Silvaria were gone before letting out a long breath.

"Do you think she means it?" Rascal asked, a smirk on his lips. "Have we really gotten rid of her for good?"

Daemon huffed. "If only." He turned to look at Wynona. "Though I have to wonder at what you were referring to. What could your parents possibly have over Celia? You obviously hit a nerve."

Wynona shook her head, her mind spinning after the tense confrontation. "I have no idea," she admitted. "I was throwing out a hunch."

Rascal growled. "It worked, but despite her declaration, I think you're right. She'll be back. If only because your parents said so."

Wynona stared at the door.

"Don't you dare," Rascal said, standing in front of her.

She opened her eyes wide. "What?"

His brows pulled down. "Don't you dare feel sorry for her. She's choosing her actions, whether they were her idea or not."

Wynona sighed and patted his chest. "I understand that, but I also understand feeling like you have no choice. My parents aren't good people. If they're hanging someone over Celia's head, she needs understanding, not a fight."

Rascal pinched the bridge of his nose and sighed. "Can we at least agree to wait for this heart to heart until there's a little less danger in your life? I know I was involved in pulling you in to help, but the more we talk to people, the more I feel like this murder case is only going to get worse before it gets better."

Wynona gave him a short kiss on the cheek. "Yes. Believe it or not, I'm not looking forward to it either. But she deserves a chance to be heard. I was given an opportunity she wasn't. My parents didn't care about me, which is the only reason I don't live there under their thumb. She never had the option."

Rascal nodded. "Thank you."

Wynona responded in kind.

"You're not what I expected."

All three of them turned to see Marsh watching them from the pool. Wynona had forgotten the quiet merman was there. "Goodness," she breathed. "Sorry, Mr. Monroe. I forgot you were there."

He gave her a crooked smile. "The blue hair stands out, but silence goes a long way in helping hide a person."

Wynona nodded.

"But that doesn't change the fact that I thought you would be much more like your sister." Gray eyes narrowed. "You're not."

"Thank you," Wynona said easily. "I've made it a goal to be their exact opposites."

"And you were really born without magic?"

Wynona shook her head. "Not technically, no. I was cursed in the womb. My powers were bound."

"And now they're not." It was a statement, not a question, and Wynona had a feeling she would be responding to it a million times before things were settled.

"No." She swallowed. "The person who cursed me passed away and the curse has slowly broken since then. It came apart fully a few weeks ago."

"Huh." Marsh looked at Rascal, who was still standing at Wynona's side, before coming back to her. "You're lucky you have such a good protector."

"Thank you," Wynona said again. She couldn't help but start to wonder where he was going with this. She needed to study the space.

"Deputy Chief, I didn't kill Ms. Roseburg," Marsh said. "But I think I might know who did."

Wynona jerked. "Excuse me?" Why in the world didn't he say this earlier?

"And?" Rascal responded, his hands on his hips.

"I believe her ex-husband, Mr. Wayde Killoran, did it."

Rascal's eyes darted to Wynona, then back to the merman. "And what makes you say that? Do you have any evidence?"

Marsh shook his head. "No. No evidence. Just a couple of...odd circumstances."

"I think you should come out of that pool and down to the station," Daemon said, finally stepping into the conversation.

Marsh nodded. "I think you're right." That crooked smile crossed his handsome face again. "This isn't the place for this little chat."

"I'd like to look around before we leave," Wynona whispered to Rascal.

He nodded. "Mr. Monroe can wait a few minutes. Take your time."

Wynona squeezed his arm in thanks and began to move along the pool. "Where was the body found?" she asked.

"According to Zander, it was floating in the deep end," Rascal provided. "When we got here, she was lying on a stretcher, already having been declared dead."

Wynona pursed her lips. "Did anyone mention where she'd been laid out on the tile?"

Rascal shook his head. "No." He tilted his head. "Does it matter?"

Wynona shrugged. "I don't know. But I wanted to play it out in my mind." She faced Mr. Monroe, who was putting away his tools. "What work did you do that day?"

Mr. Monroe looked over his shoulder. "Uh...I might not have been as...busy at work that day."

Wynona turned away, trying to hide the heat in her face. Sheesh. She needed to be less sensitive to the world around her. "So...no tools or anything that might have been left out?"

"No. Not that I can think of."

Wynona nodded, still not looking at the merman. Instead, she began to study the tile.

What are you looking for? Violet asked, scrambling down and walking slowly in the same area.

"I don't know," Wynona murmured, her focus on the floor. "Anything that might look out of place." She stepped around a lounge chair and moved closer to the pool.

Violet's nose twitched and she hesitated, one paw in the air.

"What is it?" Wynona asked, dropping to her knees.

There's something here. Violet sniffed harder.

Rascal got close to the ground and sniffed as well. "Chemicals," he offered. "Pool chemicals." He leaned back on his haunches. "That's nothing unusual. I'm sure Mr. Monroe uses chemicals almost every day."

But not on the ground, Violet argued.

"How can you be sure it was on the ground?" Wynona asked. "Are you referring to a spill?"

Violet nodded. She darted around from side to side. *It's here. Whatever was spilled hasn't been cleaned up yet.*

"Mr. Monroe?" Wynona hollered.

"Yes?"

"When did you spill chemicals?" She heard footsteps coming their way and his shadow came over her head.

"I didn't spill anything," he snapped. "I've never spilled the chemicals, not even when I first started."

Wynona frowned and turned to Rascal.

He stood and began to move around, looking at the space from multiple angles. Finally, he stopped. "There it is."

Wynona followed and gasped. There was a thin, glossy shine on the tile, evidence that something had been poured or spilled and never cleaned up.

Rascal pointed. "See how it has a line toward the water?"

Wynona nodded. She had to tilt her head just right to see it, but once the light was just right, it couldn't be missed. "It looks like someone skidded."

"Could Ms. Roseburg have fallen and hit her head?" Daemon asked. "Maybe it was an accident."

"But then why heal her?" Wynona objected, shaking her head. "That makes no sense."

Rascal pushed a hand through his hair.

"I'm telling you, I didn't spill anything," Marsh argued.

"Where do you keep the supplies?" Daemon asked.

Marsh sighed and pointed to a closet in the corner.

"And who all has a key?"

The merman deflated. "Only myself. Ms. Roseburg didn't like to deal with the mundane things."

Rascal stepped forward. "Officer Skymaw, take Mr. Monroe out to your car. I think maybe we need to speak to him about more than his suspicions about Mr. Killoran." Grabbing his cell phone, Rascal punched in a number and began to bark at someone about getting a photographer and evidence kit at the pool.

Wynona watched Mr. Monroe being escorted out, then looked back at the ground.

What are you thinking? Violet asked, coming to rest at Wynona's foot.

"You can't tell?" Wynona teased.

Violet shrugged and scrubbed her face. *I didn't want to intrude.*

Wynona ignored the obvious fib. She took a deep breath. "I don't know what to think. A slip at the pool and a healing on the back of her head don't make sense. If she wasn't alone and there was an accident, why wouldn't the person help her? If they wanted her dead, why bother to heal her at all?" Wynona rubbed her temple. "It all goes in a circle."

Violet climbed her leg and settled on her shoulder. *We need to get to the tea shop. Maybe it'll make more sense later tonight.*

Wynona glanced at her watch and gasped. "Rascal! I need to get to the shop."

He nodded and held up a finger. Finishing his conversation, he walked to the door. "Come on. I'll drop you off, then come back. Did you want to be involved with Mr. Monroe?"

Wynona nodded. "If it's not too much to ask for you to wait. I might be able to leave things with Lusgu if they're slow this afternoon."

Rascal snorted. "Just shoot me a message."

"Via cell phone or brain to brain?"

Rascal grinned. "Whatever works."

Wynona climbed into the truck, Rascal's hands on her waist to help. "How far can we be apart from each other and still have it work?"

"I guess we'll have to test it out," Rascal said. He smiled up at her. "I've never done this before either."

"Right." Wynona clasped her hands in her lap, heat infusing her cheeks. "Sorry."

Rascal stepped up and rubbed a knuckle along her cheek. "Nothing to be sorry about. We're figuring this out together, remember?"

Wynona nodded. "Thank you."

"Always."

CHAPTER 12

The day was going much slower than Wynona would have wished. There were too many patrons at the moment for her to pass everything off to Lusgu so she could help out at the station, so Wynona had sent a mental message to Rascal and focused on taking care of her customers.

"Fresh eclairs and a pot of green rooibos," Wynona said, setting the tray down with a small flourish of her fingers. She was finally using her magic in public, though in very small ways. Her customers hadn't said a thing about it, which Wynona was grateful for. She had decided she was going to start integrating it in subtle ways until everything was running like a well oiled machine. But perhaps if her family knew magic was common in her life now, they would think twice about trying to pull her back.

Except Celia saw you in action.

Wynona blew a breath out her nose. *True,* she thought back. *But I don't think Celia is as sold on Mom and Dad's plan to get me back as they are.*

Violet scrubbed her face.

"Thank you, dear," the older shifter said, smiling up at Wynona. Her hooked nose displayed her heritage as a bird, though her features were still lovely for her age.

Wynona nodded with a smile and walked away. She meandered around the room, checking on everyone, who seemed content at the moment. With a sigh of relief, she went back to the kitchen. "Finally, a little quiet," she said softly.

Violet scrambled down and ran under the stainless steel island, disappearing from view. *Lunch time!*

Wynona chuckled. "Enjoy." She had no idea what food her familiar kept under there, but Lusgu had proven to be a softie when it came to the mouse and Wynona was positive he kept Violet well stocked.

Her own stomach grumbled and she walked to the fridge to grab a bite. Wynona rarely had a sit down meal, but she was usually able to eat enough to keep her satisfied until Rascal joined her for dinner.

She pulled out a container with some leftover soup and began to walk to the microwave when Violet squeaked at her. "Right. Powers." Wynona set the bowl on the counter and pointed at it. She held her breath, trying to keep the heat minimal. She knew from past experiments that she had enough power to blow up a building, when all she wanted was hot soup.

Her shoulders relaxed when the soup began to steam and Wynona dropped her hand. She was getting better at this and that was something she needed to be proud of, though she was usually too busy trying to keep up to celebrate the milestones.

The ringing of the bell at the front door caught her attention and Wynona left the soup, walking back out to the dining room so she could greet whoever had just arrived. Her steps came to a screeching halt, however, when a woman with hair black as pitch waltzed into the shop. Her pouty red lips were pursed and her skin unblemished from wrinkles or any other problems.

For Wynona, it was like looking in a mirror, other than the look of disdain her mother sported while studying the other tables.

"Wynona!" Marcella cried, once she spotted her daughter. Arms raised, Marcella walked quickly forward, as if to embrace Wynona.

Wynona automatically stepped back, her hand up. "Hello, Mother." She was grateful Marcella stopped before touching her. She wasn't quite sure her magic wouldn't respond to her discomfort. "What brings you here?"

Marcella's press conference smile was plastered on her face. "I came to see you. Isn't that what mothers do?"

Coming!

A tiny bit of Wynona's tension relaxed as Violet climbed her leg. She always felt more in control when her familiar was with her. "Not usually," Wynona snipped. She pinched her lips together. She probably shouldn't antagonize her mother. They were in public and Wynona needed to be professional. She stuck her chin in the air, ignoring the look of annoyance on her mother's face. "I'm afraid I'm working right now. Would you like a table, or should we speak another time?"

Marcella's smile was anything but kind. "I suppose I'll take a table. Mothers should test out their daughters' work, shouldn't they? Who else will be honest with you about how you're doing?" Smiling and nodding at the other ladies, Marcella flounced across the room until she reached an empty table.

Wynona ground her teeth. She didn't want to serve her mother. In fact, she didn't want to see her at all.

How about a little rhubarb in her tea? Violet snickered.

We're not giving my mother a laxative, Wynona shot back. Instead of responding the way she wanted to, Wynona walked over. "Would you like a full tea? That includes a tray of pastries along with a custom tea. You can also order a pot of your favorite with or without the treats."

Marcella sniffed. "Might as well go for the full service." She tilted her head, batting her eyelashes. "What tea do you recommend for your mother?"

I'm starting to hate that word as much as I hate "sister".

Violet laughed again, drawing Marcella's eye.

"A mouse isn't exactly...couth," she said tightly.

"Violet is my familiar," Wynona said firmly. "She stays."

Marcella's look changed and Wynona realized she might have given her mother more information than she should have.

Let her do something, Violet growled. *I can handle her.*

Ignoring Violet's vicious streak, Wynona studied her mother. She had to set aside her own longing, hurt and pain in order to open her magic, which didn't seem to want to work for her at the moment.

"Is there a problem?" Marcella pressed. "Does it always take this long to figure out a drink?"

Violet pressed her nose into Wynona's neck and the extra focus was enough to help her finish the task. "Orange," Wynona finally said. "Orange with basil and mint." She straightened. "It'll help you handle the stress in your life." Spinning on her heel before her mother could argue, Wynona left for the kitchen, already using her magic to begin putting together the tray. She wanted her mother gone as soon as possible.

It only took a few minutes for Wynona to bring the tray out, using her magic to settle in front of Marcella. The tray landed in the middle and then Wynona placed the cup in front of her mother. With a wiggle of her fingers, she filled the cup with hot water and then dropped the infuser into it. "Enjoy," Wynona said as she started to walk away.

"Sit."

Wynona paused and turned around slowly. "I'm working," she said as politely as she could.

"I said sit." Marcella pointed at the chair next to her.

A force tugged on Wynona, trying to pull her to the seat, and Wynona felt her magic instantly come to life. Her feet cemented to the floor and the tug on her snapped back like a broken rubber band.

Marcella jerked back, blinking rapidly. There was nothing seductive about this look. She was actually shocked and Wynona wasn't sure she had ever seen it before. "How did you do that?"

I have no idea. There was no way Wynona was admitting that out loud. "Please refrain from using your magic," Wynona said coolly. "You have no right to compel anyone in here."

Marcella's lips became a thin line. "This isn't over."

Wynona knew she was right, but she wasn't going to stick around. "Please let me know if there's something else you need." She turned and walked away, hesitating when every other patron quickly turned back to their tables. A stark reminder that they weren't alone.

"I think. perhaps, your other patrons are done."

Turning, Wynona's jaw dropped. "Excuse me?"

Marcella slowly stood. "As President Le Doux's wife, I don't feel safe in this establishment while it's open to the public. While I'm here, I believe you should close the dining room to others."

Wynona's hands clenched, but she worked to control herself. She could feel the sparks of magic starting to snap against her skin. "I'm afraid that's not possible right now. They were here before you and I was unaware you were coming. If you would like to make a private appointment, I can make sure the private dining area is ready for you next time."

Scrambling behind her caused Wynona to turn. Apparently, the other women didn't believe Wynona would sufficiently protect them as each one was hurrying to leave. Wynona raised her hand to stop them, but dropped it. It was no use. They were already going out the door.

She spun, glaring at her mother. "Are you happy now?"

"If it will keep you from walking away from me, then yes."

"You had no right."

"I'm your mother," Marcella said confidently. "I have every right."

"You spent thirty years not wanting anything to do with me. I've been disowned by Dad. I don't think you get to count me as your daughter anymore."

Marcella's eyes flashed and her red magic sparkled. "Times change."

"No. Curses change." Wynona knew she was getting too emotional. Her vision was going purple and she was reacting with anger, which wasn't going to help her, but she was struggling to pull herself back. This confrontation had been a long time in coming and now that it was here, Wynona found every bad memory from her childhood, and even from recently, coming to the surface.

Easy, Violet warned. *Don't let her push you into something you don't want.*

Wynona breathed deeply, not daring to close her eyes or look away from her mother.

"Yes..." Marcella said, eyeing Wynona. "Curses. I'd like to hear the story of what happened to yours." Her eyes flashed red and Wynona knew her mother was looking for answers. One of her gifts had been to see magic. Not residual like Daemon could, but live, pulsing magic. So far, it was something Wynona couldn't replicate.

Marcella's eyes went back to normal. "It's gone. Completely gone."

Wynona nodded. "Yes."

"Did you ever find out where it came from?"

Wynona hesitated too long and her mother's eyes grew shrewd. "Tell me. Who would dare go against our family?"

Wynona shook her head. "It doesn't matter now. It's over."

Marcella pounded a fist on the table, rattling the tea service, and slowly climbed to her feet. "It's NOT over. *Someone* thought they had the right to deprive our family of your gifts and they deserve—"

"What, Marcella?" a voice interrupted.

Wynona spun, shocked to see her grandmother's ghost standing in the doorway. Her mother must have been just as shocked because she fell back into her seat, shaking.

"Saffron?"

"What do they deserve?" Granny pressed. "Death? Were you going to say death?" Granny threw up her hands. "Well, congratulations because that's exactly what they got."

It didn't seem possible for Marcella's eyes to widen any further, but they did. "You?" she breathed. "You cursed Wynona?"

Wynona felt like she was at a tennis match as her head snapped back and forth between the two women, but this wasn't a conversation she wanted to be a part of.

"I did." Granny clasped her hands and tilted her head. "And now she's free. Thank goodness."

"Free?" Marcella recovered quickly, her lips pulling into a sneer. "You cursed her in order to get her away from us, didn't you?" Slowly, she rose to her feet. "How *dare* you. She wasn't your child."

"And now she isn't yours," Saffron said with ease. "After all, you did disown her not too long ago."

Marcella's chuckle started low and it immediately put Wynona on edge. Even Violet winced and tucked deeper into Wynona's neck.

"And now what?" Marcella asked. "You're dead," she spat. "Wynona can't control her powers by herself. Who do you think she's going to turn to?"

Wynona backed up. If her mother thought Wynona would come running home, she was crazier than anyone knew.

Marcella put a perfectly manicured hand to her chest. "The only person strong enough to handle her."

"I don't need handling." The words were out of Wynona's mouth before she could stop them. Now all the attention was on her and she wanted to disappear. Instead, she forced her chest out and her shoulders back. "I've built a life without you, Mother, and I'll figure out my magic without your help." She waved her fingers at the tea tray and scooped everything up, sending it back to the kitchen in the blink of an eye. "I think it's time for you to leave."

Marcella's face tightened and Wynona prepared herself for the backlash headed her way. The problem was, she wasn't sure if it was going to be verbal or physical.

"AHHH!" Marcella screamed, throwing a hand toward Granny. "This is all your fault!" A shot of red burst from the witch and Wynona responded without thought.

Throwing her own hand between them, a purple wall blazed, stopping the red flame coming from Marcella.

The flame stopped almost instantly and Granny chuckled darkly. "Did you really think you needed to protect a ghost, dear one?"

Wynona didn't care that Granny could have disappeared and been unharmed. "This shop is mine," Wynona said to her mother. Her voice was deeper than normal and Wynona was surprised by it, but kept going. "I won't let you ruin it because of a simple tantrum. If you want a fight, take it elsewhere. This. Is. My. Home. And my friends are my family." Wynona pointed toward the door. "I will never be coming back and you will never control my magic. Now leave before I force you to."

Marcella's mouth snapped shut. "It's true. It's purple."

Wynona didn't budge. *Please don't make me do it,* she begged. *Please don't make me push you out.* Her heart was racing and sweat was trickling down her back. She wasn't sure how much longer she could hold back the waterfall of emotional magic raging in her system. If her mother didn't leave quickly, Wynona would end up hurting her without even trying.

Marcella's nostrils flared, but she spun and stomped to the door. "This is far from over," she declared right before slamming the door so hard the windows rattled.

"VIOLET!" Wynona shouted, grasping her head and dropping to her knees.

A frantic howl told Wynona that her soulmate had sensed her distress and was almost inside. Her mother's shriek meant he was at the door.

NO! Wynona screamed internally. She didn't want Rascal anywhere near her at the moment. She'd already hurt him once, she didn't want to do it again.

"Cecidimus." A finger touched Wynona's forehead and the magic faded into nothingness.

As her body swayed, Wynona fell into a large furry body. She sucked in a breath, her lungs finally working properly. Her hands came up, gripping Rascal's fur. She kept her eyes closed until her body began to relax. "Lusgu," she said weakly. She knew exactly who had stopped the outburst.

The brownie stood to the side, watching her carefully. His black eyes went up and down her body before nodding. He turned to leave, but Wynona reached out to stop him by taking his hand.

"Thank you," she whispered hoarsely. She squeezed his long fingers. "I don't know how you can do that, but I'm so thankful Granny sent you to me."

A light red colored the tips of his long ears as he snorted away her thanks. Without another word, he shuffled to the kitchen, his broom jumping to life behind him.

Turning, Wynona wrapped her arms around Rascal's large canine body. "I'm okay," she assured him, speaking out loud for her own benefit as well. "I'm okay."

Rascal whined and shifted so he was wrapped around her.

In a minute she would need to let him change back and explain, but his warm, soft fur was helping calm her down and she needed all the help she could get. "I'm okay..." She blew out a breath. "It's going to be okay." Maybe someday that would be the truth.

CHAPTER 13

Wynona wasn't sure how much time had passed before she finally let herself separate from Rascal's comforting back. She stood on shaky knees, breathing deeply. "Okay. You can change back now."

He whimpered, huffed, then flashed back into a man. "What in all of purgatory happened?" Rascal demanded, wrapping his arms around her.

Wynona melted into his chest. Considering how shaken up she still was, she wasn't about to complain about his need to touch her. "My mom showed up," Wynona mumbled into his shirt.

"Figured that one, since I snarled at her while coming in the door."

Wynona let out a humorous chuckle. "It might have been worth it to see that."

Rascal growled. "What did she do? Why was she here?"

Wynona picked her head up. "Why do you think she was here?"

Rascal cursed again and dropped his forehead to hers. "She can't have you," he said in a low tone.

"No. She can't." Wynona reached up and threaded her fingers through his hair. "I won't be going back willingly, that I can promise."

"The problem is, *unwilling* is still a way they'll take you."

Wynona nodded, breaking their touch. "I know, but I'm doing my best to not let that happen."

"I think maybe I just need to stay by you at all times. I'll chain you to my hip."

Wynona pulled back enough to straighten her shirt and skirt. "As wonderful as that would be, it's not very efficient for either of our jobs."

He pushed his hand through his hair. "Then how am I going to keep you safe? The confrontation was over by the time I got here and my wolf isn't exactly a slowpoke."

Wynona rolled her eyes. "I can protect myself," she argued.

Rascal just raised a single eyebrow.

"Okay. Fine. I'm working on protecting myself." She pasted a wide smile on. "But seriously. One of my magical accidents might go a long way in keeping them off my back."

Rascal didn't find it funny. "Where's Violet?"

Wynona reached for her shoulder, then jerked around. "I don't know!" She spun in a circle. "And where did Granny go?"

The kitchen door opened and Wynona turned to the sound, relaxing slightly when she saw Violet on Lusgu's shoulder. Their relationship was such a surprise, but right now Wynona was grateful for it. "Violet," Wynona rbeathed, reaching out her hand. "What happened?"

You nearly exploded, Violet said wryly.

Wynona hung her head. "I'm sorry." She brought the purple mouse to her chest. "I didn't mean to."

"You need control." Lusgu grunted, glaring up at Wynona. "Your familiar can only do so much."

Wynona nodded. "I know. I'm trying." She hesitated, but decided to press her luck. "Did you see what happened with Granny?"

"She disappeared," Lsugu said easily. "Will probably be back later." He put his hands on his hips. "You need a teacher."

"Do you have any suggestions?" Wynona asked, fearing his answer. She had a feeling who would be the perfect person to teach her about having such strong powers and Wynona wasn't sure she was ready to accept it.

Lusgu's eyes narrowed. "You don't need an answer." Spinning, he left.

"He meant your grandmother, didn't he?" Rascal grumbled.

Wynona nodded. "I think he did."

Another growl filled the room. He took her hand and tugged toward the door, causing Violet to squeak. "Come on."

"Where are we going?" Wynona asked.

"To the station. Somehow I doubt there'll be any more customers today anyway. Close down and come interrogate suspects with me."

Wynona huffed a small laugh. "That does sound enticing, but I need to finish up here first."

Rascal snorted. "Then I'll wait."

Wynona squeezed his arm. "Rascal. I'm fine. I'm grateful you came, but I'll be okay. Let me take care of work and then I'll come to the precinct."

He leaned his shoulder against the wall, letting her know he wasn't going anywhere. Secretly, Wynona was grateful. She didn't want to admit it, but a part of her was still struggling with the leftover adrenaline from her confrontation.

"Give me a few," she said softly, then headed back to the kitchen to talk to Lusgu again.

Half an hour later, they were on their way to the police station. Violet was tucked in Rascal's front pocket, the door of the shop was locked and Lusgu had been given the rest of the day off.

It only took a few minutes to get to the police parking lot and soon, Rascal was helping Wynona down.

"Thank you," she said softly.

Rascal gave her waist a squeeze. "Always." Letting go, he stepped back and took her hand. "Marsh is inside, waiting for us."

"You haven't talked to him yet?" Wynona was surprised. She had assumed Rascal would process the merman immediately.

Rascal shook his head while he pulled open the front door. "No. I wanted to wait for you. Plus, we had other things to do anyway. I'm trying to get a hold of the ex, as well. Skymaw should be bringing him in soon."

Wynona nodded. "Sounds good."

"Heya, Detective Le Doux."

Wynona smiled at Amaris. "I guess we'll be seeing a bit more of each other now, huh?"

"Us women have to stick together." The vampire clasped her hands and leaned forward. "The men just can't do it by themselves, you know."

"Nightshade!"

The whole room jumped and Wynona turned. "Hello, Chief Ligurio."

His red eyes flashed. "Enough gossip. I've got a merman threatening to get a lawyer if we don't let him go." His black eyebrows rose high. "Are you coming?"

Wynona nodded. "Of course. Thank you for waiting for me." She ignored his huff and walked with Rascal down the hall, waving discreetly to Amaris, who rolled her eyes in rebellion.

Wynona held back a laugh, sobering quickly as they walked into the room where Marsh Monroe was waiting. "Hello, Mr. Monroe," she said politely. "Thank you for being patient. I'm afraid I have a day job that keeps me from being available at all hours."

Bright blue eyes glared. "There was nothing stopping the officers from taking care of this," he grumbled.

Wynona nodded. "Stations can be busy places. Plus, I wanted to be here when we chatted."

Marsh leaned back in his seat, folding his arms over his chest. "I'm drying out. If I don't get to my pool soon, I'll start to get sick."

"I understand," Wynona assured. "Again, thank you for your patience."

Chief Ligurio was sitting on her right and Rascal stood on her left. Since there was no concern about the merman using magic against them, Wynona wasn't as concerned about Daemon still being gone. They could catch him up later.

"Let's talk about this chemical on the ground, shall we?" Chief Ligurio began.

Marsh held up his hands. "I haven't spilled anything. I have no idea how that got there. And even if I *did* spill something, I would clean it up."

Ignoring the explanation, Chief Ligurio examined a piece of paper. "Our tests came back showing it was a chlorine alternative. Meant to keep pool water clear and chemical free."

Marsh shook his head. "Ms. Roseburg wanted me to try that, since she hates the smell of the chlorine. She tried a spell once to get rid of the smell, but it backfired and smelled even worse."

Chief Ligurio turned to look at Wynona. "I've never heard of that, but it's plausible," she said softly.

He nodded before turning back to the merman. "The room smelled of chlorine when we were there to pick up the body."

"That's because that junk didn't work. I stuffed it in the closet and never pulled it out again. I've been using bromine, which has a bleach-like smell, and Ms. Roseburg wasn't happy with that either."

"Why didn't she just spell the water herself?" Wynona asked. Keeping a pool clean should be relatively easy for a witch like Ms. Roseburg.

Marsh shrugged. "She just always said she wasn't a water witch."

"Huh." Wynona frowned and made a mental note to look into that. It seemed odd to her. "And you didn't touch that chemical again?"

Marsh shook his head.

"You mentioned having information about Mr. Killoran," Wynona said, changing subjects for the moment. She ignored the look Chief Ligurio gave her. "Why do you feel like he killed Ms. Roseburg?"

Marsh continued to glare for a moment before leaning forward. "He's in debt."

Wynona waited. "Okay?"

Marsh rolled his eyes. "Like...a lot of debt. He's got a gambling problem."

"We don't have any gambling houses in Hex Haven," Wynona said.

Marsh laughed darkly. "The underworld does."

She snapped her mouth shut. Her only interaction with the underworld had been with Roderick Caligari, her first landlord. He'd been part of the underground mafia and attempted to woo Wynona in order to gain her magic. When she discovered his subterfuge, not to mention the fact that he killed two men, she helped bring him down, rather than falling for his lines.

Rascal's chest rumbled.

Wynona could feel that he'd had the same thought as her. "How bad is it?" she asked.

Marsh smirked. "Enough that if he doesn't pay it soon, he won't exist."

"And how do you know this?" Chief Ligurio demanded.

Marsh shrugged. "No one's afraid to talk in front of the pool boy. Plus, he came to the house the other day." His smirk grew. "No one seems to realize that mermen have exceptional hearing, even when we're under water."

Wynona's cheeks flushed. She had a habit of forgetting that many paranormals could hear well. It had gotten her in trouble a few times. "So you heard Ms. Roseburg and Mr. Killoran arguing?"

He nodded. "Wayde wanted a loan. Harmony said no. He wasn't happy."

"Unhappy enough to kill her?"

Marsh leaned back again and folded his arms. "Creatures will do anything if they're desperate enough."

"How does killing her get him money though?" Wynona asked. "Surely he's not still in her will. They were divorced years ago."

Marsh shook his head. "He could be planning to appeal to whichever of the kids ends up inheriting. Silvaria would probably give him something, but Zander..."

"Zander didn't get along with dear old Daddy?" Rascal sneered.

"Dear old Daddy felt like Harmony spoiled him," Marsh snorted. "Which was true. The guy's a class A..." He eyed Wynona and cleared his throat. "Let's just say I won't be sad when my contract runs out."

Chief Ligurio stood. "We'll be sending in our investigative unit to do a test on your hands," he said.

Wynona jumped to her feet, following the chief's lead.

"When they're done, you'll be free to go. However, I wouldn't advise leaving town, Mr. Monroe."

Marsh's lip curled, but he nodded. "I didn't kill her, I had no motive to kill her. And if you'll look into her records, you'll see that I had ordered several more products for the pool. There was no reason for me to get that particular one out when I wasn't using it anymore."

"We'll do that. Thank you for your time. We'll be in touch." Chief stormed from the room, Wynona and Rascal on his heels. They headed down the hall until entering the chief's office, where he threw himself in his chair and rubbed his forehead. "Thoughts?" he demanded.

Wynona carefully sat down in a chair, grateful that Rascal sat next to her. "I don't know. I have to agree that he doesn't have much of a motive."

Chief Ligurio stared at her, obviously waiting for more.

"He said he was having fun with Ms. Roseburg. If they weren't fighting, what would he gain by killing her?"

"Maybe he didn't do it on purpose," Rascal offered. "If he spilled that chemical, she could have accidentally been killed and he's simply covering up his mistake."

Wynona nodded. "I can't argue that one. It's very plausible." She tapped her knee. "I'm stuck on the chemical thing though. Ms. Roseburg was a talented witch, even if water wasn't her strongest element, and it seems odd she wouldn't be able to keep her pool water clear."

"I'll let you look into that," Chief Ligurio said. "It'll be more your area of expertise."

Wynona nodded. "Sure." She pinched her lips together, her mind trying to work through the puzzle. "If it was an accident," Wynona murmured, "who healed her? And why did she still die?"

Chief Ligurio huffed and leaned back in his seat. He looked at Rascal. "Ideas?"

Rascal shook his head. "Not yet. I agree with Wynona, the healing doesn't make sense."

"I did notice that Zander and Silvaria both have blue magic," Wynona offered. "I don't know what color Ms. Roseburg's was."

"Do you have a way of finding out?" Chief Ligurio asked.

Wynona looked up at Rascal. His lips pinched into a thin, white line, knowing exactly what she was thinking. "Yeah."

The chief's eyebrows pulled together. "But?"

Wynona shook her head. "But nothing. I haven't exactly been ready to speak to Granny Saffron yet, but she'll have the answers we're looking for."

The chief snorted, apparently not worried about her desire to stay away from the woman who cursed her. "You take care of that and let us know what you find." He reached for a folder and threw it across the desk at her. "You'll need to sign this, by the way."

Wynona took it and opened it. "Another contract?"

"You're an independent consultant. If you're helping in an official capacity, you need this in order to follow us around or go somewhere without us."

She clucked her tongue. "It looks like I didn't get a raise from last time."

His red eyes narrowed. "I believe you once told me you didn't do this for money."

"Ah, but *you* pulled me in this time," Wynona teased. When Chief Ligurio's eyes tightened even more, Wynona relented. "I'm joking, Chief Ligurio. As long as I don't have to shut down my shop, I'll be fine helping you."

"Speaking of..." The chief tilted his head. "How did you get here so early today?"

Wynona shook her head. "You don't want to know."

"Oh, I think I do. When my deputy chief bursts into his wolf and races through the building fast enough to start a paper hurricane, I think I have a right to know what's going on."

Wynona leaned back. "My mother paid me a visit today, then Granny...and it didn't go well."

He scrubbed his face. "They're bold. I'll give them that." He raised his eyebrows expectantly. "Is it taken care of for now?"

"For now." Wynona made a mental note to ask Granny about more than just Ms. Roseburg's magic. There were a couple other things she needed to know.

A knock on the door had all their heads turning. "Enter!" Chief Ligurio shouted.

Daemon poked his head in. "I've got Mr. Killoran."

Chief Ligurio nodded. "Interrogation room two. Ten minutes."

Daemon nodded and disappeared.

"Looks like we're still on duty." The chief stood and gathered his computer. "Ms. Le Doux?"

Wynona stood and, taking Rascal's hand, headed back out. Her detective hat would have to stay in place for a bit longer.

CHAPTER 14

Interrogation room number two looked just like all the other rooms. The room was white with no ornamentation. A table with chairs on either side allowed those inside to sit while talking, but other than that, the space was filled with...nothing.

It was made especially stark as Daemon took up his place by the door, his eyes going black, indicating that he had his powers at the ready in case Mr. Killoran decided to get defensive.

"What's she doing here?" Mr. Killoran grumbled, his brown eyes attempting to melt Wynona into a puddle.

Using her years of experience at feigning confidence, Wynona threw back her shoulders and flicked her hair the same way her mother did. "Hello, Mr. Killoran. It's been a long time."

He leaned forward, his fists resting on the table. "I said, what are you doing here?"

"She's working with us on a consulting basis," Chief Ligurio inserted. "You will treat her with the same respect as the other officers."

Wynona bit back the retort she wanted to say at that remark. It wasn't that she wasn't grateful for Chief Ligurio's comment, but Mr. Killoran didn't treat anyone with respect, so the command wouldn't go very far.

Violet's snort in Wynona's mind told her that her familiar felt the same way.

"Thank you," Wynona murmured as Rascal held a chair for her.

Mr. Killoran was leaning back in his seat, his eyes still on Wynona. "Does your father know about your activities?" One side of his lip curled. "Somehow, I don't think he'd approve."

"My choice of activities are my own, Mr. Killoran," Wynona said easily. "Now." She folded her hands in her lap. "My condolences on the loss of your ex-wife."

He huffed and looked away. "We haven't been together in many years."

"Maybe not, but we have a witness saying you visited her just last week."

His head snapped around and Wynona felt the snap of magic in the air. Unlike his children and former wife, green sparks floated through the air.

"Control yourself, or we will do it for you," Chief Ligurio said with a pointed look at Daemon.

Mr. Killoran looked over and grumbled, but his magic dissipated. "I suppose it wouldn't be sporting to use magic against someone who doesn't know how to use theirs."

He's trying to bait you, Violet declared. *It means he's scared.*

Wynona gave a subtle nod. She knew. The only reason he wouldn't like having her there was if he was worried she would do something that could hurt him. "Why were you there, Mr. Killoran?" she asked, raising her eyebrows expectantly.

He sneered. "You tell me, since you're so observant."

Chief Ligurio slid a paper in her direction.

Wynona took it and read the first few lines. "I see that you owe a few people some money." The paper the chief had given her held nothing of the sort, but the chief had given her a paper with gibberish on it. She followed a hunch that he wanted her to use it to fake out the warlock.

Mr. Killoran's face paled. "I don't know what you're talking about," he said, his voice softer than before.

"No?" Wynona pressed. "You haven't found yourself digging a deeper hole down in the underworld? Maybe a little gambling?"

Mr. Killoran jerked forward, his pale face turning alarmingly red as he hit the table with his fist. "Half of that money is mine! I was married to her for almost twenty years!"

Wynona swallowed hard, hiding the fear at his reaction. Her fingers tingled, and she forced herself to calm down. Her magic wasn't needed either. "I don't believe that's how our laws work, Mr. Killoran. Ms. Roseburg's family inheritance was hers and hers alone." Wynona tilted her head to the side. "What did you do when she wouldn't give you any? You were asking for help with your loans, correct? And since she's been killed, I'm assuming Ms. Roseburg said no."

"I didn't kill her," he ground out.

"Okay. Then what *did* you do?"

Mr. Killoran's nostrils flared as he took in a deep breath. "I walked away." He shrugged. "What could I do?"

Wynona pursed her lips. "Did Ms. Roseburg ever share with you what her will said?"

He snorted. "No. Not even when we were married. It's always been a secret." That lip curled again. "Zander, spoiled punk that he is, probably gets it all. Harmony always did favor him. Him and those cursed cats."

"You think she'd leave out her daughter?" Wynona pressed.

Mr. Killoran shrugged again. "More than likely." He looked Wynona in the eye. "Harmony knew how to hold a grudge." His smile held no humor. "Even toxic plants can be beautiful."

Unfortunately, Wynona knew that all too well. She nodded. "Where were you when she was killed?"

"Home."

"By yourself?"

He smirked. "Wouldn't you like to know?" His eyes roved her, sending a shiver down Wynona's spine. "I always did think it would be good to join our families."

Rascal's growl came so fast that Wynona jumped in her seat. She reached out and put a hand on his arm.

"Strongclaw," Chief Ligurio warned. He turned his red glare to Mr. Killoran. "Keep it relevant or I'll let you cool your ardor somewhere less favorable."

Mr. Killoran rolled his eyes.

"Why did you ask her for money if she wasn't known for being charitable?" Wynona asked.

"Who else was I going to ask?" Mr. Killoran demanded. "My family ran out of money ages ago."

"Ran out, or you spent it all?" Rascal offered.

Mr. Killoran clearly didn't appreciate the commentary, but he also didn't deny it. "Look. On the night Harmony was killed, I was down in the underworld, playing Black Jack."

"What den?" Chief Ligurio asked.

"Like I'm telling you that," Mr. Killoran scoffed. "I don't have a death wish."

"Sounds like you do," Chief Ligurio said lightly. "Otherwise you wouldn't be so desperate to get all that money."

"It's because I *don't* have a death wish that I need the money," Mr. Killoran spat. "I'm trying to save my life."

"By killing your wife."

Mr. Killoran shook his head and groaned. "Okay, I can't give you an alibi, but there is no way you can pin this murder on me. There's no evidence. Asking for a loan means nothing and killing Harmony is actually the worst thing that could have happened to help my case."

"Unless you assumed one of your children would give you the money instead," Wynona offered.

"Zander hates me," Mr. Killoran snapped. "Silvaria might have considered it, but she couldn't keep her mouth shut long enough for Harmony to even consider keeping her in the will. If she had only bitten her tongue a little, she'd be swimming in it by now."

Pity rose up in Wynona's chest. What a sad existence. His children didn't like him, his ex-wife wouldn't help him. Wayde Killoran was nothing but a washed up warlock who had power, but nothing else. And that power wasn't enough to help get him out of the pit he'd dug himself into. He was leading a miserable, lonely existence, which led Wynona to another moment of gratitude that Granny had pulled her out of that lifestyle. Wynona might not have appreciated how it was done, but she couldn't deny the results.

You might start with that when we talk to her, Violet offered.

"What do you know about pool chemicals, Mr. Killoran?" Wynona asked, ignoring Violet.

He scowled at the sudden change in subject. "Pool chemicals? What do you mean? I thought Harmony drowned." His eyes widened. "Did someone poison her?"

Wynona stood. "Thank you, Mr. Killoran. When we have more questions, we'll let you know."

"No, no, no," he hurried to say. "You have to tell me. Was Harmony poisoned?"

"Why would it matter if she was poisoned?" Wynona asked, not correcting his assumption.

He chuckled darkly, sending a shiver down Wynona's spine. "Would serve her right. She always said those cats could protect her from anything, but if someone managed to get something into her food or drink, then it only goes to show how stupid she was."

Wynona was disgusted. This man was a parasite to society. "Thank you for your time," she said quickly, marching toward the door. She couldn't stand being in the room with him for one moment longer.

Rascal was behind her, but Wynona wasn't sure if the chief had followed. She didn't care, heading straight to his office and bursting inside. She gulped in deep lungfuls of air, feeling as if she was finally able to breathe properly.

"Sorry," Rascal said, rubbing her back. "That got a little more intense than I planned."

Wynona held up a hand and shook her head. "No. It's alright." She straightened, leaning into his side. "It just hit a little too close to home," she whispered.

"I know." Rascal kissed her temple, then stepped back when Chief Ligurio came into the office.

"Skymaw will be here in a minute," he grumbled before sitting in his chair. He huffed through his nose. "Thoughts?"

"Has the date for the will reading been announced yet?" Wynona asked. She had a feeling they would learn much more at that appointment.

"It's tomorrow."

The voice came from behind Wynona and she had no idea who it was. Spinning quickly, she stopped. A handsome man, who appeared just old enough to be her father, stood in the doorway. His tie was perfectly straight, his shoes shiny and the briefcase he held looked to be genuine leather.

What shifter did he kill for that? Violet sneered.

Wynona sighed.

"Mr. Melion," Chief Ligurio said, standing up and offering his hand.

Wynona watched the newcomer approach. His sleek way of walking said he was a shifter himself, likely of the feline variety.

Leopard, Rascal provided.

That's right. She'd forgotten Rascal had told her that before.

"Chief Ligurio," Mr. Melion said easily. He looked comfortable and confident in his place at the police station. "I thought it would be best to come offer the news in person," he said, explaining his presence.

"I appreciate it," Chief Ligurio said. He turned to Wynona. "This is Ms. Roseburg's lawyer, Romulus Melion. He's been fighting the legal wall to get the will read as soon as possible."

Wynona nodded and shook his offered hand. "Will the police be allowed to sit in on the reading?" she asked.

"Probably not," Mr. Melion said apologetically. "The family has to all agree and the odds of that are..." He made a face.

Wynona nodded, a small smile tugging at her lips. Apparently, the lawyer was well aware of the family dynamics. "Do you mind asking?"

"Of course not. Consider it done." He tilted his head and studied her. "You look very much like your mother."

Wynona stilled. "Thank you," she replied, though she wasn't sure it was a compliment...at least not to her. Her mother was a beautiful woman, but Wynona wanted there to be as few connections between them as possible.

"But I hear your magic is something else entirely."

"My magic is my own," Wynona said, her voice tight.

"Of course," he said, ducking his head. "Pardon my curiosity."

Rascal's hand on her lower back had Wynona relaxing. "It's fine," she assured him. It was clear he wasn't trying to offend. It made sense that a lawyer would be the type to poke and figure things out. It was what they did, after all. Wynona blinked several times as a thought occurred to her. "Do you mind telling me how long you've been in Hex Haven? I'm pretty familiar with the lawyers who serve the upper class and I've never heard of you."

Mr. Melion chuckled. He turned to Chief Ligurio. "I can see why she's been recruited," he said with a smile. "I've been here for close to ten years, but I don't practice full time. Hex Haven was *supposed to be my retirement area.*" He shrugged. "I ended up taking on just a few clients. Ms. Roseburg was one of only three that I still share my knowledge with." His eyes twinkled. "Your parents are already well settled, so they weren't interested when I opened my small office."

Wynona nodded. Her parents' lawyer practically lived at the palace. He wouldn't give up his position easily. "It was nice to meet you. If things change about tomorrow, please let me know."

Mr. Melion nodded. "I will. It was nice to meet you as well."

Rascal's hand guided Wynona out to the hall. "I have some things to take care of here," he said softly. "Skymaw can take you home and I'll stop by later."

"You really need to just let me take my Vespa," Wynona teased.

Rascal kissed the tip of her nose. "Not if I can help it. Will you be okay for a bit by yourself? Can you put up a ward around the cabin?"

Violet squeaked and poked her head out of Rascal's pocket. *I can help with that.*

Wynona reached out and pulled her friend out, putting the tiny creature on her shoulder. "Sounds like we'll handle it."

"Good. See you soon." Another quick peck, and he disappeared down the hall.

"Ready?" Daemon asked.

Wynona nodded. "Lead the way, Officer." She touched his arm. "And thank you."

Daemon smirked. "Deputy Chief would have my head...literally...so..." He shrugged, then winked. "But it's my pleasure."

Good friends and a soulmate who loved her. This was what made her life worth fighting for. Gratitude filled Wynona while they drove to her house and she realized she just might be ready to speak to Granny.

And maybe, just maybe...forgive and move on.

CHAPTER 15

C*an you get to the Roseburg Mansion in twenty minutes?*

Wynona jolted a little at the intrusion. That wasn't Violet's voice. *Rascal?*

Yeah?

She rubbed her forehead. "I guess I don't have much use for a phone anymore," Wynona muttered. She glanced at the wall clock. The shop had opened only an hour before and her regulars were all seated in their chairs. *What's happening? Why should I be there?*

They're reading the will.

I thought we weren't allowed inside.

We are now.

Urgency hit Wynona in the gut. She had desperately wanted to watch the family's faces when the will was read, but had known better than to try and flaunt the law. Without another thought, she raced for the kitchen. "Lusgu!"

A grunt pulled her eyes to the corner.

"They're reading the Roseburg will," Wynona said breathlessly. "Can you watch the shop?"

I'm coming too! Violet shouted, racing from the direction of the office.

Wynona shook her head. "I need you here," she said to her familiar as the mouse skidded into the kitchen.

Violet put her hands on her hips and began arguing so fast it all sounded like squeaks and chitters rather than words.

Please, Wynona begged. She didn't want to say it out loud, but she didn't like leaving Lusgu in charge. He might have magic beyond the norm, but his people skills were seriously lacking. *For the shop?*

Violet stopped her protesting and chose to glare instead. *Fine. But you owe me.*

"I'll keep my mind open," Wynona said. "You can listen in."

Violet sniffed and immediately began cleaning herself as if she didn't care, but Wynona knew better.

"Thank you," Wynona whispered. She turned back to Lusgu, who had yet to give her an answer.

His glare was much more intimidating than Violet's was. "Do I have a choice?"

"Of course you do," Wynona said, her eyes wide. She might really, really want his help, but she wouldn't force it on him. "You always have a choice." And she meant it. Too much of Wynona's life had been chosen for her. She refused to do the same to others.

He huffed and turned away, but Wynona understood it as consent. If he wanted to say no, he would have. "Thank you!" she sang out, rushing to her office to gather her things.

Purse and keys in hand, Wynona practically ran to her Vespa. The scooter wasn't the speediest vehicle in the shed, but it always got her where she needed to go. And she adored the mint green color.

Plopping her helmet on, Wynona took off, weaving through traffic as quickly as she dared. Even still, she only had one minute to spare when she reached the Roseburg home.

"Cutting it a little close," Rascal said with a grin as he helped her off.

"Someone didn't give me much advance warning," she teased right back.

Rascal squeezed her hand and kissed her cheek. "Sorry. Next time I'll demand they wait for you to curl your hair."

"Hardy, har, har," Wynona said sarcastically. "Come on." She tugged on him, leading toward the house.

Rascal chuckled. "Don't think I didn't catch your surprise this morning when I popped in to say hello."

"Yeah...about that," Wynona drawled. "I think maybe we need some kind of signal. Like a knock at a front door before we just burst into each other's thoughts like that."

Rascal's chuckle grew louder. "You want me to knock on your mind before I speak." He knocked on the front door.

"Yes," Wynona said primly, sniffing for added emphasis. "Thank you," she murmured as a butler let them in. "It's the polite thing to do."

Rascal's amusement continued to rumble in his chest as he led her deeper into the house. "I'll keep that in mind."

Wynona wasn't fooled by the fact that he hadn't promised to actually "knock". *Stinker.*

His grin grew, having heard every word. "Here we are." He pushed open a door and every head spun to look at the new arrivals. "I apologize for the delay," Rascal announced. "We wanted one of our best consultants to be here."

Zander smirked, Silvaria rolled her eyes and Mr. Killoran snorted. Each person looked bored with the production and eager to be elsewhere. Only Marsh Monroe didn't make his thoughts known, though he nodded politely at Wynona.

She returned the gesture, then moved to the back and sat in a corner with Rascal standing next to her chair. She loved how he always stood. He wasn't lording over her or showing dominance, but his stance showed his protectiveness and desire to be on his guard at all times. It never failed to make Wynona feel safe and cherished.

Several cats were lazily draped around the room, their beady eyes taking in everyone and everything. Wynona watched the tail of a tabby twitch back and forth, as if it were planning its next conquest. His paws flexed, as if to show off his weapons before he began cleaning himself.

"Welcome, Ms. Le Doux," Mr. Melion said pleasantly from the front of the room, pulling her attention that direction. His reading glasses gave away his age, though his face was free of wrinkles. He was a fairly handsome man, as things stood, but the bulky wolf to her side was much more Wynona's style.

"Thank you," she responded with a smile. "I'm grateful to be here."

Mr. Melion nodded and grew more serious. "On behalf of Melion Law, I'd like to offer my deepest condolences to the Roseburg and Killoran family. Ms. Roseburg was a wonderful witch and will be sorely missed."

No one missed the lack of agreement from the family. Even the spoiled Zander didn't bother to respond to the heartfelt words. Wynona narrowed her gaze. Someone in this room was a killer, she was sure of it. But who? Who would heal a woman only to kill her? Had the death been on purpose? Was someone desperate enough for Ms. Roseburg's fortune to take her life? Did anyone actually know what was in the will?

"I have with me Ms. Roseburg's final will and testament," Mr. Melion said in an official tone. He looked over his glasses. "This will was signed and dated over a year ago and is the last official declaration from Harmony...Ms. Roseburg."

Zander shifted in his seat, then yawned. "Is this going to take long? I have better things to be doing."

"Just because you're sure the money's going to you doesn't mean the rest of us don't want to hear it," Silvaria snapped.

Zander gave his sister an unkind smile. "Maybe if you had spent a little more time sucking up to the old woman, you wouldn't be so worried about your future right now."

Silvaria cursed and Mr. Melion stood up. "There will be order," he demanded, a growl leaking into his tone. His eyes fluttered to the side before focusing again, as if taking a moment to gather himself.

Wynona watched him carefully. His animal was strong. Stronger than she would have suspected for a lawyer.

Leopard, remember? Rascal supplied. *They aren't exactly domesticated.*

Wynona gave him the side eye.

Sorry. Knock, knock...

She bit back a laugh. This wolf was going to be the death of her. *I keep forgetting, but thank you. Apparently, your memory is better than mine at the moment.* She had remembered Mr. Melion was a cat, but the exact type hadn't seemed important. Wynona made a note to remember from here on out.

Rascal discreetly tapped the edge of his nose, his eyes never giving away their conversation as they continued to roam the room.

"Any more disruptions of that nature and I will have you escorted to the jail house, is that understood?"

"Isn't that illegal?" Silvaria asked, twirling her hair through her fingers. "We have a legal right to listen to Mom's will."

"You do," Mr. Melion said with a nod. "But it can be done in a different setting if necessary." He raised an eyebrow at her. "Are you ready to behave?"

Silvaria held up her hands on either side. "I always behave. It's my spoiled brother who's the problem."

Rascal let out a long, deep growl that shook the room before Zander could respond.

Scowling, the warlock chose to glare at his sister rather than respond verbally.

Good choice, Wynona thought.

Rascal coughed, hiding his amusement.

Mr. Melion cleared his throat, giving Rascal a look saying he wasn't fooling anyone, before diving into the will.

It took a couple of minutes to get past the beginning paragraphs and finally the room was on the edge of their seats. "To my pool boy, Mr. Marsh Monroe," Mr. Melion said clearly.

All eyes turned to the merman, who stuck his chin in the air, though Wynona noticed his gills flashing rapidly with anxiety.

"I leave his contract. He may keep his contract with Roseburg House alive as long as he wishes. Neither my children nor my ex-husband or any other person who lives within these walls may terminate said contract. If at any time, Mr. Monroe wishes to be free from working on the Roseburg House pool, he may quit without warning or explanation."

Marsh folded his arms over his chest and huffed. As far as gifts go, it was an interesting one. Definitely not one worth killing for though.

Wynona wondered what his pay had been. Would working with Ms. Roseburg's children be worth the amount?

"To my ex-husband..."

Mr. Killoran perked up and smiled. "That's more like it."

"I leave my deepest condolences. I've heard of your black activities and am aware of the dwindling bank account that used to hold your family's coffers."

Mr. Killoran's face was turning a dangerous shade of red and Wynona found herself leaning back slightly. She looked sideways to Daemon, whose eyes had turned black. When no magic appeared in the room, she relaxed slightly, though she was beginning to understand why Ms. Roseburg's family hated her so much.

Zander snorted behind his fist. "Good luck, Dad."

Grumbling curses under his breath, Mr. Killoran stood and headed for the door. "I didn't come here to be insulted," he shouted.

"Sit down, Mr. Killoran," Mr. Melion said tightly, once again rising to his feet.

Daemon stepped in front of the door, his look daring Mr. Killoran to try to leave. Without magic, the witch was no match for the large black hole.

"There is nothing that says I have to stay past where my name is read," Mr. Killoran ground out, turning to face the lawyer.

"We will do this correctly now or later," Mr. Melion said. He waved toward the now vacated seat. "But it *will* happen." He paused, stilling in anticipation before his muscles moved again.

His lips pinched into a tight, white line, Mr. Killoran sat, though the veins in his neck and arms looked ready to burst at any second.

Again, not a good motive for murder.

Rascal rubbed her shoulder in agreement.

"To my daughter," Mr. Melion continued.

"Somehow I don't think I want it," Silvaria said as if she hadn't a care in the world.

"I leave a permanent place at Paranormal Rehab. Your name has been placed on the records and your stay paid for any time you finally decide to get your act together and make a witch out of yourself."

Silvaria slunk into her seat.

I didn't know she was an addict, Wynona sent the thought to Rascal.

She smells of alcohol at all times of the day, though it's fairly subtle.

Wynona frowned. Had Silvaria been worse when she was younger? Was that why she was kicked out? Most addicts would be drenched in the smell, allowing even Wynona to understand what was going on.

"And to my favorite son," Mr. Melion's voice continued to interrupt Wynona's thoughts.

"Finally," Zander breathed, rubbing his hands together.

"I leave the apartment on Luminous Street. While the home is paid for, you will need to get a job in order to pay for the utilities. I trust that at this point in your life, with as much money as I have doled out for college and graduate school, you can finally find it within yourself to get off my couch and use your hands for once."

Zander's jaw dropped and his eyes bugged. "An apartment? That's all she left me?"

Mr. Melion nodded his assent. "Yes."

"That can't be right," Zander argued while his sister chuckled rudely at his dismay. "The house, the fortune, it's all still here. She hasn't given it to anyone."

"Not yet," Mr. Melion agreed.

"Are you saying you're not done?" Zander asked.

"That would be correct."

Zander's jaw clenched. "You're reading it wrong."

The lawyer's eyebrows rose. "Excuse me?"

"You're reading it wrong!" Zander stood up. "There was no one else for her to leave it to. She had no family other than us and her boyfriend already got his stupid job. My mother would have died before giving it all to charity." He leaned onto the desk as if to intimidate Mr. Melion. "So I say again, you're reading it wrong."

"Young man, you will sit or I will have you forced into it," Mr. Melion said coolly.

Zander punched the desk. "YOU'RE READING IT WRONG!"

"Tanjin." Mr. Melion tilted his head, his body relaxed and overly still.

A man that Wynona hadn't even noticed emerged from the shadows. His craggy face and sharp lines told everyone he was a troll, which meant he towered head and shoulders above everyone else in the room. The creature dressed in black stepped up to Mr. Melion's desk.

"Please help Mr. Killoran find his seat."

Zander backed up quickly, his fingers twitching but no magic coming out. "I'm fine," he stammered, dropping into the chair. "Just finish reading the stupid will."

Tanjin stood stoically next to the desk, apparently not willing to leave his boss alone now that a threat had been made.

Mr. Melion resettled the glasses on his nose, his eyes scanning up and down the page. "As for my home, my wealth and the future payments of my investments," he read, "I leave them to Duo, my beloved cat."

"WHAT!" Zander screamed, once again jumping to his feet.

"As the only creature who ever truly loved me, I have made sure that your future is assured and any posterity you have will be taken care of for generations to come. The Kitty Kauldron will continue as your caretaker until such time as there are no more descendants to provide for. At that point, the money and properties will become the property of Rowan School of Witchcraft, my alma mater, as a trust in my name."

"Are you telling me that my wife left *millions* of dollars to a cat?" Mr. Killoran said in a dangerously low tone.

Mr. Melion removed his glasses and nodded. "She did."

"And you believe she was in her right mind?"

The leopard shifter nodded. "She was."

Mr. Killoran pointed a finger at Mr. Melion. "I'll see you in court. This will never stand." He stormed from the room, his daughter on his heels.

Zander, however, paused, studying Mr. Melion for a long moment. "We're going to fight this," Zander said calmly, a stark contrast to his behavior only a few moments before. "Don't think you'll get away with it."

Mr. Melion sighed. "I was expecting it, Mr. Killoran. Do what you must." He closed his eyes for a few seconds, obviously gathering strength.

With one last glare, Zander left the room.

Wynona slumped against the wall once they were gone. "That might be the craziest will I have ever heard."

Mr. Melion walked from the backside of the desk and picked up the tabby from the bookcase, slowly scratching the cat's ears. "Ms. Le Doux, meet Duo. The richest cat in Hex Haven."

CHAPTER 16

"Thank you so much for coming, Ms. Lupa," Wynona said with an extra loud voice. The old dragon shifter wasn't as young as she used to be.

"Call me Gendyl," Gendyl shouted, though the volume was unintentional. She leaned in and tried to whisper, but it was still far above normal speaking tones. "Calling me Ms. Lupa makes me feel old."

"I'll remember that," Wynona said kindly. "See you soon." With the shifter gone, Wynona took a deep breath. Her shop was finally empty. The day had been a long one. After the reading of the will, the fighting of the family and then having to come back to work...Wynona was exhausted.

Lusgu grumbled as he walked through the dining room, his broom, as always, in his wake. "Dark happenings," he mumbled. "Dark, dark, dark."

Wynona frowned. "Lusgu?"

He paused and turned to glare at her.

"What's dark?"

Lusgu shook his head. "Dark, dark, dark."

Wynona threw up her hands when he disappeared down the hall. Getting a straight answer from the brownie was sometimes an Olympic sport and most of the words he did mutter didn't make any sense on their own. "Dark," Wynona murmured. She opened her mind to Violet. *Any idea what he's talking about?*

The fact that it's night time?

Wynona refrained from rolling her eyes, but barely. "I don't think that's it."

Violet sauntered in from the kitchen. *How am I supposed to know?*

"You get along with him better than anyone else," Wynona pointed out.

Violet smirked and smoothed down her fur. *People can't resist me.*

A snort broke free from Wynona that Violet definitely didn't appreciate.

Is Wolfy coming tonight?

"He usually drops by for dinner," Wynona said, using her fingers to begin cleaning up. There was something so satisfying about watching all the dishes float through the air. No wonder creatures always used their magic. "Look, I remembered," Wynona said with a grin.

Violet gave her a slow clap.

"You're in a mood tonight."

Violet paused. *Something's in the air.* She shook all over. *Sorry. I'll try to be nicer.*

Wynona frowned and looked toward the window. It was dusk, Lusgu was muttering and Violet said something was in the air. Walking to the window, Wynona put her hand against it. Purple began floating like mist through the air, curling and creating beautiful patterns. It dissipated only a few inches from her hand. "I don't feel anything," Wynona said.

Maybe it's an animal thing? Ask Rascal if he feels it.

Wynona closed her eyes. *Rascal?*

Where are you? he shot back, his voice hard.

Wynona jerked back, though Rascal wasn't actually yelling at her. *The shop.*

Stay there. I'm coming.

Wynona turned to look at Violet. The mouse scrambled over, climbing Wynona.

I think he felt it, she said.

"I think you're right." Wynona waited at the window, her heart beating faster than normal, but if she worked, she could feel Rascal getting closer. Within minutes he was right in front of the building and Wynona moved to let him in. "What's going on?" she asked automatically, closing the door behind him. "Oof!"

Rascal tugged her into his chest, nearly smothering her against his uniform. "Are you okay?"

Wynona pushed against him until she could look him in the eye. "Of course. Why wouldn't I be?"

Rascal let go of her and scrubbed his face. Fine lines were showing around his eyes, letting her know he was worn out. "Zander Killoran was killed."

Wynona's knees nearly buckled. "What?" she rasped.

Rascal nodded, pulling her back in, but slowly this time. "They found him in the pool room again, but this time, his throat was slit."

Wynona wrapped her arms around Rascal and squeezed tight. "Did it have to do with the will?" she whispered.

"We don't know yet." Rascal buried his face in her hair. "But since you were at that meeting, I came straight here after hearing the news."

Wynona closed her eyes. "We need to go see the scene."

He sighed. "I know, but I need a second to hold you first."

"I don't think I was in any danger," Wynona assured him, but didn't let go. A second murder in only a few days. Something was going on with this case and it was proving to be deadly. "Lusgu and Violet both were acting funny, saying there was something in the air, but I didn't feel anything and my patrons were completely normal."

"Good." Rascal kissed the top of her hair. "Okay, I think I've gotten the wolf under control." He gave her a sheepish grin. "Sometimes he needs reassurance."

Wynona nodded and patted his chest. "I'm happy to provide it. But let's get to the scene before they move anything. It was much harder having to imagine Ms. Roseburg's murder when I couldn't see the body."

"Better lock up. I'll take you home afterward."

"I'll need my scooter for the morning."

Rascal shook his head. "I'll come get you."

Wynona gave him a look. "You can't just keep coming out to get me every day."

Rascal winked and leaned in to kiss her cheek. "Watch me," he whispered, sending a shiver down Wynona's spine.

When all this dead body's nonsense and family drama was over, she wanted some serious alone time with her soulmate. Maybe they could take a trip and visit Spell Summit or something.

"Let me tell Lusgu I'm going." Wynona headed down to her office, poking in her head. The vacuum was running while Lusgu dusted the bookshelves. "Rascal is here," she shouted, making sure she caught his attention. "We need to go do some police work."

Lusgu scowled, but nodded.

"I'll lock up behind me." Wynona stepped in a little farther and startled the brownie by touching his sleeve. "Thank you," she mouthed.

That little blush on the tip of his ears crept back in, but Lusgu, as always, simply frowned and gave a curt nod.

Wynona held back her smile until she was out in the hall. She was beginning to see that he wasn't quite as hard hearted as he wanted her to think. She grabbed her coat from the hall closet and slipped it on. "Okay, I'm ready."

Rascal held out his hand, taking Violet, who settled herself comfortably in his chest pocket. Then he grabbed Wynona's hand, intertwined their fingers and led the way to his truck, which was parked on the curb.

"You always do that," Wynona said in exasperation. "Why not just find a parking spot?"

"Why do I care about the curb when my soulmate might be in danger?"

She couldn't hold back her smile even as she tried to keep a scolding tone in her voice. "I wasn't in danger."

Rascal shrugged innocently. "I didn't know." His face split into a grin as he opened the door and helped her up. "Besides, if I can't park where I want, what's the point of being an officer?"

Wynona waited for him to walk around to his side before responding. "Oh, I don't know. Maybe solving crimes? Putting bad guys behind bars?"

"Yeah…that doesn't do it for me."

She whacked his arm, then settled down when he chuckled. "Does the family know about Zander?" she asked, her thoughts having gone serious again.

Rascal nodded. "Chief was assigning people to take care of it when I came to get you."

The rest of the ride was silent as Rascal navigated the busy streets. It took nearly twenty minutes for them to get to the side of town with the large estates and another five to pull up to the Roseburg home.

When Rascal helped Wynona down from the truck, she paused. "I can feel it," she whispered.

Rascal nodded. "Violet and Lusgu were right. There's something sinister in the air tonight."

"Is it like this every time someone's killed?"

He shook his head and led her to the door. "No. But when it *does* feel like this, the crime is almost always committed using paranormal ways."

"So you're saying he was killed with magic?"

Rascal tilted his head. "That would be my guess."

Wynona was eager to see if Rascal was correct. The heaviness she had felt outside could probably be attributed to any number of things, but if it meant magic had been used for nefarious purposes, then it was a feeling she wanted to pay attention to.

They walked into the pool wing to utter chaos.

Wynona jerked back when a group of paparazzi turned at their approach. "Ms. Le Doux! What are you doing here?"

"Does your father know you're helping the police?"

"Are you and the Deputy Chief dating?"

"What is your relationship to Chief Ligurio?"

"No comment," Rascal said loudly, leading Wynona through the crowd.

She didn't breathe easy until they finally crossed the police line, the reporters having to stay back. "I'm sure some of those creatures are lovely, but it's hard to tell when they're shoving a microphone in your face."

Rascal snorted. "You're more generous than I am. I've gotten to where I hate reporters on principle."

"Even old friends?"

Wynona turned. "Mr. Hesa!" she exclaimed with a smile. "How nice to see you." She noticed he was in his corporeal form, which meant she hadn't gotten a witchy warning of his presence.

The small man grinned. "Any exclusive tips you can offer?"

Wynona's smile stayed even as she shook her head. "Not this time. But it was good to see you."

An officer began ushering the reporter back, since he had crossed the police line. "Let me know when we can make another deal!" he shouted.

"When you have something to share, bring it to the station," Rascal retorted. He snorted and shook his head. "They never stop."

"Mr. Hesa was a huge help to us on the last case. Go easy on him."

Still grumbling, Rascal turned back to the scene. "There's Chief."

"Stronglaw, Ms. Le Doux," Chief Ligurio said with a nod. He was surrounded by men and women in uniform, grouped around two more people on the floor.

Wynona braced herself. Seeing the bodies was always the hardest part for her.

Zander's face was slack, his eyes closed, though Wynona had to wonder if the emergency workers had done that, since his body seemed to be in a state of shock.

"He looks..."

"Surprised?" Chief Ligurio offered, jotting something down on his phone.

Wynona nodded.

"More than likely, the killer caught him off guard."

"Interesting." Wynona noticed the placement of the warlock's hands. His fingers were curled and his arms lay near his throat, which, just like Rascal said, had been cut open. She tried not to pay too much attention to the blood staining the floor, but Wynona had learned from experience that every detail mattered. She looked at the worker who was still taking measurements. "May I?"

The man looked at the chief, then nodded and backed up, giving her extra room.

"Thank you," Wynona said before squatting down. She forced herself to notice the pale skin and the odd edges of the wound. Zander's clothes were the same suit he had been wearing that morning, though his shoes were gone. "Any idea where his shoes are?" Wynona asked.

Chief Ligurio shook his head. "Not yet."

"Is the coroner coming?"

"He's on his way," Daemon's deep voice broke into their circle. He nodded at the chief. "What do you want to tell the reporters?"

"To go home," Chief Ligurio snapped.

Wynona hid a grin. She tilted her head to get a better look at the body. "Was he wet at all when he was found?"

"No. Best we can tell, he never made it into the pool."

"So he more than likely was simply meeting someone here," Wynona murmured. "I'm assuming there was no forced entry?"

"No," Rascal responded. "Nothing indicates he was with someone at all. His sister was at her apartment. Dear old dad is being pulled out of the underworld. Our pool boy was at home." He looked at a page in his notebook. "Leaving Zander home alone, unless he invited a friend we don't know about."

"But he couldn't have done this to himself," Wynona said.

"I don't disagree that he didn't kill himself, but you sound as if you have evidence," Chief Ligurio pressed.

Wynona pointed to Zander's neck. "Look at the ragged edges of the wound. If he was cutting his own throat, he wouldn't have done it in several swipes." She looked around. "And where was the weapon? If he was alone, it would just fall to the floor."

Chief Ligurio smirked. "We have already figured all that, but it's good to see my begging hasn't gone to waste." He glanced up. "Azirad's here," the chief said, referring to the coroner.

Wynona waited for the elderly creature to arrive. The red cap was knobby kneed and looked as if he hated the world, but she knew he was good at his job. "Daemon?"

"Hm?"

"Have you looked for residue?"

Daemon nodded. "Yeah. There's nothing there."

"Nothing?" Wynona's eyes bugged out.

He shook his head. "Nothing."

"Excuse me, missy," Azirad huffed as he moved her out of the way to get to the body.

Wynona stood and stepped back, allowing the red cap room. "CHIEF!"

The room buzzed with interest as an officer raced across the pool house, his hands full. "I found his shoes and socks."

Wynona frowned.

"Good work, Aldor," Chief Ligurio said. "Bag 'em and put them with the rest of his belongings." He paused. "Where were they?"

"Tucked under that lounge chair," the officer said, pointing to a spot on the far side of the room. They were harder to see because it's canvas instead of slats." The creature shrugged. "The socks were folded inside the shoes, as if he took them off in order to dip his toes in the water."

Chief Ligurio nodded and scowled as the noise from the reporters grew louder. "SKYMAW!" the chief shouted.

"Yes, sir?"

"Get them out of here. I want the whole pool house closed off, no matter what the family says."

Daemon nodded and turned to do exactly as he'd been told.

"Chief," Wynona said softly.

"Hm?"

She waited until he looked at her expectantly, his red eyes impatient. "I think you need to send those shoes to Evidence."

"Oh? And why is that?"

"Because those weren't the ones he was wearing this morning."

CHAPTER 17

Wynona sat on her couch, staring into the dark room. "Granny?" she called. "Are you there?" The normal prickling sensation that accompanied ghosts was absent and Wynona realized that although she could sense them, she had no idea how to call to a person who had passed on.

Try doing it mentally? Violet suggested.

Wynona pinched her lips together. "Okay." She closed her eyes to concentrate better. Her mind wanted to be anywhere but in this room. Rascal had brought her home and then gone back to the station in order to go over the evidence, leaving Wynona to her worries and thoughts.

She wished she was still at the station with him, but her presence wasn't going to help anything go faster. Rascal would help her know what they found, and Wynona was supposed to be getting some rest. She had been too keyed up to fall asleep, however, and had decided now was a good time to talk to her grandmother about all things witches.

Granny? Can you hear me?

Wynona waited, holding her breath. Subtly, something flicked on the edge of her consciousness. She waited, the sensation growing slightly stronger until finally that hair-raising sensation began to crawl across her neck. Wynona opened her eyes, blinking until the room turned purple. "Granny?"

"I'm here." The purple blob spoke, then slowly took shape and Wynona turned off her ghostly vision.

"Thank you for coming," Wynona said softly. She folded her hands in her lap. This was the first time they had met since Granny's confession and Wynona wasn't sure how to break the ice.

"Either you've forgiven me, or you want something." Granny tilted her chin down as if she was still looking over her glasses, like she had in life, though there were no glasses sitting on the edge of her nose.

Wynona sighed. "Sort of both, to be truthful."

Granny sat in a chair. "Go on."

"I don't like holding onto a grudge," Wynona explained. "And after dealing with my family a couple of times in the last few days, I can understand why you did what you did." She rolled her eyes. "You saw what happened with my mother the other day."

Granny nodded, but didn't speak.

Wynona braced herself. "I forgive you."

Granny slapped the chair. "Well, thank heavens for that. Now we can get down to business."

Wynona shook her head. "I didn't call you here to talk about any kind of possible future."

Granny narrowed her gaze and sat back down. "Then what do you need help with?"

"I'm helping the police with a murder investigation—"

"You're not wasting your talents on catching petty criminals," Granny snapped.

"Now, what a minute," Wynona said, jerking upright. "You don't have a say as to how I use my talents."

"It's that wolf," Granny muttered. "I know he's your soulmate, but he's influencing you. You have a great future ahead of you in running Hex Haven."

"I DON'T WANT TO RUN HEX HAVEN!" Wynona shouted, jumping to her feet. Her fists were clenched and her face flushed. She could feel her pulse beating in her throat and Wynona's stomach was so clenched she thought she might be sick. She hated yelling. She hated confrontation. It reminded her too much of her family and the way they handled everything from family dinners to politics.

Granny's eyes nearly bugged out of her head. "You don't mean that. You can do so much good."

Wynona forced her knees to bend so she could sit back down. She didn't like standing over her grandmother like some kind of dictator. "I am doing good," Wynona said in a softer tone. "And I'm doing it in a way I'm comfortable with."

Granny shook her head. "Why did you call me here? If you don't want to take the city back and reform our system, why am I here?"

"Because I need someone who can teach me about witches."

Granny didn't move. "You *are* a witch."

Wynona bit back a sarcastic retort. "Yes, thank you, I'm aware. But I'm also well aware that my education is severely lacking." She held up a hand to stop her grandmother from responding too soon. "I know you did your best and you taught me a lot, but the practical side of being a witch is beyond me. I didn't use magic to clean my room or do my hair. I don't understand all the differences in magic or how to determine what one witch can do and another cannot."

Granny waved a dismissive hand through the air. "It's all practice and learning. Nothing you can't handle."

"Granny, Harmony Roseburg was killed a couple of days ago. Her will was read yesterday and now her son has also died."

Granny's eyebrows shot up. "Zander? The little blond devil?"

Wynona nodded. "Yes. Zander."

Granny frowned. "What happened to Harmony? Have they figured out who killed her?"

Wynona shook her head. "Not yet. I'm helping with the case."

"Why?"

"Because I've discovered I'm good at thinking outside the box." Wynona sat up straighter. She didn't like having to defend herself, but perhaps if Granny understood what it was all about... "I've helped on a couple other cases and been able to pinpoint evidence and situations that the police don't always see. And now Chief Ligurio has asked for me to help on a more permanent basis. He thinks my powers will be of use."

Granny snorted. "Of course he does. And I'll bet he's paying you pennies."

"I don't do it for the money."

"Have you ever noticed there are no witch officers?" Granny pressed. She tsked her tongue. "He's trying to get a hold of an advantage. That's all you are to him."

"And Rascal?" Wynona asked tightly. "What about him? Do you think he's abusing my good nature as well?"

Granny deflated. "He's your soulmate and a wolf. I'm actually surprised he would be willing to let you get involved in something so dangerous."

"Rascal supports me," Wynona said with a huff. "He doesn't control me."

Granny pushed a stray hair out of her face. "What do you need from me, Wynona?"

"I already told you. I need a tutor."

Granny let out a harsh breath and leaned back in the seat. "Tell me about Harmony."

Wynona knew better than to get too excited. While Granny Saffron had been Wynona's salvation, there was also a reason why the older witch had been one of the most feared and respected paranormals in the world. "Harmony drowned in her own pool."

Granny's white eyebrows shot up.

"The family has been pointing a finger at the pool boy, who's a merman, but there are a few...points of interest that make it seem odd."

"Such as?"

Wynona leaned forward. "First, can you tell me about powers? Mr. Monroe, the mer, said Ms. Roseburg couldn't clean her own pool. That she claimed she wasn't a water witch."

Granny nodded. "It's true. Often witches have a specialty that is stronger than all their other powers."

"So not all witches can use the five elements?" Wynona reached up to rub Violet, who had been particularly quiet during the little chat.

Granny shrugged. "I wouldn't say that, but the word 'use' can be pretty vague. A witch might be able to create a spark and you can say she's using fire. But that spark might not even be enough to light a piece of paper on fire."

Wynona nodded thoughtfully. "Do you know anything about Ms. Roseburg's powers?"

"Harmony was an air witch."

"So she could control the wind?"

Granny nodded. "She could create a hurricane like no one else." Granny smirked. "Of course, that's about all she could do. Her family powers were never very well rounded."

"Do you know what color her magic was?"

Granny pursed her lips, her eyes off to the side. "Blue, I think?" She shook her head. "I'm not positive. It was never something I paid a lot of attention to."

"What causes a witch's magic color?" Wynona asked. "I've read it's genetic, but our family all has different colors."

Granny tilted her head back and forth. "It's both genetic and power driven. Our family has been bred to have full powers that are stronger than others. So we rarely pass down colors genetically. Instead, they're a show of what we're capable of."

"So the Killorans being blue was genetic. But ours is power based."

Granny nodded, her eyes sparkling as if she knew the question Wynona wanted to ask next.

Apparently, color wasn't going to be a very helpful tool. However, she couldn't help but wonder why her own magic was purple, a color she had never seen on anyone else, but Wynona held the question back. She had a gut feeling that it wasn't something she would be ready to deal with anyway, so it was better, in this case, to stay ignorant for a little while longer.

"Ms. Roseburg had a spot on the back of her head," Wynona said, changing the subject. "There was residual magic there, indicating that she had been healed."

"Yet she was dead."

Wynona nodded.

Granny scowled. "That doesn't make sense. Who would heal her, then drown her?"

"Could she have healed herself?"

Granny shrugged. "Possibly, but like I said, air was her strength. Most witches that aren't skilled in healing need to be able to see the wound. If it was in the back of her head, she wouldn't have been able to do that."

Something was tickling at the edge of Wynona's brain, some clue that she knew she should be putting together, but it wasn't coming to her. Instead of dwelling on it, she stood. "Thank you. I appreciate your help."

Granny stood up as well. "You said you wanted a teacher."

Wynona nodded.

"I'll agree to come give you witch lessons if you'll agree not to throw away the idea of someday taking over."

Wynona automatically began to shake her head, but her grandmother intervened.

"Think on it," Granny said firmly. "The palace is a corrupt place, to the point where even the president's own children aren't sacred anymore. They're merely a means to an end." Granny stepped forward Wynona. "Do you really want to see Celia take over someday, a spoiled warlock at her side, and for her children to be treated like chattel? The same way you and your sister are?"

Wynona was frozen. "What do you mean Celia is treated like chattel?"

Granny's face softened, sadness making her look weary. "Your sister's life isn't the glamorous one you expect it to be." Granny looked down, as if gathering her courage, and then backed up. "She's just as much a prisoner as you were."

Despite the fact that it was something Wynona had suspected for a while, the words still felt like knives to her chest. They might have nothing in common, other than their heritage, but the idea of Celia being kept a prisoner sat in Wynona's stomach like a lead cauldron. It wasn't right, no matter who was being held back. "Why didn't you help her the way you helped me?"

Granny shook her head. "Because you were the greater priority. I only had so much time in order to save you. Celia can last a little longer."

"She shouldn't have to."

"Then do something about it," Granny snapped, her fiery personality coming back. "Hone your powers and put your father out of the castle."

"I'm not staging war against my own family."

Granny stepped back, her body starting to fade. "Then you'll doom Celia to remain a pawn forever."

Wynona reached out, meaning to stop Granny from leaving, but the ghost was gone. Even the feeling on the back of Wynona's neck only lasted a split second before dissipating.

What do you make of that? Violet asked.

Wynona slowly shook her head. "I'm not sure, but at least she answered our questions."

Are you going to take her up on the lessons? She didn't say you actually had to declare war, just be willing to think about it.

Wynona plopped back down on the sofa. Her head was spinning so badly, it seemed as if the room was actually moving. "I can't think straight." She gripped her head. "It's all just too much. When will I ever get a chance to breathe?"

When you take over the government.

"Not funny, Violet," Wynona murmured. "I don't think war is going to help me sleep better at night."

Violet sniffed. *Well, it would help me sleep better at night. Your sister is a terror.*

Wynona let her head fall back and she closed her eyes. "I need to just get through this case. It's one of the things on my list I actually have some control over. Solve the case, then worry about Granny's offer."

Probably wise. Violet scrambled down and rushed across the floor. *See you in the morning.*

Wynona waved a lazy hand, but didn't bother to respond otherwise. It felt like too much. If she put one more thing in her head, Wynona was positive it would explode. "Sleep," she muttered to herself. "A good night's sleep and then some good tea." Groaning, she rose to her feet and headed to her bedroom. "That's the best medicine I can think of." Now she just had to hope that it would actually be enough.

CHAPTER 18

The next morning seemed to drag on. Wynona was feeling more and more weighed down by her personal life and it was making it difficult to keep going in public. She needed those lessons from Granny...badly. But Wynona wanted nothing to do with taking over the presidential seat and she absolutely did not see herself ever declaring a siege on her father.

But if I can help Celia...

The argument in her head went in circles. She wanted a certain result, but wasn't willing to take the path that would lead to that result.

Forget your family, Violet scolded. *If you don't start paying attention to your customers, they'll all walk out and then it won't matter one way or another.*

Wynona nodded. "Right." She shoved her worries aside, focusing on the here and now, and managed to make it through the afternoon. By the time she set the 'Closed' sign on the door, Wynona was ready to collapse. "And yet the day is only beginning," she murmured. She had yet to speak to Chief Ligurio or Rascal today about Zander's body. Tired as she was, Wynona wanted to know what they'd discovered.

Standing in the middle of the dining room, Wynona began to clean up the space as quickly as she was comfortable with with her magic. Trays and dishes began to fly through the air and Wynona held perfectly still, afraid that the slightest break in concentration would cause her to break something.

As the organized chaos began to wind down, she found herself relaxing slightly. Stepping forward, Wynona smiled, proud of how far she was coming in her skills. As her left foot moved forward, she found her balance moving backward. Instead of landing on the floor, her shoe slid and Wynona fell in a heap on the hardwood.

The crashing of dishes rang through her ears, just as a heavy pulse rang through her head. "Ow," she whined, closing her eyes. "How many dishes did I break?" she muttered.

Don't ask, Violet said wryly. She sniffed. *We're just lucky you didn't hit me with anything. Then where would you be?*

Wynona sighed. "Sorry. I must have stepped in something." Gingerly, her head pounding, she sat up. Sure enough, a puddle of tea was on the floor, causing the slippery surface.

"Messy, messy, messy," Lusgu snapped. Shaking his head, he snapped his fingers and everything in the room began to put itself back together, the broken dishes dumping themselves into the trash.

"Sorry," Wynona said again. She climbed to her feet and took a deep breath to help the pain. A goose egg on the back of her head let her know she'd whacked it pretty hard.

Do you have a concussion? Rascal's voice came through her head.

Biting back her squeal of surprise, Wynona took an inventory of herself. *I don't think so. Just a headache and a bump. It's nothing.*

I've got something you can take, Rascal continued. *Want me to come pick you up?*

No. Thanks. I'll grab some chamomile and ginger tea, then come over. That way I have my scooter when we're done.

You know I don't mind.

Wynona smiled. His stubborn desire to protect her was endearing to say the least. *I know. But this will be quicker anyway. I'll be there soon. Love you.*

Love you too.

Violet was giving Wynona a smug look when she came out of her thoughts.

"Don't say it," Wynona warned. "I know we're cheesy, but it's the one thing in my life that's like a fairy tale. Let me have it."

Violet held up her hands. *I wasn't going to say anything.*

Wynona snorted and shook her head, then winced. "Tea," she reminded herself. She left Lusgu to do the heavy lifting, who was better at cleaning up anyway, and headed to the kitchen to brew herself a concoction. The spicy scent of ginger tickled the back of her throat and Wynona hummed in enjoyment as she drained the cup. Slowly, the pain in her head ebbed, but the bump still remained.

What if you tried to heal it? Violet suggested.

Wynona paused. "Granny said most witches need to see a wound to heal it."

Violet shrugged as only a mouse could. *You're not most witches.*

Wynona chewed on her bottom lip, her mind whirling. Healing would definitely be a useful skill, but dare she try it? What if it went terribly wrong and she hurt herself instead? "Lusgu?" She went back out to the dining room to find the brownie directing the broom.

He huffed at her.

"I'd like to try healing this bump." Wynona hesitated when he stilled. "Would you be willing to stand by in case I do it wrong?"

"I'm not a miracle worker," he snapped.

Wynona nodded. "I know, but you've also shown me time and again that you have the ability to stop my magic." She frowned. "I don't know why and I don't get the feeling you want to share, but I...I need your help."

Lusgu folded his arms over his suspenders and stared her down.

Wynona held his gaze. It was disconcerting, but she had nothing to hide. She wasn't trying to use him, but she didn't want to do this alone. She appreciated Lusgu and knew she would have hurt herself and several others multiple times if it wasn't for his interference. "Please."

The slight softening of his jaw was all Wynona needed to see. Brownies weren't often seen as strong or powerful and therefore often got the short end of the stick in the paranormal world. But Wynona knew better. There was more to Lusgu than met the eye.

He gave her a curt nod and the broom crashed to the floor, letting her know she had his full attention.

"Okay." Wynona took in a slow, deep breath through her nose and focused her mind. She hadn't ever healed anything, let alone a wound she couldn't see. Reaching back, she put her hand on the tip of the bump and let the electric tingle of her magic slide along her fingertips.

A touch on her ankle said that Violet was adding her own help and Wynona was grateful for the extra bit of focus and strength.

She winced when the magic first hit the goose egg. The spot was tender and the shock felt like a sharp prick from a live wire, but she knew she wasn't hurt and kept going. Slowly, ever so slowly, Wynona focused on making the bump shrink. Several excruciating minutes later, it had done just that.

She was panting with exertion, but the task was complete. "I did it," she breathed. A laugh broke free. "Oh my goodness, I did it!" The smile on her face was wider than normal and Lusgu's snort said he was unimpressed.

"About time," he muttered before going back to his cleaning.

As far as compliments went, that was about as good as it got from the grumpy brownie. Not allowing his pessimism to bother her, Wynona grabbed her keys. "Come on, Violet. Time to go."

The fifteen minutes to the police station were soothing and Wynona found she could barely keep herself from smiling the entire way. She was like a little kid at Christmas. Every time she conquered something in her magic, she felt different, better, more capable. And since she had no idea what all her magic could do, it was like opening a present with each skill.

A present that sometimes blows up in your face, Violet said.

"Thanks," Wynona murmured as she parked. "I suppose I need someone to keep my ego in check."

Violet snickered, but crawled into Wynona's hand in order to go inside.

"Hey, Amaris," Wynona said as she walked through the lobby.

The vampire spun around, her purse in her hands. "Oh, hey! You're coming in awfully late. I was just headed home."

"I know, but I had to wait until I could close the shop," Wynona explained.

"Gotcha." Amaris tilted her head toward the hallway. "I suppose that explains why Chief and Deputy Chief haven't budged yet."

Wynona shrugged. "Probably."

"Go on back. I don't know whose office they're in."

"Thanks! I'll figure it out." Wynona navigated her way through the changing of the guard and knocked on Rascal's door.

I'm with the chief.

Wynona wanted to smack herself. One of these days, she would actually remember to use her gifts. She could have avoided this altogether by simply asking. She could hear Rascal's chuckle as she walked down the hall. *Watch it, Wolf,* she teased. *I might throw out all the steaks sitting in my freezer.*

Rascal gave her a mock glare when she entered Chief Ligurio's office. "You wouldn't dare."

Wynona smirked and raised an eyebrow. *Try me.*

"I don't want to hear about your lover's spat," Chief Ligurio snapped. He waved toward a chair. "Have a seat and let's see what we can get done tonight."

Wynona followed his directions. "Is Daemon coming?"

"Skymaw will be here soon. He's on dinner break."

Wynona nodded. She clasped her hands in her lap. "So...catch me up."

Rascal growled low and began to pace. "We haven't gotten much farther than you saw last night. The shoes, which you said were the wrong ones, had his DNA in them and were the same size."

"So they *are* his shoes," Wynona murmured.

Chief Ligurio nodded. "Yes. He more than likely just changed them at some point during the day."

Wynona pressed her lips together, not convinced, but not having any real evidence either.

"Zander's throat was cut by an object that was not excessively sharp," Rascal continued. "It required more of a jagged scratching, than one smooth slice."

A shiver ran down her spine. This was the worst part of working a case. The deathly details never sat well with Wynona. "And there were no signs of a murder weapon?"

Rascal shook his head.

Wynona pursed her lips and leaned back in the seat. "We're missing something," she whispered.

"But what?"

Wynona shook her head. "I don't know. But I just feel like something is right in front of us." She began to tap her foot absentmindedly. "Why do you think his shoes were on the far side of the pool from his body?"

Rascal leaned a hip against the desk and looked to his chief.

"Maybe he took them off where he was sitting," Chief Ligurio said gruffly. "He had legs. It's possible he was walking around."

"But his pants weren't wet, right?"

"No, they weren't," Chief Ligurio admitted.

"And they weren't rolled up."

Again, the Chief confirmed her words.

"Then why take them off?" Wynona's foot grew faster. "Zander was too prissy to simply walk around barefoot. Have you asked the rest of the family and Mr. Monroe?"

"Yes," Rascal said with a huff. "They all have an alibi, just like they did for Ms. Roseburg's death." His eyes went to the floor. "Are those the shoes you slipped in?"

Wynona glanced at her flats and forced her foot to stop moving. "Yes. Why?"

He shrugged. "Just curious. It seems weird that you would slide in flats. I guess I expect it when you wear those heels, but not usually something like this."

Wynona paused. Slowly, she brought her foot up and looked at the bottom of it. "Rascal..." She craned her neck. "Do you see anything on the bottom of my shoe?"

He frowned. "What?"

Sticking her leg straight out, Wynona could feel the stirrings of excitement. "Can you see anything? Tell me if you can see any kind of liquid stain."

Still giving her a weird look, Rascal bent over until he could see the bottom of her shoe.

"This better have to do with the case," Chief Ligurio said, his tone betraying his curiosity.

"I can see a dark stain. Yes."

Wynona snapped her leg down and leaned forward. "Have those shoes tested for pool chemicals."

"What?"

"Have the bottom of the shoes tested for pool chemicals," Wynona repeated.

Black eyebrows pulled into a fierce V. "Are you telling me you think..." He trailed off, shaking his head.

Wynona nodded. "I do."

Chief Liguirio closed his eyes and pinched the bridge of her nose. "You heard her, Strongclaw. Get them tested. Now."

"On it." Rascal had his phone to his ear within seconds. As he headed into the hallway, he squeezed Wynona's shoulder.

She patted his hand before he let go and disappeared.

"But why?" Chief Ligurio asked softly.

Wynona shook her head. "I'm not sure yet."

The chief leaned back. "If your hunch is right, things just took a sharp turn."

"I know."

"They'll let us know within the hour," Rascal said as he came back inside. He stopped by Wynona's side.

"Can you have them check something else?" Wynona asked, another idea coming into her head.

Chief Ligurio nodded.

"Have them check for sock residue on Zander's feet." Wynona tilted her chin down. "And then compare it to the ones found in the shoes."

Chief Ligurio growled. "Do it," he said to Rascal.

Rascal had the phone to his ear immediately.

A knock on the door broke Wynona's concentration.

"Chief?"

"Enter," Chief Ligurio said, waving Daemon inside.

"Did I miss anything?"

Wynona looked at the chief, who sighed. "Maybe."

Daemon opened his mouth, but Rascal's exclamation stopped the coming question.

"They still need to run a couple other tests," Rascal said, holding his phone out to the side, "but from smell alone, they're almost positive that the same clear pool chemical is on his shoe."

Daemon's head bounced around from person to person. "I'm lost. What does this mean?"

Wynona slumped in her seat. "It means...that Zander killed his mother," she said softly.

"What?" Daemon shouted, then cleared his throat.

"It also means he staged the scene," Wynona continued. "Which might be even worse."

CHAPTER 19

"You think this was premeditated murder?" Rascal asked, dropping into the seat next to Wynona.

Wynona breathed slowly, buying time. "I'm not sure." She shook her head. "What I don't understand is, why? If it was premeditated, why kill her at all? He had access to her wealth and everything he wanted. Killing her actually took that away."

"But he didn't know that," Daemon inserted, stepping farther into the room. "Zander was convinced he was the sole heir."

Wynona nodded. "I know. But if he already had the money, why bother to kill her for it?"

Chief Ligurio's long fingers tapped an erratic rhythm against his desk. "Something had to be planned, however. Otherwise he wouldn't have the pool chemical on his shoe."

"We need to check Ms. Roseburg's shoes," Wynona said. "My guess is we're not going to find anything, but the DA will want to know for sure."

"Agreed." Chief Ligurio grabbed his desk phone. "Give me a moment for a search warrant. At this time of night, the judge should be home." He grinned, his sharp canines flashing. "He won't be happy to be bothered at home, but I'm pretty sure I can convince him this is an emergency."

Wynona smiled and shook her head. Men and their egos.

So did Zander heal his mom?

Wynona and Rascal both looked at Violet. "That's a good point."

"Interpret," Daemon said with his eyebrows raised.

"Violet asked if Daemon healed his mother," Rascal responded.

Daemon scratched his chin. "Some of it doesn't make sense. Why the healing if he was going to kill her? Why kill her if he already had the money?" He shook his head. "It just doesn't make sense." He frowned. "Is it possible that Zander stepped in the chemical when he was pulling his mom from the pool?"

"He didn't pull her from the pool," Rascal pointed out. "She was still in the water when emergency services got there."

"Which also doesn't make sense," Wynona murmured. "Even if he was sure she was dead, any son should have pulled his parent out of the water." She gripped her head. "I thought we finally had an answer, but it's only bringing more questions."

Rascal massaged her neck and Wynona relaxed into it. His warm touch was exactly what she needed, especially since she was still a little sore from her earlier fall. "The chemical only had one slip through it," Wynona murmured, her eyes still closed in bliss. "Which means Zander was the only one who went through it." Her eyes popped open. "Was the chemical bucket tested for magical residue or fingerprints?"

Rascal looked at Daemon, whose ears turned pink. "I don't think so," the black hole admitted.

The phone landed on the cradle. "Then it sounds like we have more work to do than we thought." He stood and began to gather his papers. "The warrant will meet us at the house."

Wynona stood and followed Rascal when he took her hand, leading her out of the room and to his truck. "I should take my scooter," she said, even knowing his response.

"No. You should ride with me." He opened the passenger door.

"You're getting awfully bossy," Wynona said, putting her hands on her hips.

Rascal's egotistical smirk was as appealing as it was annoying when he leaned in nose to nose. "My wolf calls it protective. You can't override his alpha-ness."

"I don't think that's a word," Wynona teased, poking him in the chest.

Rascal growled. "It is if the alpha says it is."

Wynona held up her hands. "I bow to your logic, O Great One." She laughed when Rascal growled in her ear again as he helped her inside.

Let's keep him forever, Violet said, fanning her face.

Wynona's smile was wide. "I think I can handle that," she whispered. It felt so good to enjoy a moment with her soulmate. She always came away feeling better...lighter. And with everything going on in her life, these moments were especially precious to her.

Rascal slammed his door and the truck roared into the street. He rested his elbow against the window and propped his head on his hand as he drove. "Any thoughts you didn't say inside?"

Wynona shook her head. "No. Chief Ligurio has actually been really open to all my suggestions." She huffed a laugh. "I've actually been really surprised."

Rascal snorted. "Me too, even though he's the one who pulled you in." His golden eyes flashed in the darkness. "I'm glad he's finally seeing what I see."

Wynona's cheeks grew hot and that dang smile refused to budge. "I'm just as confused as everyone else," she insisted. "I don't know why you think I'm so good at this."

"Almost every lead we've followed has been yours," Rascal pointed out. He tapped his nose. "You have a knack for seeing things."

Wynona shrugged. "Either that or I'm just too detail oriented for my own good. Some might call that obsessive compulsive."

"Maybe we should hire detectives like that more often," Rascal responded.

Wynona shook her head with a soft laugh. The few minutes to the mansion were quiet but comfortable. She never tired of Rascal's company and things were rarely awkward between them, especially not now that she understood the connection they had.

When they arrived at the mansion, Chief Ligurio was walking down the driveway toward a limousine. He leaned into the window, stayed a moment, then straightened just as the vehicle left.

Wynona whistled under her breath. "The judge travels in style. Though I'm surprised he came out personally to deliver the warrant."

Rascal smirked. "He didn't. That was the assistant."

Wynona's head whipped around, watching the taillights. "How do you know?"

Rascal tapped the side of his nose. "She's a druid. The smell of wet forest never really leaves."

"Huh." They headed up to the house. "I bought my house from a druid."

"I know," Rascal said casually. "Your house reeked of it for weeks."

"It did not!" Wynona protested.

"Just be grateful you have a human nose," he said, tapping the end of hers.

Wynona glared, then headed inside just behind the chief. She tried to let go of what Rascal said, but the conversation irked her. She had cleaned that house thoroughly when she'd bought it and there was no way it had smelled of wet forest.

Maybe he was actually smelling the Grove of Secrets, Violet offered. *It's not far out in the backyard.*

Wynona nodded. That could have been it. Druids got their magic from the earth and the one who had owned Wynona's house liked privacy. The Grove of Secrets was the type of place that held untameable magic. Creatures went in, but no one ever came back out.

Normally, it provided just enough protection that people left Wynona alone, though they'd gotten braver lately with her name being involved in several murder cases. Still…most of the time it was a sanctuary she was grateful for.

"Where to first?" Chief Ligurio asked.

"Let's check Ms. Roseburg's shoes," Wynona said. "I think that'll be the easiest one to knock off the list."

Chief Ligurio nodded and they had the butler lead them to Ms. Roseburg's old room. As they were walking down the hall, they heard a screech of outrage.

"What are you doing here?"

Wynona spun, along with the officers, to see Silvaria standing with her hands on her hips. She was in silky pajamas, an eye mask propped just above her forehead and some kind of green concoction coating her cheeks.

Chief Ligurio held up the document in his hand. "We have a search warrant for the entire premises. We'll be starting with your mother's room."

"Isn't it enough that Zander's dead?" Silvaria asked through clenched teeth. "Mother, I don't care about, but now Zander? Why aren't you out there finding his killer instead of digging through family heirlooms?" She jammed her manicured finger toward the door.

Wynona stepped back, letting Rascal crowd her a bit. She wasn't about to get involved in this confrontation. Let the law handle it.

"We're working on that," Chief Ligurio said calmly. "And the leads have led us back here." He turned and Silvaria screamed for the butler, but the man ignored her, leading the group farther into the house.

"President Le Doux will hear about this!" Silvaria bellowed.

Chief Ligurio's red eyes darted to Wynona. "The law is on our side," he whispered.

Wynona nodded, though the words unsettled her. Her father didn't always play by the rules and if he decided to stick his nose into this case, she was a little afraid of what would happen. As they walked, that same feeling she'd had before crept up her spine. They were being watched.

"Cats," Rascal hissed.

Filthy beasts, Violet agreed. *They're everywhere.*

"How many did she have again?" Wynona asked, craning her neck to spy the pets.

"Twenty-three," Daemon said dryly. "Enough to give anyone the heebie jeebies."

Wynona's conversation with her grandmother came back to her. Ms. Roseburg's magic wasn't nearly as strong as her family's had been. Was that why she kept so many cats around? Did she utilize them to help her keep the pretense of power?

"It's a thought," Rascal agreed.

Wynona whacked his arm. "Would you stop reading my thoughts?"

"Would you stop broadcasting them like prime time television?" he teased back.

"Whatever." Wynona put her focus back on the case. She refused to admit *again* that Rascal was right. Her block hadn't been up at all.

He put his hand on her lower back. "You'll get the hang of it," he whispered, nuzzling her ear. "Time and patience, love. Time and patience."

"Any more time and my family will realize just how weak I am."

His hand flexed. "Not happening."

"If you two would stop whispering sweet nothings, we can get to work," Chief Ligurio drawled.

Wynona cleared her throat and stepped away from Rascal's touch. "I need Ms. Roseburg's closet." She began opening doors until one of them finally led to a closet the size of Wynona's bedroom. Her eyes were wide as she took in the beautiful gowns and clothes and shoes.

"You look starstruck," Rascal commented. "Your family must have rooms like this."

"My family did, sure," Wynona murmured, her eyes still roaming. "But there was no reason to give me a wardrobe to impress. I wasn't allowed out in public."

"And yet now they're clamoring for your attention," Chief Ligurio said curtly. He gave her a meaningful look. "All that shimmers isn't gold."

Wynona nodded, grateful for his support. "Okay. Shoes." She looked at the rows upon rows of footwear. "Do we know which ones she was wearing the night of her death?"

Rascal held up a finger. "Just a sec." He scrolled through his phone until he had a picture. "Most everything was waterlogged, of course, but it was given back to the family."

Wynona studied the picture, then scanned the wall. "They're not here."

"Got it." Daemon picked up a box. "This is from the station." He opened it and began pulling out Ms. Roseburg's personal effects. Apparently, no one had been in a hurry to put them back.

Wynona and Rascal walked over and Rascal took the shoes, smelling the souls. He shook his head. "There's nothing but the smell of pool water."

"Could that have hidden the chemical?" Chief Ligurio asked. He walked over with his hand out, sniffing the shoes as well. He made a face. "Wrong chemical."

"Yeah, but it's not as strong as the one that was spilled," Rascal pointed out.

Chief Ligurio nodded. "Agreed." He held the soles up to the light. "And no sign of her stepping in anything. I'm sure the DA will want a forensics report though." He bagged the shoes and set them aside. They were now evidence again, rather than simply personal effects.

"Daemon, can we check on the bucket?" Wynona asked. "I'd like you to look for residue."

He nodded and they all walked through the mansion until they reached the pool room, the invisible eyes following them the whole way. Wynona gave a delicate shudder as they entered the door. The cats apparently didn't like water because the eyes seemed to go away once the door closed.

However, another feeling overtook the sensation of being watched. "Someone's here," she whispered.

All three officers stopped. Rascal and Chief Ligurio both sniffed, then looked at each other.

"I only smell cat and pool," Rascal said.

"Agreed," Chief Ligurio responded. He narrowed his eyes at Wynona. "What do you see?"

Reaching up to touch Violet, Wynona blinked until her vision went purple. She scanned the room but she didn't see any specters. "I..." She snapped her mouth shut. "It's the oddest thing." The hairs on the back of her neck continued to stand up. "It's the exact same feeling I get when the ghost reporters go invisible," Wynona said. "But now I can't see them." She turned another full circle. "What's going on?"

Rascal rubbed her back. "It's okay. Your powers are still new. Maybe you just don't understand this one yet."

"But it worked with Mr. Hesa," Wynona pointed out. "I can see him every time. And Granny!"

Daemon made a face. "I don't sense any magic except what's coming from you."

"And you don't smell anything unusual at all?" She first looked at Rascal, then Chief Ligurio. Both men slowly shook their heads. Her chin fell to her chest and Wynona blinked away her ghost vision. "How could I have been so wrong?" She rubbed her suddenly aching forehead.

"Hey, now," Rascal cooed. "You're doing great. Just because one power went wonky doesn't mean we can't figure it out." He gave her a cheeky smile. "Now might not be the right time though. We have a killer to catch."

Wynona nodded. "Right. Let's find that chemical bucket."

Daemon opened the side closet and rooted around until he found what they were looking for. He pulled it out carefully, not adding any more fingerprints to it than were already there.

"Do you see any magic?" Wynona pressed, doing her best to forget her flub with the ghosts.

Daemon's eyes went pitch black and he leaned in and around. "It's...huh..."

"Skymaw," Chief Ligurio barked.

Daemon's eyes went back to normal as he looked up at them. "There's the slightest hint of blue," he explained. "But it almost looks like the residue of a residue."

"What's that supposed to mean?" Chief Ligurio growled.

Daemon shrugged. "What's there is too thin to have been a real spell. Almost like the spell had been on something else and then that touched the bucket." He scrunched his nose. "This is a new one for me," he admitted. His eyes went to Wynona. "You have an idea, don't you?"

She nodded, biting her lip.

"Out with it, Ms. Le Doux." The chief was obviously losing his patience.

"I think Zander healed his mother, touching the wound on the back of her head," Wynona explained.

"And then brought the bucket out to cover up her death," Rascal finished, his eyes turning a bright gold.

"But why heal her?" Chief Ligurio folded his arms over his chest. "Why bother?"

"I can answer that question," a deep voice said from the doorway.

Wynona's breath froze in her lungs. She knew that tone all too well and she wanted nothing to do with it. When Rascal closed ranks, hiding her from sight, she closed her eyes, knowing it wouldn't be enough.

"Oh, come now, daughter." President Le Doux sneered, Silvaria holding the same expression directly behind him. "Too afraid to face your old man?"

Wynona's entire body was tight with tension, but she forced her fingers to unlock and pulled any and all emotion from her face. Ignoring Rascal's warning growl, she stepped around. "I didn't realize I had been granted the privilege of being called your daughter again," she said stoically.

Niiice, Violet said with a laugh.

Guilt trickled down her spine. This wasn't who Wynona wanted to be, but a strong defense had been her first reaction. *But I'm better than that.*

No question. Rascal took her hand, a move that didn't go unnoticed by the president, if his scowl was anything to go by.

"Come, Wynona. Enough games. Come back to the house and I'll share with you what I know."

"If you have information, you're required by law to share it with the police," Wynona said tightly.

Chief Ligurio's chest rose ever so slightly. "No one is above the law, President Le Doux." His red eyes narrowed. "Especially not you."

President Le Doux rolled his eyes. "No need for theatrics, Deverell. We've been through this circus before." One side of his mouth curled. "And you lost."

Wynona snagged Chief Ligurio's arm before he could move forward, but she knew full well the only reason he was in the same spot was because he chose to be. She couldn't have stopped him by herself.

"You seem to be losing your touch, President." Chief Ligurio let a slow, predatory grin cross his face. "One daughter works for me and another doesn't seem to be happy under your rule." The chief tsked his tongue. "What will it be like when all that power just...slips...through your fingers?"

President Le Doux growled every bit as impressively as Rascal or the chief and brought his hand up, but there was nothing there. His glare jerked to Daemon, standing quietly with pitch black eyes. Realizing there was nothing he could do, the president straightened his suit coat, tugging on the sleeve cuffs. "If you would like to talk to me, I'm afraid you'll have to get a hold of me the same way as everyone else." He stepped aside, showing the man he was hiding.

Mr. Melion gave Wynona a sympathetic glance.

"Through my lawyer." Without another word, President Le Doux made a dramatic exit that would have been at home on any stage in the world.

"Melion," Chief Ligurio ground out. "We'll meet you back at the station."

Mr. Melion sighed, weariness written all over his features, and nodded. "I thought as much." He turned to leave and soon the group stood alone.

"Bring the bucket," Chief Ligurio snapped. "And anything else you think might be useful." He stalked toward the door. "We're not leaving here until every bit of evidence has been accounted for. Zander might have killed his mother, but someone else killed Zander." Chief Ligurio stopped at the door, his hand on the knob. "And even if it's the president himself, I want them caught."

CHAPTER 20

"So we're headed back to the station?" Wynona clarified.

Chief Ligurio paused before fully leaving the room. "No. We're turning this house upside down." The red in his eyes glowed brightly, his predator side obviously close to the surface. "If Ms. Killoran is calling in favors, it's because she's afraid we're going to find something." The chief's smile was sharp as broken glass. "I intend for us to find it."

Wynona felt a little thrill run up her spine. Her curiosity and the part of her that found enjoyment in outsmarting villains was answering the chief's call to action. "Can I go through Zander's room?"

The chief stepped back, holding open the door. "After you."

Wynona let her fingers brush Rascal's arm as she walked away.

"I'll be up in a few minutes," he called out as she passed. "I want to help Skymaw finish up here."

Wynona acknowledged his response, then left with the chief. They had to track down the butler in order to find Zander's room, but a few minutes later, they'd made it. Wynona's eyes widened as she looked around.

Chief Ligurio snorted. "I don't think he ever left the college frat boy stage of life."

"I don't think he ever had to," Wynona murmured. If his mother spoiled him as much as everyone claimed, then Zander would have had no reason to grow up or become responsible at all.

She kept her eyes averted from the walls, not wanting to see any more than she already had. But the desks and flat surfaces were almost as bad. Standing beside the desk, Wynona used a pencil to move around papers and magazines, scanning each one. "Hello..." she said softly when she found a small black notebook.

"You might not want to open that," Chief Ligurio said from his search across the suite. "I doubt any of the creatures inside are really out for a good time."

Wynona shook her head. "If Zander spent time with them, then they might know something we don't."

"Touche."

She thumbed through the book. The first several pages were exactly what she would have expected. Numbers from different women, each with a unique rating that Wynona definitely had no desire to interpret. But as she got in deeper, she realized Zander had used the book to take notes. "Chief."

The vampire was at her side before she could take another breath. *Dang, vamp speed,* Violet grumbled after clinging to Wynona's neck.

Wynona found herself grateful that the vampire couldn't read minds, though she was positive she'd heard Rascal snorting in the back of her head. "He took some notes in here."

Chief Liguri snatched the book from her hands and began reading them. "They're just snippets. None of them make sense."

Wynona nodded. "They don't make sense now, but something might if we get this all figured out."

The book landed on the desk with a thump. "I'm still hung up on something."

"What's that?" Wynona dug carefully through the garbage can.

"The why of it all." Chief Ligurio paced the book shelves. "The healing. It throws everything off." He paused. "You're sure she didn't heal herself?"

Wynona shrugged. "It's possible, but Granny said it's unlikely. Ms. Roseburg's specialty was wind. Healing would have been difficult and she would more than likely have needed to see the wound."

Chief Ligurio pushed a hand through his hand, his normally smooth 'do becoming much more messy. "Did Skymaw say if there was any way to tell how old the healing was?"

Wynona shook her head again. "No. He said it looked recent because the color was vibrant."

"But it was the same color that runs in the family," he grumbled. "Both of the kids have the color, as well as Ms. Roseburg."

"Right." Wynona knew he wasn't really looking for a response, but she answered anyway. She straightened, the garbage being a bust, and put her hands on her hips. She frowned and took a deep breath. Something was different in this room. But what?

It's messy? Violet offered.

Wynona pursed her lips. This space was messier than the rest of the immaculate home, but that wasn't it. Something was nagging at her...she just couldn't place her finger on it.

The door opened and Rascal came inside. "Ah..." he said with a sigh. "A breath of fresh air."

Wynona stilled. "What did you say?"

Rascal's eyes widened. "What?"

She waved him on. "What did you just say?"

"A breath of fresh air?" Rascal looked at the chief, then back at her, confusion written all over his handsome face.

"Fresh air." Wynona smiled grimly. "That's it."

"Explain," Chief Ligurio barked in his usual demanding tone.

"Take a deep breath, Chief Ligurio," she said. "What's missing?"

"The smell of cats," Rascal said automatically. He folded his arms. "None of the cats were allowed in Zander's room."

"He was allergic."

All heads whipped around. Silvaria stood in the doorway, the same tabby in her arms that had been there before. It was the cat Mr. Melion claimed had inherited the entire Roseburg fortune. Its tail whipped from side to side and its green eyes were narrowed, as if it knew its worth.

Wynona stared. She couldn't help it. The cat just looked so...human.

There's something wrong with that thing, Violet muttered. *Not right in the head.*

The hairs on the back of Wynona's neck rose and she frantically looked around. *I'm going crazy,* she told Violet.

No...I can feel what you're feeling. Violet chittered. *Something is off in this house. Weirder than normal.*

"Zander was allergic to the cats?" Chief Ligurio asked, his eyebrows high. "And yet your mother kept so many?"

Silvaris made a face. "Like Mother cared about anyone but herself." Her eyes lazily moved to Wynona. "You've got guts," she said, her tone slightly envious. "But I wouldn't want to be you when your dad catches up." The glee in her voice overtook any sympathy that Wynona might have harbored for the woman.

"That one was your mother's favorite?" Wynona asked, nodding toward the feline.

Silvaria held the cat up to look at its face, then brought it back into her arms. "Yes." She snorted. "It's crazy really. She rescued this one when I was a little girl. Not really sure how he's still so healthy and alive."

Wynona had to agree. Maybe that was the weird sensation she was getting? Could Ms. Roseburg have spelled the cat to live longer than normal?

"I'm surprised to see you holding him," Rascal said, reminding Wynona he was in the room.

"Why? Because he had the love I always wanted?" Silvaria laughed harshly. "Mother was right. Duo loves you no matter what. No person does that."

"Not even your brother?" Wynona's attention began to wander. Silvaria was just a neglected, bitter woman. Wynona felt sorry for her, but she also had no power to change it. Her eyes fell on a painting, a particularly lewd one, that was a little off balance. *Do you see that?*

Might as well check it out, Violet responded.

Rascal headed that way, a testament to the fact that he had been listening in. With a small burst of strength, he pulled the painting away from the wall, revealing a safe.

"Bingo," Wynona whispered, ignoring Silvaria's outraged cry.

"Ms. Killoran," Chief Ligurio said with a loud voice. "Either help us open it or please remove yourself from the area."

"Anything in that is private," Silvaria argued.

"Anything in that is evidence," Chief Ligurio argued back. He waved his warrant. "President Le Doux has no power to stop me from taking anything that might prove our case."

Rascal put his ear to the safe and turned the level. He leaned back. "I've always wondered if a person can really open one just using their ears."

"SKYMAW!"

Wynona winced as Chief Ligurio shouted down the hallway. Apparently, Silvaria had decided to leave. She obviously wasn't going to help.

"Yeah, Chief?" Daemon's head came into view.

"In the room, now."

Wynona pointed at the wall. "Are there any booby traps?"

Daemon smirked, then his eyes went black. He shook his head. "No. Just a regular safe." He scratched the underside of his chin. "Curious. I'd think a warlock would have warded it."

Wynona bit her tongue. The fact that the Roseburg family magic was weakening wasn't pertinent to the case...at least not yet. "Chief, with your permission?"

Chief Ligurio nodded.

Wynona walked forward, resting her hand on the safe. She wasn't totally convinced she could do this, but if there were no other spells, she felt mostly confident that she wouldn't hurt anyone by trying.

Close your eyes, Violet instructed. *Imagine the safe in your mind. Let the magic run through it.*

Wynona took in a long breath through her nose, centering herself. She did as Violet said, letting the purple mist move through the metal door. Slowly, a picture began to build in her mind. "I can see it," she whispered. Gears and locking mechanisms, which meant nothing to her, came to view. "What do I..." She trailed off. Something shimmery caught her attention and Wynona moved her mental eye closer to check it out. "There was a spell," she said softly.

"How do you know?" Rascal asked.

"I can see the residue."

"I didn't see anything." Wynona recognized the voice as Daemon's.

"It's inside the safe," she said. "I don't think it's visible from the outside."

A huffing sound let her know what the black hole thought of that.

"Can you break through it?" Chief Ligurio pressed.

"The spell has faded," Wynona said, shaking her head. "It must have been Zanders and it broke at his death."

"Just like a curse," Rascal agreed.

"Right." Wynona moved through the leftover magic. "What do I pull?"

"Can you make the gears move so the level rises?" Rascal asked.

Wynona scrunched her eyes and tilted her head. It took a couple of tries, but she finally got things moving. A soft clicking sound let her know she'd done what she'd set out to do. She opened her eyes. "Okay. Try pulling."

Rascal gave a heave and the lever shifted, the heavy door slowly swinging open.

"What's in there?" Chief Ligurio demanded.

"Mostly papers," Rascal said, pulling several files out. He began passing them out. "Take a look. See if anything's interesting." He handed Wynona one marked **Insurance**.

She made a face, but didn't complain out loud. Maybe she could find a money angle on life insurance. If Zander had taken out a policy on his mother, it would explain why he killed her.

And maybe why someone killed him.

Wynona nodded and pulled out the thin document. Her eyes widened. "Chief!"

Once again, he practically flew to her side. "A will?" he asked, taking it from her.

Wynona pulled it back just long enough to point at the bottom of the page. "It's a copy of Ms. Roseburg's will. See the note about Mr. Marsh inheriting everything?"

Chief Ligurio frowned. "But this is a copy. Why?" He flipped over the manilla envelope. "And why was it marked insurance?"

Wynona tapped the papers. "Because he found out about the will before it was read?" she suggested.

Rascal put his fists on his hips. "So he killed her? Why wouldn't he have tried to change her mind?"

Wynona rubbed her forehead. "I don't know. Killing her while the will was not what he wanted it to be seems foolish. But the evidence is there that he did the deed."

"Perhaps whoever killed him will have those answers."

Wynona sighed. "Maybe I'm completely bonkers. Maybe he didn't kill her."

Chief Ligurio shook his head. "No...I think we're on the right track. But there's still something missing."

"I sure hope so," Wynona murmured.

"Do you think your dad really has the answers?"

Rascal's question brought the room to a sudden silence. Wynona considered the question. "I don't know," she admitted. "But..." She sighed. "I wouldn't put it past him." She made a face. "But if he knows, it's because someone told him." She raised her eyebrows. "Which means someone else knows what happened."

There was a beat of silence. "Skymaw. Bring Ms. Killoran down to the station." He began to walk away. "I think we might have some more questions for her."

CHAPTER 21

"Have a seat, Ms. Killoran," Chief Ligurio said in a measured tone as they entered the interrogation room.

Silvaria stuck her chin in the air, but Wynona could practically smell her fear. Silvaria's hands were shaking and she kept swallowing as if she couldn't bring moisture to her throat.

"Silvaria," Wynona said softly, then smiled when the woman turned to look at her. Wynona waved at the chair. "We're not here to hurt you. Please...sit down and try to relax."

Silvaria cackled. "Relax?" She threw herself in the chair. "As if anyone could relax when they're being questioned by the police. Or when their brother and mother are killed within days of each other."

Wynona sat down as well, grateful for Rascal's strong presence by her side. "I realize these aren't ideal circumstances and we all understand that your family has had a difficult week, but—"

"A difficult week?" Silvaria snorted. "You don't even know what that means, Ms. I'm the president's oldest daughter."

Wynona had to pause. Anger was instantly boiling inside of her and she could feel her magic electrifying her entire body.

Easy, Violet cooed. *She's an idiot, yes. But that doesn't mean she deserves to be shishkebabed.*

I know! Wynona shot back, then immediately gave into the guilt that comment sent through her system. Letting herself feel bad about her behavior helped pull her off the ledge and Wynona was able to take a deep breath and force herself back to calm. It was moments like this that she completely understood why Granny might have been worried for her. Left unchecked, Wynona knew there was a part of her that could definitely be everything she despised...and more. It was a side to her emotions that frightened Wynona. She didn't like to think about the person she could have become if her parents had encouraged that type of behavior, rather than her grandmother teaching her the exact opposite.

The unrepentant smirk on Silvaria's face did nothing to help Wynona's ire, but she kept herself under control, pushing the magic down and earning a respectful nod from Daemon. She nodded back. "Ms. Killoran, all we want is the truth." Wynona leaned forward. "If my father knows what happened with Zander and your mother, it's only because someone told him about it."

Silvaria's jaw clenched.

Wynona sat back and waited. The tension in the room built to uncomfortable proportions, but she didn't speak. Let Silvaria sweat it out a little. Something would eventually break her. They just had to find the right button.

Spoken like a true cop, Rascal said.

Wynona had to clench her muscles to keep from looking at him. *You're breaking my concentration.*

A thousand apologies, Miss President's Daughter.

That did earn him a glare, but it didn't last long. The uncontrollable urge to stick out her tongue was making Wynona want to laugh. The topic of her father wasn't a funny subject, but Rascal's teasing always had a way of lightening the mood.

Silvaria frowned slightly, looking back and forth between her and Rascal before shaking her head. She folded her arms, thrusting her chin in the air. "I don't have anything to say to you."

"Are you aware that your brother had seen the will?"

Silvaria winced, giving away an answer before she could speak.

The question had come from Chief Ligurio, but Wynona jumped in. "Did he offer you part of the inheritance if you helped him kill your mother?"

"What!" Silvaria screeched. "Absolutely not!"

"So he just wanted to keep it all himself," Wynona said with a slow nod.

"He killed your mother for the inheritance and then you killed him," Chief Ligurio responded conversationally.

"How can you say that?" Silvaria demanded. "We all heard the will. You were allowed to sit in. The money was left to the stupid cat."

"The one you were cuddling with just an hour ago," Wynona pointed out.

"And your family was planning to contest the will," Chief Ligurio added. He looked at Wynona. "By killing Zander, there was one less person to share it with."

"Maybe her father was next?"

Silvaria thrust her hands through her hair, screaming. "You have it all wrong! I would never kill my brother! I was helping him hide the murder!" She gasped and slapped her hands against her mouth.

Wynona leaned back, feeling slightly exhausted as well as relieved. Her theory had been correct...and she hated herself for it. "What happened?" she asked softly. "Did you heal the spot on her head or did Zander?"

Silvaria was frozen for a split second before she burst into tears. Her alabaster skin turned bright red and her nose began to run. Between her sniffles and gasping for air, she began blubbering words that not even the most skilled linguist would have been able to interpret.

Wynona shared a look with the chief, then sighed. "Daemon, would you please bring me some hot water, a mug and some hawthorn and lavender?"

"Hawthorn and lavender," he grumbled, shaking his head as he headed out of the room.

"We're in a police station," Chief Ligurio said under his breath.

"Amaris has some up front," Wynona said easily.

Rascal covered his laughter with a cough.

One side of Chief Ligurio's mouth curled and he shook his head. "Ms. Killoran," he said over her blubbering. "If you would simply calm down, we'll get this whole thing settled."

Her crying only grew harder.

Wynona felt bad for the woman, but the sound was starting to wear on her nerves, making her extra grateful when Daemon made it back with the requested items. Taking them with a "Thank you," Wynona set them on the desk and brewed the tea. She was grateful her magic had reached a point where she could have it ready almost instantaneously.

Standing, she walked around the desk. "Ms. Killoran," she said gently. "Try some of this."

Silvaria nodded, her bottom lip still shaking, and took the mug, sipping it carefully. Within thirty seconds, the woman had calmed down and seemed to be breathing easier. "Thank you," she whispered hoarsely.

Wynona nodded and grabbed a nearby metal folding chair. It wasn't comfortable, but she'd live. She sat next to Silvaria and took her hand. "Tell me what happened. Why did Zander kill your mother?"

Silvaria let out a shaky breath. "It was an accident," she said, her voice still gravelly.

Wynona nodded encouragingly.

"He didn't tell me until after it had all happened, but he found the will." Silvaria pulled away from Wynona's hold and wiped at her face. "He tried to confront Mother about it, but she refused to listen. Instead, she headed toward the pool house." Silvaria sneered. "Her and that...merman...were always meeting in there."

Wynona pinched her lips together. How many people had been hurt because of one person's choices? Did Ms. Roseburg have any idea how her affairs hurt her children? Maybe if she'd spent more time with them instead of entertaining men, there wouldn't be such a fight over the money. It all seemed so senseless.

"But Zander didn't back off. He followed, still arguing." Silvaria paused to drink more tea, then narrowed her eyes at Wynona. "How did you know this would help?"

Wynona shrugged. "It's a gift I have."

Silvaria's mouth turned down and her gaze went to her lap. "Our family magic is dying with each generation," she admitted.

Wynona nodded again. "I know."

"How?" Silvaria shook her head. "Never mind. It doesn't really matter now anyway." Pushing a hand through her hair, she went back to the story. "Anyway, Zander wouldn't back down and Mother finally spun around to confront him, and she slipped." The tears began again. "She fell hard and hit her head against the tile floor." Silvaria's voice was barely audible. "The fact that she didn't use her magic to catch herself tells me she had to have been drunk or something," Silvaria said.

Wynona's eyes darted to Chief Ligurio, who nodded that he understood what she wanted him to check.

"And the hit to the head killed her?" Wynona pressed.

Silvaria nodded while taking another drink. "She didn't try to stop herself at all. Zander said he heard the hit echo through the room. By the time he reached her side, there was a huge puddle of blood and..." She choked on the words. "And she was gone."

Wynona gave her a moment to breathe before pressing for more. "What we're trying to figure out is why Zander healed her. If she was already gone, why not just call it in?"

Silvaria snorted. "Zander was under the impression that Marsh was getting it all."

A lightbulb went off. "So he healed your mom and pushed her in the water so that it looked like Mr. Monroe did it." She straightened and looked at the chief. "He was trying to frame the pool boy to get him out of the way to the inheritance."

"But in the end it didn't matter," Silvaria snapped. "It wasn't even Marsh who got the money. All of Zander's set up with the pool chemicals didn't even work."

Wynona shook her head. What a tangled web of deceit. False wills, angry children, framed innocents... "Wait," she said. "But then...why was Zander killed? Your mother's accident was covered up and the money was given to the cat. But why kill Zander?"

Silvaria grew depressed again and she sunk into her chair. "I don't know," she whimpered. "He, Dad and I were going to fight the will together, and it looked like he had gotten away with Mom's death. I just can't..." More tears spilled. "I have no idea why someone would want to kill him."

Wynona leaned back, pursing her lips in thought. "What happened after the reading of the will?"

Silvaria shrugged. "We went out to lunch and discussed fighting it."

"What lawyer were you going to use?" Wynona asked. "You couldn't use Mr. Melion."

Silvaria dropped her gaze again. "That's, uh..." Her blue eyes darted up, then back down. "That's when I went to your dad."

Here we go, Violet said dryly.

It took a lot of concentration for Wynona to stay still.

"I told him what was going on with the will, and figured he could help us."

"Which is how my dad knew about Zander's role in your mother's death." It wasn't a question, but at least Wynona knew she wasn't going to have to face her dad again anytime soon. He didn't know anything she didn't know.

Silvaria nodded. "He said he could help us with the lawyer."

"But..." Wynona paused. What was in her mind might be something better to discuss without Silvaria around. "Is there anything you haven't shared with us?" Wynona asked, suddenly anxious to be done. Her questions had been answered, and Ms. Roseburg's death solved. Now they needed to focus on Zander's death and Wynona was almost completely positive that Silvaria was innocent in that.

Silvaria shook her head. "That's everything," she said with a sigh.

"Thank you for your cooperation, Ms. Killoran," Chief Ligurio said firmly. "I'm sure it will go a long way in helping the judge figure out your sentence for aiding and abetting a murderer."

"What!" Silvaria's mug went flying as she jumped to her feet. "You can't be serious!"

"Did you or did you not just admit to knowing who killed your mother, but keeping the information from the police?"

"Yes, but—"

"But nothing." Chief Ligurio gathered his things and stood. "You may want to call that lawyer the president offered you." He paused at the door. "You're going to need it."

Wynona followed wordlessly. She felt bad for Silvaria, but the chief was right. She had had crucial information and hidden it from the authorities. They reconvened back in the chief's office.

"Does anyone think she was involved in Zander's death?" the chief immediately asked.

Wynona shook her head, noting that Rascal and Daemon did the same.

Chief Ligurio nodded. "I feel the same." He sat at his desk with a groan. "So we're still at square one."

"Not necessarily," Wynona said, stepping closer.

Chief Ligurio's eyebrows shot up.

"If my father was helping her get a lawyer to go up against Mr. Melion, then why did he hire Mr. Melion?"

Chief Ligurio tapped the desk, his long, white fingers rapping a frantic rhythm.

"Didn't Mr. Melion once tell you that he wanted to work for your family but hadn't been invited into the circle?" Rascal asked.

Wynona nodded. "Yes. He did." She turned back to the chief. "My family has used Mr. Bizana since before I can remember. Why did he suddenly hire Mr. Melion? And who was he sending to help the Killorans?"

"Do you believe your father could be trying to influence Mr. Melion?" Chief Ligurio asked.

Wynona shrugged, relaxing slightly when Rascal's hand landed on her lower back. "I don't know. But the circumstances are odd. I can't say that I'd put it past him though."

"Hmm..." The chief tapped his fingers a few more times. "Looks like we better go have that chat with Mr. Melion." He stood. "It's going to be a long night, everyone. Grab what you need because I want this case off my desk before another body shows up."

CHAPTER 22

"Hello, Mr. Melion," Wynona greeted. The lawyer jumped to his feet, straightening his tie. He had been waiting quite a while and Wynona was beginning to feel sorry for him. Not only was he caught up in the Roseburg and Killoran family drama, but now that her father was intervening, the poor lawyer might actually be in danger.

"Ms. Le Doux," Mr. Melion said kindly. He held out his hand and she shook it. "Chief Ligurio." The lawyer greeted every member of the party the same way, then held his tie to his chest and sat down. "I have to admit that I didn't expect to be sitting in on a meeting like this," he said with an easy smile. His brown eyes turned to Wynona. "It was just a couple days ago I was asking you to give my name to your family, and now..." He held his hands out to the side. "Here we are."

Wynona held back the explanation that she had nothing to do with his hiring. That, unfortunately, had everything to do with a spoiled, young witch who didn't know how to handle her own life. "Here we are," she agreed. She folded her hands in her lap. "I didn't realize my father was looking for a new lawyer."

Mr. Melion tugged at his tie. "Yes, he mentioned that I would be a second in his employ." He shrugged. "But we all have to start somewhere." He turned to Chief Ligurio. "I've been instructed to answer your questions. What would you like to know, Chief?"

Chief Ligurio's smile was far from friendly. "Tell me what President Le Doux promised you if you worked for him."

The room grew deathly silent. Wynona hadn't realized the chief would go straight for the jugular, but she kept her eyes on the lawyer.

His brown eyes grew shrewd and the kind middle-aged man was gone.

"What makes you think he promised me anything?"

Chief Ligurio's lip curled. "No one works for someone like the president without a kickback."

Mr. Melion leaned back, looking completely at ease. "My job is an easy one," he said. "I'm to help get this murder finished, protecting those who need it, and do my best to convince Ms. Le Doux that her family has her best interests at heart."

Wynona's eyes widened and Rascal growled.

Mr. Melion held up his hand. "Easy, wolf. There was nothing that said I could use force. I was to put in a good word."

The back of Wynona's chair squealed slightly from the grip of Rascal's hand and she wished she could pry it off and hold onto it. His strength would be welcome right now, but she also needed Mr. Melion to know she wouldn't be cowed. "That may be your job," she said in a soft tone. "But what was your reward?"

He nodded at her. "Caught that, did you?" Clearing his throat, he crossed his leg over his knee. "He'll introduce me to other wealthy families who enjoy keeping a lawyer on retainer."

"And your retirement?" Wynona pressed.

He shrugged. "It doesn't take much to make me happy, Ms. Le Doux. The income from two or three families would have me living well and the workload would be minor."

"And you're not afraid that my father will go back on his word?"

Mr. Melion chuckled. "I'm sure he will, if it suits him. I plan to not put him in that position."

Huh. Maybe he's not in danger after all, Wynona sent to Rascal and Violet.

Actually, I think he might be trying to take advantage of your dad. Good luck to him.

Wynona gave a slight nod to Rascal's response. If the shifter lawyer thought he could pull one over on the president, it would be at his own peril. "When was Ms. Roseburg's will written?"

The change in topic had every head turning her way.

"Excuse me?" Mr. Melion asked. "You don't have questions about President Le Doux and the murder?"

"We already know that Ms. Roseburg's death was an accident and that Zander took advantage of it," Wynona responded.

Mr. Melion's eyebrows rose high. "I suppose I should have been representing Ms. Killoran this evening instead of your father."

"Ms. Killoran cooperated willingly," Chief Ligurio said. "She had nothing to hide."

The shifter leaned forward. "Are you saying that you aren't charging her with anything?"

Chief Ligurio grinned. "If she's your client, I suppose you'll have to ask her."

Mr. Melion chuckled, then sighed. "Back to your questions, Ms. Le Doux. Ms. Roseburg wrote her will several years ago. It was signed and dated at that time."

"Then why did Zander find a different one?"

Mr. Melion shrugged. "It's not uncommon for wealthy people to change their minds." He smirked. "Though I have to admit that I feel better about the money going to the cats than to the pool boy."

"When did she write the one with Marsh in it?"

Mr. Melion shrugged. "She never actually gave me that one, or asked for it to be official. She could have typed it up herself one evening on a whim, never planning to verify it. Or perhaps it was something she wanted to use to keep her children in line."

Wynona's stomach churned in disgust. This family might actually be worse than hers. The Roseburgs and the Killorans seemed to manipulate each other at every turn.

"Did you ever ask her why she left the money to the cats?" Chief Ligurio asked. "Rather than her son, whom she seemed to dote on?"

Mr. Melion tapped his fingers on his knee. "When she wrote it, she told me that she was tired of being seen as nothing more than a check. Even though she spoiled Zander, she knew the type of warlock he was. She also knew that without her money, the family was nothing. Their magic is dying with each subsequent generation and the only reason they've managed to survive was the Roseburg fortune. She decided it was time to let the empire fall." He scratched under his chin. "Her cats were her solace, when she wasn't…entertaining. They hid in the home from visitors, but when Ms. Roseburg was around, she was constantly swarmed. And Duo was her favorite. She didn't want to leave them out in the cold."

"Were the cats a way of enhancing her magic?"

"Perhaps," the lawyer drawled. "But it wasn't her main goal." His face softened. "They were companions for a woman who was surrounded by people and still lonely, but refused to admit it."

Wynona felt something inside her shift. She knew that feeling all too well. It was the theme of her growing up years. Even with all the trouble Wynona was going through right now, she wouldn't trade being free of her family for anything.

"Is this kind of thing done often?" Rascal asked.

Mr. Melion nodded thoughtfully, the sympathy leaving his gaze. "In those who tend to be more…eccentric in their tastes, it happens often enough."

"How many wills did Ms. Roseburg have before this one?"

Mr. Melion shook his head. "That I can't answer. I haven't lived here that long, remember?"

Wynona pursed her lips. "Fair enough." She tapped her foot, her brain scrambling to figure out what direction to go next. *Have you visited the Kitty Kauldron yet?*

Rascal's eyebrow went up. *No. It didn't seem important. It's just a cat shelter.*

I'd like to see why Ms. Roseburg picked that place over other places. He nodded subtly.

"Thank you for your time, Mr. Melion," Wynona said.

His eyes widened and he looked from person to person. "No more questions? No accusations or threats?"

Chief Ligurio didn't look amused and Daemon shifted uncomfortably.

"Well." Mr. Melion slapped his knees. "I'm not going to feel like I'm earning my keep if it doesn't get a little harder than this." He grabbed his briefcase from the floor and stood. "Gentlemen, Ms. Le Doux." With a nod of his head, the lawyer left.

Chief Ligurio turned to Wynona. "I don't like dead ends, Ms. Le Doux."

Wynona pinched her lips. "I know, but we weren't getting anywhere. At first I was worried he was being taken advantage of, but now I'm seeing that Mr. Melion is sharper than that." She took a deep breath. "I think we need to visit the cat shelter."

The chief's dark eyebrows pulled together. "Why?"

"Because I want to see why Ms. Roseburg picked it. And maybe they'll have some more insight into Ms. Roseburg's frame of mind and her relationship with her cats."

"We're not looking for her murderer anymore," Daemon pointed out. "We're looking for who killed Zander."

"Right, but I think Zander's death had to do with his mother's." Wynona turned in her seat so she was addressing the officer. "I think someone besides Silvaria knew about Zander's involvement and that it somehow led to his death."

"You don't think it had to do with the will?" Chief Ligurio asked, leaning back in his seat.

Wynona shook her head. "No. Killing Zander would have been ridiculous. He wasn't inheriting and there was no guarantee that he ever would. Why kill him?"

"Perhaps their father thought to get rid of anyone else to share with? He was the most desperate, after all," Rascal murmured.

"No…" Wynona scrunched her nose and shook her head. "I don't think Mr. Killoran would kill his kids. Honestly, the odds of a judge giving him that money even if the kids were gone, was small. Their prenup would have taken care of that."

Chief Ligurio sighed and pushed a hand through his hair. "First thing in the morning, I expect you three at the shelter. Let me know what you find."

Wynona nodded and stood, stretching carefully. Violet had fallen asleep, which left Wynona without the snarky commentary she'd become used to.

"Let's get you home," Rascal said. He took her hand, giving it a squeeze. "Welcome to the life of crime fighting," he said with a grin. "Late nights…early mornings…no dinner…"

Wynona laughed softly. "And you all wonder why I didn't jump on board immediately."

"I didn't wonder at all," Rascal said easily as they stepped into the cool night. "But that doesn't mean I don't appreciate having you here." He wrapped his arms around her, careful not to bump Violet. "Work is much better with a pretty face to look at," he said against her mouth as he kissed her.

"Is that all I am to you? A pretty face?" Despite her teasing, Wynona was smiling. Rascal continued to leave kisses all over her face and she closed her eyes, letting herself drown in the sensations.

"If you need to ask that, then you haven't done much digging through my brain," he said with a low growl. He tightened his hold, his next kisses a little more fierce.

"You're right, I don't dig through your brain," Wynona said, pulling back just slightly. "I respect your privacy."

"Where's the fun in that?" he asked with a smirk.

Wynona ran her hands up his chest and around the back of his neck. "Since I'm not going to be doing that any time soon, why don't you just show me how you feel?"

Still holding her with one hand, Rascal very gently picked up Violet and set her in the front wicker basket of the Vespa, then pulled Wynona in tight. His lips hovered only a centimeter above her own and Wynona could feel her anticipation building as her magic began to hum.

"It would be my pleasure," he said in that low gravelly tone that sent sprites fluttering through her stomach. Wynona would have responded, but apparently, Rascal didn't need one because there were no words between them for a long, long time.

CHAPTER 23

Wynona yawned and took another long pull of her tea. She needed to wake up and do it now. Rascal was coming to pick her up so they could visit the Kitty Kauldron to try to figure out why Mrs. Roseburg would leave all her money there.

A knock on her door caught her off guard and she jumped, almost spilling her tea. "That'll teach you to stay up late smooching," she muttered to herself. With a flick of her fingers, the front door opened.

"Good morning," Rascal said with a grin, followed by a chuckle when she gave him a glare. "You don't look happy to see me." He walked over and left a peck on her cheek. "Any particular reason?"

She's regretting your little make out session last night, Violet offered, scrambling up his leg.

"Violet!" Wynona cried.

Rascal laughed and brushed her skin when he tucked a piece of hair behind her ear. "I should probably be offended by that, but for some reason it's kinda funny. I'll have to up my game if you're regretting it."

Wynona rolled her eyes and sent her tea cup to the sink. "I'm not sleeping well, okay?" She sighed and rubbed her temple. "This case has me in knots and I keep looking over my shoulder, afraid that my dad is going to show up and drag me back to the castle."

Rascal's humor was gone. "I won't let him."

"Do you really think either of us could stop him?" she pressed. Wynona closed her eyes and shook her head. "I'm sorry. I'm being pessimistic and it's not like me." Her shoulders deflated. "Sometimes it all just feels too heavy."

Rascal pulled her into a hug and rubbed her back, resting his cheek on her head. "It'll all turn out okay," he cooed. "We can do this and Chief promised the power of the station to keep you out of their clutches. You just keep practicing that magic and we'll make it through both your family *and* the case." He pulled back. "We're close," he said with a firm nod. "I can feel it. Something's going to give in this case very soon."

Wynona gave him a tired smile. "Thanks. I needed that."

He gave her a quick kiss. "I know." Pulling back, he winked while tapping his temple.

"PRIVACY!" she hollered after him when he walked away smirking.

"Keep your guard up!" he retorted. He stopped at the door. "Come on. Daylight's wasting."

Wynona held up a finger and used her magic to grab her purse and keys. "Ready."

Rascal held out a hand and led her to the truck, making sure she was settled before walking to his own side. "Have you ever been to this place?" he asked, putting the truck in reverse.

Wynona shook her head. "Nope. I've seen it a couple times while running errands, but I'm not exactly in the market for a cat."

Violet snorted.

"Between a wolf and a mouse as permanent fixtures in your life, it's no wonder," Rascal said with a grin.

Wynona laughed softly. "I suppose so. I always did wonder what some witches saw in them." She tilted her head in thought. "Though I figured it had to do with my bound magic, which was obviously not the case."

The cab grew quiet as they drove through town. The Kitty Kauldron was on the opposite side of Hex Haven, as it needed quite a bit of land in order for the animals to roam.

They pulled into the small parking lot and Rascal shut off the car. "Skymaw's here." He tilted his chin toward the officer stepping out of his vehicle.

Wynona nodded. "Great. Let's go."

They got out of the truck and the group walked inside. A bell rang over their head, announcing their arrival.

"Coming!" A feminine voice came from the back of the office.

Wynona looked around, taking a moment to scan the entrance. It was plain, as far as businesses went. Concrete floors, a simple front desk. The walls were lined with pens or pallets of food. A small area to the right looked like a playground, presumably where guests could play with the kittens or adult cats.

"Hi, there," a woman said, stepping through a swinging doorway. The noise of animals caught Wynona's ear before the door swung shut. "Oh." The woman paused. Her hair was pulled up in a messy ponytail that was half falling out. Her clothes were slightly baggy and had smears on them that Wynona had no desire to know where she'd gotten them. Nervous green eyes darted around the group. "How can I help you, Officers?"

"We're looking for Miss Valence Tailorson," Rascal said politely, but with a clear air of authority.

The woman ran her hands down her shirt. "That's me. Is there a...problem with a cat? Did someone complain about an adoption or something?"

Rascal shook his head. "No. We're here about Ms. Roseburg's will."

The woman blanched. Her lips thinned into a white line. "I guess you better come back to the office then." She guided the group to a tiny space that was messy, but just as unadorned as the front of the shelter.

Cat toys littered the space, covering every surface, with climbing posts built all along the side wall.

Talk about obsessed, Violet said. *This lady really likes her cats.*

She DOES run the shelter, Wynona responded.

"I'm sorry about the mess," the woman said, scrambling to clear a few chairs.

"It's fine," Rascal said. "We can stand."

She paused, hugging several files to her chest, then nodded. "Okay. Do you mind if I sit though?" A sheepish grin crossed her face. "As you can imagine, I don't get off my feet very often."

Rascal nodded. "Of course." His eyebrows went up. "I'm assuming you're Ms. Tailorson, then?"

She nodded, jerking her chair closer to her desk. "That would be correct." Clasping her hands in her lap, Ms. Tailorson looked up expectantly. "What do you need to know about Harmony's will?"

The fact that Ms. Tailerson used Ms. Roseburg's first name wasn't lost on Wynona. She was clearly stating her relationship with the deceased witch had been close.

"Tell us about Ms. Roseburg's relationship with the shelter," Rascal pressed. "Are all her cats from here?"

"Goodness, no," Ms. Tailorson said with a laugh. "Harmony rescued quite a few cats, it's true, but she had money, so she had several pure breeds."

"And you were hired to help take care of the cats?" Rascal continued.

Ms. Tailorson nodded, leaning back in her seat. Apparently, her initial wariness had worn off. "As you can imagine, the shelter sometimes struggles for money, like most institutions who do this type of work." She paused for just a second before her eyes lasered in on Rascal. "I have over two hundred cats at the moment, Officer. Do you have any idea how much it takes simply to feed them? Let alone take care of pet vaccinations or any illnesses."

"Can't say I do," Rascal said easily. "But I'd still like you to continue answering my question."

Ms. Tailorson's cheeks flushed. "Sorry. Getting caught up in my soapbox is a hazard of this type of work." She pushed out a harsh breath. "I have a side business where I hire myself and my workers out to help do clean up and onsite well care checks for those who prefer not to have to bundle their fur babies into boxes or cages."

"I'm assuming that means your clients are mostly witches," Wynona inserted, causing Ms. Tailorson to finally take note of her. "And that they're wealthy."

A slight smirk pulled at the woman's lips. "You could say that. A luxury like in-home visits doesn't come cheap." She spread her hands to the side. "Though it does pay for this posh office you see."

Wynona made sure her smile was warm. "It's clear you care a great deal about these animals, Ms. Tailorson."

"I'm sorry." She leaned forward. "Who are you? You aren't an officer."

"I'm Wynona Le Doux," Wynona supplied. "I own Saffron House of Tea on Haven Main."

"Oh, yes." Ms. Tailorson's eyes became guarded again. She leaned back and her eyes became unfocused. "I've heard of you."

Violet snorted. *And just what has she heard?*

A tingle ran up Wynona's neck and she stiffened. *Violet?*

I feel it, her familiar assured her. *What do you see?*

Rascal subtly stepped in front of Wynona, giving her a little space to do what she needed to do. "Ms. Tailorson, how long have you been working with the Roseburg cats?"

Wynona turned to the side, blinking until her vision went purple. She noted that Daemon jerked, obviously having felt her magic, but to his credit, his face stayed stoic. *I don't see anything!* Wynona thought in exasperation. Why did she keep getting this feeling? Was a ghost following her, but able to somehow hide itself? What good was this power if the specters could still stay invisible?

"Were you surprised by the will?" Rascal asked, pulling Wynona's attention back to the conversation.

She pushed down her ghost vision. She could still feel the presence. Someone was there and Wynona couldn't see them. But why?

"Not really," Ms. Tailorson said, letting her right hand fall over the side of her chair. "Harmony and I had talked about it before." She smiled. "I suppose you could say we were kindred sisters in a way."

"You're a witch?" The question was out of Wynona's mouth before she could think better of it. With creatures who looked human, it could be hard to tell what type of paranormal they were, but flat out asking wasn't really considered polite. "Sorry," Wynona immediately said. "It was just the way you said sisters that made me wonder."

Ms. Tailorson nodded. "Yes. I'm a witch."

Everyone in the room could tell that Ms. Tailorson wasn't thrilled to have Wynona there, though Wynona didn't know why. They'd never met before. It made no sense for the woman to dislike her.

Instead of dwelling on it, Wynona smiled. "You must have an animal affinity." *In for a penny, in for a pound*, she thought. She'd already crossed the polite line, might as well simply find out what she needed to know.

Ms. Tailorson looked less than amused. "I suppose you could say that."

"Did you know that Ms. Roseburg was a wind witch?" Wynona offered. "Her specialty was air."

Ms. Tailorson nodded. "Yes. I knew that." Her eyes narrowed. "Are you planning to share your strength next?"

Wynona shrugged. "I make custom teas," she said. "I suppose you could call me an earth or plant witch."

Those green eyes grew even smaller. "Hm." After what seemed an eternity, she must have decided Wynona was no threat, because the witch straightened and smiled widely. "Did you have more questions? Or do I get to give my spiel about adopting a cat?"

Rascal coughed. "I don't think a cat and I would get along," he said with a chuckle.

Ms. Tailorson shifted and raised her eyebrows at Daemon, who gave one quick shake of his head. "And you, Ms. Le Doux? I happen to know your mother has a few."

Wynona kept that smile plastered on, though it was wavering at this point. "Sorry, but no. It wouldn't get along with my familiar."

"You have a familiar?" Ms. Tailorson turned contemplative. "And it wouldn't get along with a cat, huh?" Her eyebrows shot up. "Is it a wolf perhaps?"

The humor fled the room so quickly that Wynona almost felt as if the air had been sucked from her lungs. She got the distinct impression that Ms. Tailorson was sending a message. *But why? And what exactly is she trying to convey?*

She knows about us, Rascal said through their link. *The question is, who told her? And why does it matter to her?*

"That's one way to look at it," Wynona said. "Thank you for your time, Ms. Tailorson." Wynona turned to the door. She needed a few minutes to think things through. This visit hadn't gone the way she had planned.

"We'll be in touch," Rascal said in a low tone. Bringing his hand to Wynona's back, he led her out of the office.

Footsteps followed them and Ms. Tailorson hurried around the group, picking up the foldable counter so they could pass through. "Thanks for stopping by," she said in a perky tone. "If any of you decide you'd like a pet, just let me know."

Wynona stopped. "Where did you get that?" she asked, pointing to a long, jagged red mark on the woman's arm.

Ms. Tailorson smirked. "Hazard of working with wild animals, Ms. Le Doux." Her eyes flashed to Rascal and back. "You ought to know that."

"Some of your cats are wild?" Wynona continued, ignoring the woman's low blow.

"We're a shelter," Ms. Tailorson said slowly, as if Wynona were simple minded. "We take in all cats, no matter how feral."

Wynona nodded. "Try some ginger or golden root," she offered. "It'll help keep it from getting infected." With a completely insincere smile, Wynona led the way outside, breathing much easier once they weren't contained within those concrete walls.

"That wasn't quite what I expected," Rascal said, stopping at the side of the truck to look back at the building.

"Me either," Daemon agreed. "At first I thought she would faint at our appearance, but then she practically threatened you, though I'm not quite sure why."

"She's scared," Wynona said thoughtfully, looking back as well.

"Why?" Daemon asked. "We weren't here to arrest her. She's not even considered a suspect." He dropped his voice. "Though now I'm starting to think we should."

"What would she gain though?" Wynona asked. "We're looking for Zander's killer. Ms. Tailorson would have no reason to kill Zander."

"Revenge?" Rascal offered. "For a friend? Or maybe she was afraid he would stop the monthly income she relied on, if the will was changed over?"

Wynona nodded. "It's worth considering, but..." She shook her head. "Something doesn't quite fit."

"Why were you asking about the scratch?" Daemon asked. He grinned. "I'm pretty sure you knew exactly what it was."

Wynona nodded. "I did, but I needed her to confirm it."

"And the reason?"

Rascal's eyes widened and he turned to Wynona. She nodded, knowing he understood the possible significance. "The scratch on Zander's neck," he said. "Her scratch was jagged like the scratch on his neck."

"Can a cat kill a human?" Daemon scoffed. "That seems unlikely."

"It does," Wynona mused. "They're small, even if they can be vicious. Zander should have been able to push it away before it could do anything that severe."

Rascal growled. "So she is involved."

Wynona ticked her head side to side and up and down. "Maybe, yes, no? I'm not sure. But I do think she knows who did it." She grinned at the gentlemen. "And that's enough to help give us something to run with."

CHAPTER 24

"So let me get this straight," Prim said around a mouthful of dinner. She swallowed and leaned forward onto the table. "Zander Killoran accidentally killed his mother."

"Right," Wynona said with a nod. She pushed the salt container toward Rascal, knowing he needed it before he could ask.

Daemon snorted and shook his head. Everyone's mouths were full of food and they were all eating as if it was their last meal on Earth. The day had been long after their morning at the Kitty Kauldron.

Wynona had gone to work and the men had gone to the station. It wasn't until dinner time that they were able to get together again to talk about what they had learned that morning.

"He tried to cover up the death by healing her head wound and framing the pool boy...uh, man."

Wynona nodded again.

"You figured that out because Zander tried to use a pool chemical to frame the merman, but it was only on Zander's shoes, not his mother's. Meaning he smeared it to look like someone slipped, when no one actually did."

Wynona kept nodding. "We have the added bonus of Daemon seeing the residual magic on Ms. Roseburg's head," Wynona pointed out, holding back her smile when Prim stiffened. "Not to mention we also have Silvaria's confession."

Prim rolled her eyes. "Right. The Princess was covering for her brother. How convenient."

"Prim," Wynona scolded.

"What?" Prim widened her eyes and brought her shoulder up to meet her pink hair. "Mother cut her off from all that lovely family money. Boo hoo. Why can't she just work a job like all us normal creatures? Contrary to her belief, it's not going to kill her."

Wynona tilted her head to the side. "Have you been working with poison ivy or something today? You're not usually quite so…"

"Refreshing?" Prim supplied, batting her pink eyelashes. "Honest?" She glared when Daemon coughed a laugh.

Daemon's cheek turned red and he put his focus back on his dinner container. He was twice Prim's size, but apparently he was still afraid of her.

"Mean," Wynona finished softly. "What's going on?"

Prim slumped in her seat. "I don't know. I just…you guys all go off and get to solve these cases, looking cool and bringing in the bad guys, and I'm stuck in my greenhouse dealing with temperamental Madagascar dragon trees who refuse to spread their leaves properly."

Wynona had nothing to say. She had no idea that Prim was interested in sleuthing. Wynona had only gotten involved because it had been forced on her when she'd found a dead body in her office just before her grand opening. In fact, she'd been dragged into almost every case she'd been a part of, except this one. She'd chosen to be involved, but only after a decent amount of coercion.

Now that she stopped to think about it, however, Wynona could see how Prim would feel left out. Intentional or not, most of their group was working together and only one was not. That would hurt anyone's feelings.

"Prim, I'm sorry," Wynona said softly. "I didn't mean—"

Prim held up her hand. "No. I'm sorry. I need to shut up." She sighed. "The last couple weeks have been hard and I guess I got jealous that everyone seems to want to be your best friend, and I'm over here like…" She waved. "Hello! Best friend's position is filled!"

Wynona stood and walked over to Prim and pulled her out of her chair. She squeezed the small woman tight. "If I had the authority, I'd totally have you help us on the case," she whispered to Prim.

Prim sniffed. "I know. I'm just being a baby."

"And you *are* my best friend. No one else could ever take your place."

WHAT! Violet squeaked.

Prim poked her head out of the hug and stuck her tongue out at Violet.

Usurper, Violet muttered.

Wynona groaned. "Can a witch not have multiple best friends?" She shook her head and sat down. "You two are ridiculous."

Rascal put a hand over his heart. "I'm feeling left out of this little magical moment. Should I complain that as your soulmate I should be your best friend?"

Prim glowered. "Not if you value your house plants, buddy."

"I don't have any."

She smirked. "Maybe not, but when you get home, you might find yourself with new roommates." The fairy wiggled her fingers. "Ever seen what shrubbery can do when given free reign?"

Rascal held his hands in the air. "I'm outgunned. Got it."

"You know..." Daemon tilted his head to the side. "I think she means business."

Wynona couldn't stop the laugh when Prim's jaw dropped. Daemon usually gave the fairy a wide berth, but he must have decided it was time to start closing the distance.

Oooh, Violet said gleefully, rubbing her paws together. *Things just got interesting.*

"Violet," Wynona muttered under her breath.

The purple mouse waved her off. *Leave me to my entertainment.*

"Why does it feel like I'm constantly trying to wrangle a room full of nymphs?" Wynona asked no one in particular.

Prim's tinkling laugh drew a smile from everyone. Who could resist a fairy laugh? "Because you are," she replied. "Not one of us has grown up except for you."

"Well, at least you admit it," Wynona retorted.

Prim settled back into her seat. "Okay. Back to the case." Her tone was much perkier now that they'd cleared the air between them.

Wynona made a mental note to share more with her friend. Maybe she wouldn't feel so left out if they had more discussions like this.

"Zander killed Mommy, sister hid the truth. Daddy's in debt, but no one can pin him to anything. Pool man seems fishy, but again, no evidence actually marks him as involved."

Wynona nodded, picking up her teacup. It had cooled and she gave it a quick warming up.

"Will is read, cats get it all, except pool man gets contract, aaaaand...now we have a dead son." Prim made a face. "Does that about sum it up?"

"That and the fact that the owner at the Kitty Kauldron seemed to be threatening us, though no one can figure out why," Daemon inserted.

Prim gave him a nod, which was more than she usually did. Her status quo thus far had been to ignore him at all costs. His snarky remark must have caught her attention. "Right. But we have nothing that says she was anywhere near the house when either murder went down?"

"Nothing," Wynona agreed. "Both murders were at night. Her appointments to take care of the cats all happened in the morning hours and only every other week. As far as we can tell, she wasn't even on the same side of town."

Prim pursed her lips and nodded slowly. "But if she was acting like she was scared...then there has to be a reason."

"Exactly what we thought," Rascal said.

Prim's long fingernails drummed against the tabletop.

"We also can't think of a motive," Wynona continued. "As far as we know, Ms. Tailorson didn't know about the will. It would have been a lovely surprise. So why kill the son? She already had the support she needed."

"Unless Zander threatened her," Prim offered. "Maybe he'd decided to fight the will?"

"Oh, he was fighting it." Daemon scoffed. "All three of the remaining family members were. They announced it in the office right after the will reading."

"But their quarrel would have been with Mr. Melion," Wynona said. "Not Ms. Tailorson."

"Maybe Zander thought if he went directly to the Kitty Kauldron, he could talk Ms. Tailorson out of taking the money."

Wynona shook her head. "That doesn't make sense. She has no power over the will. The Kitty Kauldron was given the power to use the money, but it was technically left to the cat. So Ms. Tailorson wouldn't have been able to turn it down."

Rascal scratched under his chin. "She probably could have refused the contract, but otherwise, the money doesn't technically belong to her."

"And Zander was killed at the house," Daemon pointed out. "Not at the shelter."

Prim scowled. "Maybe you need to pull the pool man back in. After all, that's two deaths in his area."

"Yeah, but neither was a drowning," Rascal muttered. "I'm guessing, in Zander's case, he was killed there because no one else would be able to hear anything. The pool is a full wing away from the living part of the home."

Wynona nodded. "I thought the same thing."

"Someone has to profit from Zander's death," Prim said. "Otherwise, he wouldn't have been killed."

"Did Zander have a will?" Wynona asked Rascal.

The wolf shifter shook his head. "No. I'm sure at his age, he didn't figure he would need it."

Wynona leaned forward. "Hey, Prim. Are there any plants that can kill people? Or make animals crazy strong?"

Prim frowned. "Any plant can kill, if you have someone with the right affinity." She waved at a purple heart vine in the corner of the room. The vines began to stretch and dance their way across the space. "I could wrap someone's neck in this and strangle them if I wanted to." She shrugged. "Not that I would ever do that, you understand."

Wynona laughed softly. "Put my plant back."

Prim preened a little, but did as she was asked. "So yes. A plant can kill someone. As for making an animal go crazy, catnip has a fun effect on cats, but wouldn't cause them to be so crazy they could kill someone." She raised her eyebrows. "At least not that I've ever heard. Most of the time if an animal doesn't get along with a plant, it makes them sick, not deadly."

Wynona nodded and turned when she felt Rascal's questioning gaze. "I was just trying to come up with an explanation for the cut on Zander's neck. It looked similar to the cut on Ms. Tailorson's arm, but I just don't see how a cat could kill a healthy, grown man. Not unless the cat had super strength or something."

Rascal returned her nod. "Agreed. I don't think it could have been the house cats. Most of them won't even come near us. I can't imagine they'd take down one of the inhabitants of the house. They knew Zander."

"And he's allergic to them," Daemon added. "He purposefully ignored them. Why would one kill him?"

"Could someone have controlled it?" Wynona asked.

The room paused.

"Like Prim controls the plants?"

Rascal stared into space, his golden eyes glowing. "It's a good thought, but the only person we know with that affinity is Ms. Tailorson, and we've already determined that she wasn't nearby." He turned to Prim. "How far away can you be and still control a plant?"

Prim pressed her lips together. "I have to see it. I don't know anyone who can control an object without being in the same room."

Wynona ticked her head back and forth. "Powerful witches sort of can." She took a deep breath. "I can move something in the kitchen, even if I stay in here. I know other witches who can do the same." She shrugged. "But controlling a live animal without seeing it? I have no idea if that's possible."

"Doesn't seem likely," Rascal murmured.

Prim's fingernails were drumming again, her eyes staring into space.

"Prim?" Wynona asked.

"Hm?" Prim blinked and came back to the present.

"You look like you're thinking hard."

Prim squished her lips to the side. "It's just...something's bothering me."

"What's that?" Daemon asked, bringing himself into the conversation.

Prim kept her gaze on Wynona. "You said the pool chemical was on Zander's shoes, found in the pool room. Right?"

Wynona nodded.

"But you also said those weren't the shoes he had been wearing earlier that day."

"Right, again."

Those nails were tapping a frantic rhythm. "What color were the shoes?"

"Brown," Daemon replied.

This time Prim actually turned to acknowledge him. "And what color was his suit?"

"Gray."

"That's it." Prim leaned back.

"What's it?" Daemon asked, frowning. "I'm lost."

Wynona's eyes widened. "Oh my gosh. How did I not see that?"

Prim pointed at Wynona. "You just needed a little fairy dust."

Wynona laughed.

"Would one of you women please inform us obviously non fashionista men what's going on?" Daemon asked tightly.

Prim wiggled just a bit in excitement and Wynona waited. She'd let Prim have the limelight this time.

"No one of Zander's social status would wear brown with gray. It would go against every fashion rule under the sun."

"He's a guy," Rascal inserted. "Maybe he didn't care."

"He might not have," Prim agreed. "But his stylist would have."

Rascal scratched behind his ear. "He had a stylist?"

"Trust me," Prim said, dropping her tone dramatically. "Zander Killoran would have had a stylist."

"Okay, but what does that have to do with his death?"

"If he didn't wear those shoes," Prim said slowly, "then someone else had to have put them in the pool house." She paused, waiting for the men to catch on.

Rascal coughed in surprise. "So someone wanted us to realize that Zander killed his mother."

Prim nodded. "Yep."

Daemon whistled low. "That's a pretty good way to divert attention away from your dirty deeds."

Prim nodded at him as well.

"Silvaria said no one else knew except them and my father," Wynona added. She huffed out a breath. "She was wrong."

CHAPTER 25

The night was slow as Wynona tried to get some sleep after their group dinner, but it eluded her. Her mind wouldn't stop spinning out different scenarios or ideas or trying to piece together the puzzle pieces that simply didn't fit.

There's some piece we still haven't discovered yet, she kept thinking.

Maybe so, but we'll never think of it if you don't let me get some sleep, Violet grumbled.

Wynona smiled slightly into the darkness at her familiar's complaints. Not that she could blame the mouse. It was late. Wynona needed sleep, or she'd be dragging tomorrow, but it simply wouldn't come.

Finally, she pushed back her covers and padded to the kitchen, turning on the dim light above the sink to guide her way. Taking a deep breath, Wynona directed the kettle and tea ingredients, using her magic to create something that should help her calm down enough to get some rest.

"You're getting good at that."

Wynona yelped and spun, covering her mouth to stop her shock. "Granny," she breathed. "What are you doing?" Wynona frowned, reaching for the back of her neck. She hadn't felt the telltale sensation, letting her know a ghost was around.

Her heart fell to her stomach. No wonder she had looked so ridiculous lately. Something was wrong with that power. It had been going off when no one was there and now it hadn't gone off at all.

"Your powers are working just fine," Granny said, waving off her granddaughter's concern.

"How do you know what I was thinking?"

Granny raised a white eyebrow. "It's written all over your face, Wynona. Only a fool would miss it." She walked to the table and sat down with a groan. "Your ghost radar, as you like to refer to it, only works when a ghost is here." She spread her hands. "Right now I'm corporeal. I didn't sit in the specter stage, so your alarm didn't go off."

Wynona nodded and warily joined her grandmother at the table. The tea supplies made their way there, Wynona making the cup without much conscious thought, which should have impressed her, but she was too caught off guard with Granny's arrival. "You're here awfully late."

Granny nodded. "I thought it best if we talk...without distractions."

Violet snorted and crawled into the room. *Not without me, you don't.*

Wynona waited until her familiar had climbed her leg and settled on the table before bringing a cookie over and settling it in front of the mouse.

Violet immediately began to nibble.

"What would you like to talk about?" Wynona asked, lifting her cup for a sip of hot tea.

"Have you decided whether or not you'd like to take out your father?"

Wynona choked on her drink and barely managed to set the cup down without it shattering. Turning to the side, she coughed until she was able to breathe normally. "Nice of you to put it so bluntly," Wynona finally managed.

Granny looked less than amused. "I don't have time to beat around the bush, Wynona."

Wynona frowned. "What does that mean?"

Granny leaned forward. "Your father is ruining this city. Crime runs rampant in the underbelly and as you yourself should have noticed, criminal activity is on the rise among the common folk as well."

She raised an eyebrow. "How many murders have you helped solve at this point?"

Wynona pressed her lips together. "I don't want to rule Hex Haven," she said softly.

"Then who else will?" Granny splayed her hands to the side.

"Look, I promised I would think about it," Wynona responded. "And I have, but right now I'm also trying to solve the Roseburg-Killoran case." She leaned in. "I do believe you have yet to fulfill your end of the bargain."

Granny grinned. "I thought you didn't want to go into politics."

Wynona leaned back. "Gran...I don't know how else to say this to you, but I'm not interested in running Hex Haven. Staging a coup against my father would be disastrous and possibly even deadly. If I can learn to control my powers, I might survive, but what about the others with less magic? Aren't their lives important as well?"

Hear, hear! Violet inserted. She folded her arms over her chest and glared Granny down, not that the witch noticed.

Granny tapped her black fingernails on the table. "I can see we're not going to agree right now. We can come back to this topic another time." She stood and straightened her robes, then paused, staring at Wynona. "Well? You wanted to learn, didn't you?"

Wynona frowned and slowly stood up. "Now?"

"Now." Granny straightened her shoulders and thrust her chin in the air. "What all can you do?"

"I've had a little experience reading tea leaves, and—"

"Show me." Granny nodded toward the cup.

Wynona hesitated.

"First rule of being a powerful witch," Granny said firmly. "Never hesitate."

Wynona shook her head. "Hesitation can save lives."

"Hesitation means losing your own life," Granny shot back. "Magic equals power in our world and if you want to survive, you'll have to be willing to use it."

"But I don't want to use my powers," Wynona said with a shrug. "At least not outside of normal living."

"Not using them means they'll become out of control," Granny insisted. "When they were emerging from the curse, how did it feel?"

"Like a dam was breaking."

Granny nodded. "Right. Not using them will be the same way. They'll be bottled up, and eventually spill over." She raised her eyebrows. "In other words..." She made an explosion with her hands.

Wynona hung her head. "So I'm just always going to be a danger to those around me?"

"No. You will learn to use your magic and you will control it," Granny stated. She threw her shoulders back again. "That's why we're here. Now...read the tea leaves."

Violet chittered, reaching for Wynona.

"No," Granny interrupted. "Let her learn to control it herself. This is a small skill. You'll be useful when she's using something stronger."

Wynona pinched her lips. Okay...she could do this. She raised her hand toward the cup, calling on the constant bubbling of powers within her belly. The electric feeling spread down her limbs and the cup began to rattle in its saucer. She closed her eyes to concentrate better.

"Open them!" Granny barked.

Shocked, Wynona opened her eyes and the magic shot out into the room, knocking things off the walls and breaking a few plates. Still wide eyed, Wynona looked around. She turned back to her grandmother. "Was that really necessary?"

Granny put her hands on her hips. "It is if you want to survive. Magic isn't just useful, it's defensive. Reading tea leaves might seem benign, but being able to do it quickly can save lives. Never close your eyes. It gives anyone the ability to sneak up on you."

Violet grumbled. *That's what I'm for.*

Granny pointed at the mouse. "You won't be enough."

"Can you hear her?" Wynona asked, her jaw dropping.

Granny shook her head. "No, but I don't have to to know what she's saying. Mice are notoriously cranky."

That really set Violet off. She was chattering so fast even Wynona had no idea what she was saying.

Wynona rubbed her forehead. "Maybe tonight isn't such a good idea."

"Grow up, Wynona," Granny snapped. "The world won't wait for you to decide the best day." Her eyes hardened. "Your father won't wait either."

Wynona hated to admit it, but Granny was right. The dead witch might be handling things with an iron fist, but she was correct. Her dad wasn't going to wait for her to be ready. In fact, he would more than likely show up when she was least expecting it, doing his best to gain an advantage. She imitated Granny and threw back her shoulders. "Okay. Fine." Reaching out, she funneled the magic faster than before. Her hand shook as she struggled with control, but Wynona refused to let it win. *She* was in charge, not her gifts. They would bend to her will.

The teacup rose up, twirling in the air, just like it had always done before. Wynona noted that several other pieces of pottery began to spin as well, but she stayed focused on the cup. When the timing felt right, she brought the cup to her hand and rested it in her palm. The other items floated back down to the tabletop and Wynona tipped the cup to look inside.

"A cross...a dragon..." Wynona tilted her head to the side, still staring, waiting for the images to reveal themselves. "A hammer...and...a snake." She took a deep breath, the magic draining slowly, bringing Wynona back down to Earth.

Granny rolled her eyes. "With magic that flashy, you'll never be able to sneak a reading."

Wynona huffed. "You're the teacher, Gran. If you want me to do it differently, then teach me."

Granny ran her hands over her face, suddenly looking tired. "I'm too old for this," she muttered.

Wynona bit her tongue on another sharp retort. She was going to have to get a hold of herself if they were going to survive these lessons. It was already clear it wasn't going to be all fun and games.

"Can you tell me what they mean?" Gran asked, slumping into a chair.

Wynona nodded. "I think so. The cross is trouble...or death."

Violet snorted.

"That means there are sudden changes coming." Wynona swallowed hard. One of the things she wished for the most was for her life to settle down and be easy. She had yet to see that particular wish come to pass. "The hammer means there will be challenges to overcome and the snake means to be cautious or wary."

Granny nodded. Her already pale skin was pallid. "That's just fine. I'm glad to see those lessons stuck."

Wynona frowned. Granny was a ghost. Why did she look so...worn?

"We'll continue this later." Without another word, Gran was gone.

"But!" Wynona reached out, though it was to an empty chair. Growling, she turned to Violet. "That's it?"

Violet shrugged and began cleaning her face. *The old crone certainly didn't do much, did she?*

"She looked...sick," Wynona said softly. "Can ghosts get sick?"

Violet shook her head. *Not that I've ever heard. Come on.* She scrambled down the table leg. *I might not need beauty sleep, but you definitely do.*

"Gee, thanks," Wynona grumbled. But the mouse was right. It was time for bed. Using her magic still tired her out, so Wynona had high hopes that she'd be able to actually sleep now.

She groaned, sinking into her bed and immediately closing her eyes. Her thoughts still swirled, but with each filling of her lungs, Wynona could feel her body growing heavier. Her breathing deepened, her limbs slacked and blessed darkness took her.

Her last thought was that tomorrow she'd have to go back and talk to a few people about the Roseburg case...and she would start with Silvaria.

CHAPTER 26

"You're sure about this?" Rascal asked, helping Wynona down from the truck.

She nodded. "Yes. I think Silvaria is our best bet. Someone else knew about Zander's situation with his mother. We know she told my father, but he didn't step in until after Zander was dead. Plus, he had no reason to kill Zander. He was going to help them, whatever that looked like. Maybe Silvaria told a person, or maybe Zander did, it really doesn't matter. The point is, she's our starting point."

Rascal nodded. "Skymaw's on his way, but he was running double duty this morning. Do you want to wait for him?"

Wynona shrugged. "Only if you do. I don't mind filling him in."

"You aren't worried about Silvaria using her powers against us if she gets mad?"

Wynona shook her head. "No. Their family powers are dying, remember?"

He grunted and together they walked up the front steps. Silvaria had moved into the mansion and was currently refusing to leave, though the property technically belonged to Duo, the cat.

As of yet, the authorities hadn't been called in, but Wynona felt confident that Mr. Melion would eventually put his foot down in order to fulfill the will. He was probably allowing Silvaria a bit of a mourning period.

Wynona knocked and smiled politely when the butler answered. "Hello, we'd like to see Ms. Killoran please."

"Ms. Killoran is in a meeting," the man intoned. "Please come back another time."

Rascal stepped up and flashed his badge. "We'll wait, thanks."

The butler, to his credit, didn't bat an eyelash. Nodding graciously, he stepped back and allowed them inside.

"Please tell her we're here," Rascal said with a tight smile.

The butler left and Wynona turned to Rascal. "Pulling out the big guns, I see," she whispered.

Violet chittered from Rascal's front pocket.

He smirked and leaned down to her ear. "Sometimes a wolf has to flex a little or other creatures forget who they're dealing with."

A shiver ran down Wynona's spine and she wanted to snuggle in closer. What she wouldn't give for a little alone time with her soulmate.

"Ms. Killoran will see you now," the butler said, interrupting their little moment, and Wynona jumped back as if being caught with her hand in the cookie jar.

Rascal's flashing golden eyes were laughing and Wynona stuck her nose in the air, walking past him, which must have only amused him more since he chuckled while he followed behind her.

The butler led them to a large salon and closed the door as he left.

Wynona sat carefully on one of the sofas. The place was so clean she was afraid of touching anything. She scanned the room. Everything was perfectly in its place. Not a speck of dust to be found.

"How do they keep it so nice with all the cats around?" Wynona murmured.

Rascal snorted. "They must not be allowed in here," he said. "It doesn't smell like them at all."

"Huh." Wynona allowed herself to lean back. "With Ms. Roseburg being so close to her cats, I would have expected the whole house to be open to them."

"She kept some rooms cat-free in order to help Zander with his allergies," Silvaria said curtly as she came into the room. She sighed. "What do you two want?"

Wynona straightened. "We'd like to talk to you."

Silvaria shook her head. "I have a lawyer hired. You'll have to talk to him." She glared at Rascal. "The police have made my life a living purgatory ever since I helped you."

Wynona didn't back down. "Ms. Killoran, we're trying to figure out who killed your brother. We think we have some leads, but we need you to clarify them." Wynona raised her eyebrows. "Don't you want to help us catch your brother's killer?"

Silvaria walked farther into the room with a disgusted scrunch to her nose. "Zander doesn't care if his killer is caught. I'd rather have the police stop breathing down my neck." She threw herself onto a chaise lounge.

And this is why dearest Mumsy cut her off, Violet grumbled.

"You're certainly welcome to have your lawyer present," Rascal said from his place behind Wynona.

She couldn't see him, but his tone said he was bored, though Wynona knew better. His wolf was on edge and ready to spring at any moment. He didn't like moody witches.

"But cooperating with us can only help your case in court." His smile was a sharp flash of fangs. "Judges tend to look kindly on those helping to keep the peace."

Silvaria rolled her eyes. "Whatever." She turned her blue eyes to Wynona. "What do you want?"

Wynona tilted her head. "Did you tell anyone else about Zander's cover up of your mother's death, besides my father?"

Silvaria stared at her nails, then began picking at the peeling polish. It was apparent she hadn't had a manicure in a while. "No."

"Are you sure?" Wynona pressed.

Silvaria kept her head down, but her eyes came up glowering. "I already answered your question."

"Yes, but I have reason to believe you're lying," Wynona said bluntly.

Silvaria jerked. "Excuse me? Who do you think you are?" She blanched as soon as she said the words. "I...mean...You're the president's daughter, but..." Silvaria trailed off and huffed, folding her arms over her chest. The pouty child was back. "I'm not lying."

"Do you know if Zander told anyone else?"

Silvaria shook her head. "No. He said he came straight to me."

Wynona's eyes narrowed. "How close were you and your brother? You had been kicked out of the house, so I wonder how often you spent time together." Wynona leaned back slightly. "It must have been hard to have your mother lavish him with attention and access to her money, but keep you out in the cold."

Silvaria laughed harshly. "Sounds familiar, doesn't it?" She sneered.

Wynona frowned.

"Celia told me all about how much of a disappointment you were to your family," Silvaria stated with a satisfied smile, which fell almost immediately. "Though you don't seem too put out by it."

Wynona sent soothing vibes to Rascal, who was struggling to hold his wolf at bay. Neither of them liked Wynona being degraded, but Rascal was also trying to let her stand on her own two feet, which she appreciated. His protective side was wonderful, but sometimes she needed to prove she could take care of herself.

Wynona smiled, knowing it wasn't exactly warm. "I'm not," she said bluntly. "And I wasn't kicked out. I escaped." She leaned in. "Because sometimes family isn't what it's supposed to be, no matter how much power or money they have."

Silvaria blinked. "I..." She snapped her mouth shut and gave a small lip curl. "Still looks like you landed on your feet. Are you telling me that was all your own doing? You didn't use your family's influence when opening your little tea shop?"

"I had a little money from my grandmother," Wynona admitted. "Just enough to get started, which she left me right before she died."

The smug smile starting on Silvaria's face fell.

"Never once have I used my family's name to get ahead. In fact, I really didn't mind when they refused to claim me as a member of the Le Doux family at all." Wynona snorted. "Life was actually easier then."

Rascal made a noise of agreement.

"But now that my powers are emerging, they want me back." Wynona tilted her head to the side. "Tell me, Silvaria. Do they really want me? Or just the power I can bring them?"

Silvaria dropped her gaze, picking at a thread on the sofa. "What do you do when you have nothing else to recommend you?' she asked softly. She looked up from under her eyelashes. "I wasn't raised to stand on my own two feet. Without my family money, I'm nothing."

"Without your family money, you're poor," Wynona corrected. "But that has nothing to do with your worth." She held her breath. Wynona hated confrontation and wasn't usually so bold when she spoke to someone, but Silvaria was pushing all her buttons. And truthfully, in some ways, she reminded Wynona of Celia. Spoiled and pampered, these ladies were never taught what life was all about.

The anger Wynona had been harboring against her grandmother dissipated as if it had never existed. She had understood before, she had grasped what her grandmother had said about her upbringing, but right in this moment, Wynona knew not just in her head, but deep down in her soul that Granny had saved her life the day she bound Wynona's powers.

Silvaria scoffed. "Easy for you to say."

Wynona shook her head, but didn't argue. The witch wasn't ready to hear anything else. Unless she *wanted* to make a change, there was nothing Wynona could do. "Did you tell anyone about Zander, Silvaria?"

Silvaria shook her head. "No."

That stupid tingling which began on Wynona's neck was back. Surreptitiously, she tried to look around, but there was nothing there. She knew her eyes were glowing, but Silvaria was still too caught up in her pity party to notice.

Blinking, Wynona was caught off guard when the large tabby cat jumped from behind the sofa and settled onto Silvaria's lap. "How did..." Wynona looked at the door, frowning. "I thought the cats weren't allowed in here?"

Silvaria shrugged, her fingers digging into the thick fur. "I don't see why it really matters now."

"I suppose." Wynona pinched her lips together. Silvaria didn't seem surprised to see the cat, so there must be a way for the cats to roam the house as they wanted. "Is this the famous Duo?"

Silvaria nodded. She seemed to have calmed down with the cat in her lap. Funny how pets were such good therapy at times.

Violet huffed. *I'm not a pet.*

Never said you were, Wynona corrected. *And you're also not always a good form of therapy.*

Rascal snorted, then covered his laugh with a cough.

Nice, Violet responded. *We'll see how helpful I'll be next time you're about to blow the world up.*

Wynona held back an eye roll. "How long has he been with the family?" Wynona watched Duo's tail swish back and forth. The intelligence in the cat's eyes was remarkable. Once again, Wynona had to wonder if Ms. Roseburg used them for more than just companions.

She glanced down at the cat's feet, but couldn't see any claws through the fur on its large paw. *No...there's no way something that small could have killed Zander.*

Not likely, Rascal agreed.

He has killer eyes, Violet offered. *You never know. Sometimes the small ones are the worst.*

"Since before I was born, if you can believe it," Silvaria said with a small smile. "I'm really not sure how he's survived this long, but..." She shrugged. "I'm sure that's why Mother left everything to his care. She had him since the beginning."

"How did he get his name? Do you know?" Wynona pressed. Over twenty years was an awfully long time for a cat to live. The question of a spell came to mind.

Silvaria laughed softly, her face easing dramatically with the movement. "Duodecim is his full name, which I'm sure you caught at the will reading." Silvaria grabbed one of his paws and splayed it for Wynona. "He has six toes on each of his front paws. Mom named him after that. Duodecim means twelve in Latin."

Wynona blinked. "Six toes on each front paw?"

Silvaria nodded. "Yep. It's called polydactylism. It's genetic."

Wynona nodded, her head spinning. "I've heard of it before." Something wasn't right here. She tried to picture the cat sitting on the shelf during the reading of the will. His paws were hanging over the edge of the shelf. She shook her head. No. Wynona was positive that the cat had normal sized paws. There was no way it had six toes.

Looking at Silvaria's lap, the paw was larger than normal. It was easy to see something was different.

Wynona jumped to her feet. "Thank you for your time, Silvaria. We're done for now, but we might be back." She walked quickly to the door, letting herself out.

"But..." Silvaria's voice faded as Wynona practically ran down the hall.

"What's going on in that pretty little head of yours?" Rascal said in a low tone as he followed. "You're blocking me."

Wynona nodded curtly. "Not here."

Rascal fell silent until they got out to the truck. "Okay. What?"

Violet poked her nose over the top of his shirt pocket, twitching with excitement.

"Do you have pictures of the cat?" Wynona asked breathlessly as she attached her seatbelt. "From earlier in the case?"

"Maybe." Rascal put the truck in gear. "Why?"

"I'm not sure," Wynona said, chewing on her bottom lip. "But if I'm right, I think we might have found something important."

CHAPTER 27

"So..." Rascal parked in the precinct parking lot and put the truck in park. "What's going on?"

Wynona glanced at her phone, watching the clock. "In about an hour, we'll need to go back." She began to mutter to herself. "Gotta get Lusgu to open today." She ignored Violet's snort. "He can handle things for an hour or two...I hope."

"Wy!"

Rascal's call pulled her from her thoughts. "Hm?"

He shook his head, a half grin on his face. "What's going on? You're still blocking me."

"If you weren't always poking around in my brain, you wouldn't be so upset by that," Wynona pointed out.

Rascal rolled his eyes. "What's the point of having a soulmate if I can't dig around for information I wouldn't get otherwise?"

"Why, indeed," Wynona grumbled. She grabbed her door. "Come on. Let's find those pictures."

"Wy," Rascal warned, climbing down as well. He came rushing around the front of the truck. "What do you know that I don't? And why are we going back?"

Wynona kept walking, smiling at Rascal when he still opened the doors for her even though she was moving past him quickly. "The cat," Wynona said. She waved at Amaris, but didn't stop to chat. "I'm almost positive that the cat in the office, the one everyone called Duo during the will reading?"

Rascal nodded when she waited to make sure he understood.

"He didn't have six toes."

Rascal frowned. "So what does that mean exactly? Could they just have mixed up the cats?"

Wynona shrugged, pausing outside the chief's door. "It's possible, but don't you think that would be weird? Supposedly Duo has been around since before the kids were born. So not knowing what he looked like would seem odd."

"Not any weirder than a cat having six toes one minute, but not the next," Rascal pointed out. "Magic can do funny things sometimes."

"True, but I don't think someone is casting a spell on the cat at random times."

"Then what do you think is happening?"

Wynona knocked on the chief's door rather than answer Rascal's question. It was better if they didn't worry about explaining all of this twice.

"Enter!"

"Good morning, Chief," Wynona said with a wide smile. "Can we look at the pictures from the house? The ones from Ms. Roseburg's murder?"

Chief Ligurio glared. "And why are we pulling those out? Ms. Roseburg's murder has been solved."

Wynona nodded. "Right, but there's something we need to check on."

Sighing and rubbing his forehead, Chief Ligurio pushed a button on his phone cradle. "Nightshade. The photos from the Roseburg case. Stat."

"On it, Chief," Amaris responded.

Chief Ligurio folded his long fingers and glared at Wynona. "Explain."

Wynona glanced at Rascal, who nodded. "We were just talking with Silvaria when a cat came into the room."

Chief Ligurio raised an eyebrow. "There are over twenty cats in that house, Ms. Le Doux. This isn't a surprise."

Wynona sat down, leaning forward. "Except this room has always been off limits to cats," she explained. "Why would one suddenly think it was okay to come in?"

"Why not?" Rascal argued. "No one was stopping them anymore."

"Maybe not, but it's not like you can just say 'You're now allowed in here' either," Wynona pointed out. "The cats wouldn't know they were allowed." She held up a finger. "And! Where did the cat come from? The door was closed and it came waltzing around from the back of the sofa as if it owned the place."

Just as Chief Ligurio opened his mouth, a knock came at the door.

"Chief?" Amaris stuck her head inside. "I've got those pictures."

He waved her in and Wynona scooted her chair forward, reaching for half of the stack. They spent the next few minutes studying everything until Wynona found what she was looking for. She looked at the cat's paws. "This is it."

Rascal leaned over her shoulder. "Okay...so that cat has normal paws." He straightened. "What does that have to do with anything?"

Wynona blew out a breath and leaned back in the chair. "I'm not sure."

They already think you're a little crazy, Wynona. This isn't helping.

Wynona shot Violet a look, but the mouse wasn't coming out of her cozy place in Rascal's pocket. She held up a hand before the chief could chew her out. "I'm aware that this could be nothing, but something about it is just...off."

"There could be two cats that look just like this," Chief Ligurio snapped. "Just because they called him Duo doesn't mean they had it right. It could have been a simple mix up."

Wynona leaned forward again. "But is that what your gut says?" she asked. When he didn't respond, she pressed forward. "I've only seen a few of the cats in that house, but only one has been a striped tabby. I've seen Silvaria holding him several times, and he's slunk around during our conversations, watching and waiting as if he were intelligent enough to know what's going on. Everyone at the house calls this one cat a single name, and yet the cat in this picture..." She held it up. "Is *not* the one that Silvaria was convinced belonged to her mother."

"Fine. Great," Chief Ligurio said. "You've found a mistake in the cat count. But again, I ask, what does this have to do with the case?"

Wynona shook her head. "And I'll answer again, I don't know, but it *has* to be relevant."

"Why?"

"Because it's an oddity," Wynona pressed. "Either someone is lying to us about the cat, which begs the question why, or the family and servants have no idea that two different cats are parading around as the same one. Their mother's *favorite* one. The very one that was left millions of dollars and has supposedly lived for well over twenty years. Don't you find that a little coincidental?"

Chief Ligurio grumbled under his breath and Rascal let out a low growl. Red eyes glared up at his officer. "Careful, Strongclaw."

"With all due respect, Chief," Rascal said tightly, "you asked her here. I agree with her, it's something weird and weird things can lead to other things. Instead of insulting her, why not let us chase down the lead?"

Chief Ligurio sighed and plopped back against his chair. "Fine. It's not like we have anything else to go on anyway." He waved them off. "Go find this cat and figure out why it's important."

Wynona jumped to her feet. She was grateful for Rascal's interference. This wasn't one of those times where standing on her own two feet would have produced any results. Apparently, the chief just thought she was crazy. "Can I have this picture?"

"Don't lose it," the vampire snapped.

Wynona nodded and she and Rascal hurried out. "Whew. I don't think he's had his morning blood yet," Wynona whispered. She glanced at her phone. "When we get back to the truck, let me call Lusgu and then we'll go back to the mansion. I wanted to give the cat enough time to switch."

Rascal shook his head. "This might be the weirdest thing I've ever done." He helped Wynona into her seat and then walked around to his own.

Meanwhile, Wynona had Lusgu on the line. "Hey, Lusgu. Can you please, please open today?" Wynona paused, listening to his instant complaints... "Yes, I'm aware that the regulars will be waiting, but we're following up a lead this morning and the chances of me making it in time to open the doors are slim."

"This isn't my shop," her janitor muttered.

Wynona sighed. "I know, but you're my favorite employee." She winked at Violet, who instantly looked peeved. "I can't trust the shop to anyone else."

Drop me off, Violet demanded.

"Uh...If we brought Violet by, would that help?"

There was more grumbling on the other side of the line before Lusgu finally agreed.

"Thank you! You're the best! I owe you one." Wynona hung up and pursed her lips. "What is it with you and Lusgu?" she asked Violet. "You two are thick as thieves sometimes."

Violet sniffed and didn't answer.

Wynona shook her head. "Okay. We'll talk about it later." She looked at Rascal. "Can we drop Violet off before going to the house again?"

Rascal nodded, his eyes on this phone. "Yeah. I'm just getting Skymaw caught up, hold on." A moment later, he turned off his screen and set the phone on his dash. "He'll meet us there. I figure it might take a few of us to find that cat."

Wynona nodded. "Agree." She buckled up and the truck pulled into traffic. When they arrived at the tea shop, Wynona winced. Some of her regulars were already waiting outside. While she was grateful for their patronage, it made her feel bad to be abandoning them.

She reached out, letting Violet climb onto her hand, then opened the truck door. "Hello, ladies," Wynona said with a smile. "I have some errands to run this morning, but Violet and Lusgu will open the doors in a few minutes and get you all settled."

There were a few grumbles and Wynona knew the women weren't thrilled about working with Lusgu, but they could all handle it for one morning. She opened the door, set Violet down, then ducked back out. *Good luck. And thank you.*

I live to serve, Violet said, her tone slightly sarcastic.

Wynona laughed under her breath. It was times like this that she understood why the cranky janitor and passive agressive mouse got along. She climbed back into the truck. "Okay. To the mansion."

Rascal chuckled. "You sound like a superhero calling us to action."

"Should I say to the bat cave? Would that get us moving faster?"

Rascal raised an eyebrow. "You want us to move faster?" He made to press down on the gas pedal and Wynona cried out.

"No, no!" she yelled. "I was teasing!"

Rascal laughed again and Wynona gave him the stink eye.

"Soulmate, shmoulmate," she grumbled.

Rascal reached over and squeezed her knee. "Sorry, sweetheart. You're stuck with me."

Wynona took his hand. "Thank goodness."

They arrived at the mansion a few minutes later and Daemon was already waiting for them. He got out of his car as they parked. "What's this all about?" he asked. "I thought you spoke with Ms. Killoran earlier."

Wynona nodded. "We did. We're here for the cat."

Daemon stumbled before catching himself. "I'm sorry, what?"

Rascal slapped his officer on the back. "We're here to catch Duo, the tabby that inherited the mansion and money."

Daemon's dark eyes were wide. "Can I ask what for?"

Wynona made a face. "I think there are two Duo's and we need to prove it."

"And just how is that going to work?"

Wynona explained about the six toes and the picture.

"And what will this do for us as far as solving the case?"

Wynona's eyes dropped to the ground. Seriously, the detective business should be easier. "I don't know," she muttered. Braving Daemon's reaction, he stared at her before finally shrugging.

"Okay. Well, let's catch a cat, then." He waved an arm toward the front door.

Wynona gave him a grateful smile. "Thank you." She took in a deep breath and led the way. This was her idea and even though she didn't know what it was going to lead to, she was certain that figuring out the case of the two cats would help bring them closer to Zander's killer.

She knocked and the butler arrived again.

"Ms. Le Doux," he said, his tone slightly disapproving. "Did you forget something?"

Wynona shook her head. "I'm sorry to intrude again, but we need to see Duo."

The butler frowned, breaking his stoic facade. "I beg your pardon?"

"The cat? Duo?" Wynona insisted. "We need him."

The butler blinked. "Please wait here." He shut the door and Wynona could hear hurried footsteps on the marble floor.

Rascal leaned in. "Should I use my badge to worm our way in again?"

Wynona shook her head. "Nope. This time we'll do better if they aren't mad at us. We might need their help with the cat."

"Fair enough." Rascal straightened just as the butler came back.

"Ms. Killoran would like to know why you need...Duo."

"How about we just speak to Ms. Killoran," Wynona said. She started walking, forcing the butler to step back. "I'm sorry to be pushy, but this really is important."

"So important you'll break in without a warrant?" Silvaria snapped, walking into the front entryway.

Wynona smiled, trying to keep the peace. She hadn't wanted Rascal to muscle his way in, but she was doing the exact same thing. "I have reason to believe that Duo isn't actually Duo."

Silvaria stopped and frowned. "What? That doesn't make sense."

"Can you help us catch him?" Wynona asked. "It'll help us explain everything."

Silvaria pursed her lips, then shrugged. "Whatever. He was in the office last I saw." She led the way and sure enough, the large tabby was lying on the same bookcase as before, his tail twitching from where it hung over the shelf.

"Come here, baby," Silaria cooed, picking up the cat. "Now...what is this all about?" she asked Wynona snippily.

"Look at his paws," Wynona said.

Silvaria raised her eyebrows, but pulled up a paw. "I don't under..." Her voice trailed off. "Wait a second." She shifted the cat and looked at his face. "You're Duo, aren't you? You have to be." She looked again at the paws, shaking her head. "This doesn't make any sense. Mother only had one tabby. She said he was special."

"He was," Wynona said. "And I believe if we look around, we'll find the real Duo."

"Two Duos?" Silvaria's eyebrows were pulled together in confusion. "I'm so lost."

"I actually don't understand myself," Wynona admitted quietly. "But something is going on and I'm trying to figure it out." She pointed to the cat. "And it starts with him."

"Miss?" the butler intoned from the doorway.

"Yes, Heqere?" Silvaria asked with a huff.

He tilted his head down the hall. "I believe the cat Ms. Le Doux is looking for is down there."

The entire group scrambled to the doorway, nearly knocking the butler flat on the floor in their haste to see the cat.

A large orange tabby with extra wide paws was strolling down the marble hallway. He hissed and pulled back when the group spilled into the space, eyes widening when he spotted the cat in Silvaria's arms.

Duo number one hissed in return and the hair on his back stood up on end, while Duo number two turned and began to run.

"Stop him!" Wynona cried.

Rascal dropped to all fours in a flash of fur, giving chase. Right before he reached the cat, however, the animal disappeared into thin air.

A sharp sting hit the back of Wynona's neck. "Ouch," she muttered, rubbing the now sore skin. Her eyes widened. "The cat..."

"How did he—?" Silvaria stood in one place, trying to calm the cat in her arms while her mind tried to process everything that had just happened.

Rascal came trotting back, a scowl on his wolfy face.

Wynona rubbed his ears and he leaned into her side. Sighing, she turned to Silvaria. "Can you put that cat in a carrier? We'll need to take him with us."

"Where?" she asked, squeezing the cat tighter.

Wynona looked down at Rascal, then back up. "To Mr. Melion's office."

CHAPTER 28

It had taken some finagling to convince Silvaria to stay behind. When Wynona had mentioned Mr. Melion's name, the young witch had been furious, her magic sparking out of control until Daemon had stepped up, his powers quickly negating Silvaria's.

Wynona stared at the road ahead while Rascal drove.

"You're sure it's the lawyer?" Rascal asked as he maneuvered them quickly through the streets.

Wynona sighed. "Reasonably sure?" She glanced down at Violet, who was sitting on her lap, glaring at the fake Duo, who was meowing unhappily in his carrier. "He makes the most sense. He's a feline shifter, so it could have been his claws that hurt Zander."

Rascal growled. "We considered that, but he had an alibi and no motive."

"I believe he's been essentially running the Roseburg fortune for years," Wynona said tightly. "Manipulating Ms. Roseburg through her cat fetish."

Violet began cleaning her face. *Don't trust people who like cats.*

Wynona nodded. "Duo, or the fake Duo, was in Mr. Melion's office the day of the will reading. I remember him sitting on the bookcase, watching the whole proceedings." She turned to Rascal. "There's no way he didn't know."

"But why kill Zander?"

Wynona shrugged. "Maybe Zander figured it out. Remember when Zander left that day? He made a threat that the situation wasn't over. I thought he was talking about them fighting the will, but if Zander had figured out what Mr. Melion was doing, then his words mean something completely different."

Rascal nodded. "Right. But why not just say something? The police were there."

"Because Zander himself was covering up a murder," Wynona argued. "I mean, not exactly a murder, but he was working to frame someone and had been privy to his mom's death."

"And the shoes," Rascal added with a sage nod. "Someone had to know about the shoes in order to plant them and Mr. Melion would have been the most likely."

"Right," Wynona agreed. "Plus, telling your lawyer about your crimes is commonplace. Besides his sister, it makes the most sense for Zander to tell Mr. Melion."

They arrived at the large office building and Rascal pulled onto the sidewalk with a wink at Wynona.

Despite the tenseness of the situation, she laughed softly. "I believe you became an officer just so you could break the rules without repercussions."

"At least now you know who you're stuck with," he teased. Leaning over, Rascal left a quick peck on her cheek. "Hang on while I call for backup. I should have done that before we left."

Wynona watched the building, waiting for Rascal to finish his phone call.

"Okay. Let's go in."

"You don't want to wait?" she asked.

Rascal shook his head. "I don't think he can do too much. Between Skymaw and myself, we'll have the kitten cornered in no time."

Wynona was a little nervous, but she knew Rascal and Daemon were both competent in what they did, so she climbed out of the truck, setting Violet on her shoulder. "We might need to work together if things get out of hand," Wynona whispered to her furry companion.

Violet chittered. *Let's do this.*

Wynona snorted quietly. Sometimes the mouse could be a bit frightening.

"Not that I don't believe in your abilities," Rascal said in a low tone as they walked into the building. "But I'd feel a lot better if you let Skymaw and I lead."

"Lead away," Wynona said. "I hate this part of the investigation." She blinked a few times, working down the lump in her throat. The last time they had been toward the end of a case, they'd been caught off guard when the witch they were investigating arrived home early. If she closed her eyes, Wynona could still hear Rascal choking and see the purple color of his face. The witch had Wynona caught in a magical trap that Wynona had been unable to break as she slowly watched her soulmate die.

"None of that," Rascal said gruffly. He reached back and took her hand. "This time we're going in with our eyes open. Melion won't catch us off guard and he doesn't have that kind of magic."

"Right." Wynona swallowed. "It'll all be fine." Still, she couldn't help but worry. *If you corner a frightened beast, they can do terrible things in their desperation.*

The elevator seemed especially small as they traveled up to the fifteenth floor for Mr. Melion's office. The soft music made Wynona cringe. She didn't want to be calm right now, she wanted to be prepared and ready for whatever fight might come their way. If Mr. Melion had been manipulating the funds for his own disposal for years, he wouldn't go down easily.

The door opened and they walked into a lobby with a desk facing them.

"We're here to see Mr. Melion," Rascal said, flashing his badge.

"Oh, dear," the secretary muttered. "Um..." She stood up. "I'll just..."

"Have a seat," Daemon said. "We'll let ourselves in."

The woman sat down, her eyes darting around the group and her bottom lip trembling.

Facing away from her, Wynona was still sandwiched between Daemon and Rascal as they burst into the lawyer's office.

Mr. Melion held the phone to his ear. "Thank you, Mrs. Kobold. I have it from here." Slowly, Mr. Melion put the phone back in its cradle. "Deputy Chief Strongclaw." His eyes went to Wynona. "Ms. Le Doux. Officer." Mr. Melion nodded. "You appear to be in a hurry today. Is there something I can help you with?"

"Let's have a chat about Zander Killoran, shall we?" Rascal asked, coming to sit in a chair placed in front of the desk. He settled back as if he hadn't a care in the world, but the bright flashing of his golden eyes told a different story. "And while we're at it, we can also talk about Duo."

Mr. Melion's eyebrows rose high. "Ms. Roseburg's cat?"

"The very one."

Mr. Melion chuckled, his eyes going around the group. "What's this all about, Deputy Chief? You're not making sense."

"How long have you been keeping Duo alive?" Wynona asked, stepping up to stand by Rascal's chair.

Mr. Melion frowned. "I'm lost."

"The cat," Wynona clarified. "The one that sat on your bookcase during the reading of the will."

Mr. Melion nodded. "Duo is the cat that Ms. Roseburg left her fortune to, in the care of—"

"Under the care of the Kitty Kauldron, right," Wynona interrupted. She leaned in. "But tell me, Mr. Melion. Who controls the money allotted to the shelter?"

"I do," he said, leaning back with a wary eye. "It's a common enough place for a lawyer to be."

"Maybe, but most lawyers don't swap out dead cats for live ones so that the money doesn't stop," Wynona said. "They also don't kill their client's children in order to keep the secret."

Mr. Melion's mouth dropped open and then began to chuckle. "You don't really believe that I'm hiding the fact that a cat died, do you? Or that I killed Zander? Why would I do such a thing? Ms. Roseburg was a friend of mine."

"I think the will tipped Zander off," Wynona said. She pointed to the bookcase. "I think he figured out your scheme with the cat and was going to call you on it, but you killed him to keep it quiet."

Mr. Melion held up his hands. "Duo is healthy and safe. He's home with Silvaria right now. You can check."

Wynona shook her head and Rascal slowly climbed to his feet. "No...the imposter is in Deputy Chief Strongclaw's truck. The six-toed cat, Duo, is a ghost." She raised a single eyebrow. "We saw him while Silvaria was holding the fake in her arms. The cat she was holding only had five toes. The ghost..." Wynona shrugged. "Imagine our surprise to see those extra large paws."

Mr. Melion hesitated for only a split second, but every paranormal in the room caught the movement.

Rascal's muscles tensed as Mr. Melion smiled.

He spread his hands out to the side. "I do believe we can work this all out, lady and gentlemen. It's not what you think."

"What isn't?" Rascal growled. Claws began to emerge from his hands as he walked the two feet to the desk. "The fact that you've been swindling a woman out of her money? Or that you killed her son to keep him from blabbing about your thievery?"

Mr. Melion's smile dropped and the predator made an appearance. Like Rascal's, the lawyer's eyes flashed brightly. "That ignorant pup thought he could blackmail me," Mr. Melion said with a sneer. "Thought he had it all figured out." Mr. Melion shook his head. "But he knew nothing," the shifter hissed. Slowly, Mr. Melion stood up, his skin pulsing as his shift came closer to the surface. Fangs began to grow in his mouth, making his words harder to understand. "Do you have any idea how much money it takes to hobnob with the elite?" he asked. "The rising cost of a mortgage or even a trip to the human world?"

Wynona slowly stepped back. She was grateful to have Rascal in front of her and could feel Daemon coming from behind. Violet's tail wrapped around her neck and Wynona brought her magic to her fingertips. She didn't want to startle the creature in front of her, but she wanted to be prepared for anything. She wouldn't be caught off guard again.

"Stand down, Melion," Rascal demanded, the strength of his alpha voice ricocheting through the room.

"I'm not one of your cronies," Mr. Melion said with a deep laugh. "Cats don't answer the call of the hounds."

Rascal began to move to the side of the desk and Daemon moved the opposite so they would catch Mr. Melion in the middle.

Mr. Melion stood his ground, not looking worried in the least. His smug smile worried Wynona.

"Romulus Melion," Rascal said. "You're under arrest for the murder of Zander Killoran. Also, embezzlement of the Roseburg fortune."

Mr. Melion laughed. "I'm afraid, gentlemen, I won't be going to jail."

Wynona wiggled her fingers. *Be ready, Violet. I have a feeling things aren't going to go well.*

Really? Violet drawled. *Whatever gave you that idea?* Even with her snark, Violet tightened her hold on Wynona's neck.

Her magic sat at the ready, thrumming under her skin. She wouldn't let Rascal or Daemon be hurt.

"This will go better for you if you'll cooperate," Rascal said, still moving forward. "We'll do it the hard way if we have to, but judges look more favorably on prisoners who don't fight back."

Mr. Melion burst into laughter. "Oh, really? Think he'll let me live when they find out what I was forced to do?"

Rascal grabbed an Old Hag's thread from his back pocket. "Easy does it, Melion."

Mr. Melion shook his head and shifted back until there were several more feet between him and the officers. "I'm afraid I can't do that, Deputy Chief. You see...I didn't really murder him."

"You know your rights," Rascal stated. "You can tell a lawyer what happened and I'm sure he or she will be happy to help you."

Wynona paused. Something was tickling at the back of her mind, but she wasn't sure what. Mr. Melion had already said he'd been involved in the killing. So what was he talking about? What did he mean, he hadn't actually been the killer?

"Aren't you the least bit curious about who was really pulling the strings?" Mr. Melion asked. His eyes went to Wynona. "And there she is now."

Wynona jerked back. "What?"

"Right on time, darling," Mr. Melion called.

It was then that Wynona realized he wasn't looking at her, but over her shoulder. A curse word came to mind just as a very familiar voice spoke from behind.

"As usual," Ms. Valence Tailorson said from the doorway.

Wynona began to spin, her hands up and ready, but before she could make any kind of defensive move, a large object flew over her head, landing next to Ms. Tailorson.

By the time Wynona was facing the door, five dozen cats and a leopard were blocking the exit with one very smug witch standing in the middle. Ms. Tailorson grinned. "We'd love to stay and chat, but I'm afraid we have a plane to catch." She shrugged. "A bit more money would have been nice, but Romulus and I can live very well on what we already have." She waved. "Thanks for the laughs." With a snap of her fingers, the cats all hissed and moved forward to attack.

Wynona screeched and held up her hands, while squeezing her eyes shut. Angry meowing and hissing continued, but she hadn't been shredded just yet, so she dared to look. A purple wall of magic stood between her and the angry horde.

Rascal hurried up behind her with Daemon on his heels.

"Come, Romulus," Valence said. She snapped her fingers again and the wild cat trotted at her side.

"She's controlling him," Wynona whispered. "Her cat affinity allows her to control all of them."

"Stop her magic!" Rascal shouted at Daemon. The shifter was toe to toe with the purple wall, waiting to make a move.

"I can't," Daemon said in a tortured tone. "Not without taking out Wynona's wall. We won't make it to the door without being shredded first."

"They're just cats," Rascal growled.

Wynona shook her head. "No..." She tilted her head, too afraid to bring down her hands and lose the wall. "Look closely." The eyes of every cat there were glowing as they clawed at her protective bubble. "These are *all* ghost cats and she's not just controlling them anymore...they're under a spell. They're corporeal right now, but if I let down my wall and they turn into specters, we'll have no way of protecting ourselves at all. I'm almost positive that's what I kept feeling was the ghost cats, but for some reason I can't see them like I can human-like creatures."

Rascal held up a fist with a shout, but didn't actually hit the wall. "So what now?" he demanded. His wolf was barely contained at this point.

Wynona shook her head. "I don't know." Her heart was in her throat and she doubled down on her hold on the wall. This was not how she'd expected this morning to go.

CHAPTER 29

The cats began pressing up against Wynona's bubble, as if testing for weak spots. "If any of them decide to go ghost, I won't be able to stop them," she said softly. Her heart was about to beat out of her chest at this point. Rascal might be angry that the murderer was getting away, but Wynona was more worried about them all making it out of there alive. Magic or not, there was no way for them to defend themselves against so many cats.

"Yes, you can."

"Granny!" Wynona shouted.

"The wall, Wy!" Rascal growled.

She closed her eyes, realizing that she had become distracted. Violet's tail wrapped around her neck.

Focus, Violet said firmly. *I'll be mouse tartare if you don't.*

Wynona nodded and managed to open her eyes again. "Can you help us?" she asked.

Granny pinched her lips. "You have to send the cats over."

Wynona's eyes widened. "What?"

"She doesn't have that power," Rascal argued. "Can't she find a way to put them to sleep or something? So we can catch that witch before she escapes?"

Granny shook her head. "She does have the power." Her ghostly form was floating above the cats and it flickered in and out. "It's the same power you use to read the tea leaves. You're looking into the beyond when you tell a future. In this case, you're pulling the beyond to you. Open a gateway, Wynona. Then herd the cats toward it."

Daemon snorted. "Herd the cats? Are you even listening to yourself?"

Granny scowled. "Do you want to survive this or not?"

I want to survive. Listen to the witch.

Wynona nodded. "Okay. I'll give it a try." A sudden thought occurred to her. "Wait...I won't suck you into the portal, will I?"

Granny shook her head. "Keep it contained. *You* are in control of your magic, Wynona."

"Right." She reached out and took Rascal's hand. It helped keep her feet anchored while drawing on so much power. Opening up the floodgates, she allowed more power to travel through her body and imagined a portal to the afterlife. A tug on her core let her know something was happening and Wynona opened her eyes.

Daemon cursed and Rascal growled.

But Wynona's gaze was fixed to the small hole in the floor. It was shimmering. *Come on*, she pressed. *Time to go home, kitties.* More and more she fed her magic into the hole and the cats started to twitch. Some began hissing, others jumped and made their displeasure known with extended claws and scratches on her shield.

She felt each claw mark as if it were personally being done on her body, but Wynona forced herself to stay focused.

"Gather them together!" Granny shouted, her voice sounding shaky.

It took all her concentration not to see why Granny was struggling, but Wynona knew if she looked away, she would lose the portal. Sweat began to drip down her spine and she pulled the hole into the center of the group.

Use the shield, Violet suggested. She also sounded strained. *Capture them with the shield.*

The idea was brilliant and gave Wynona a burst of confidence. Slowly, she pushed the shield away from her and the men, stretching and pulling until it enclosed around the cats like a bubble.

"SKYMAW!" Rascal shouted.

Without another word, Daemon took his freedom and raced out of the room, chasing down the criminals.

Wynona's body shook, but she mechanically removed each finger from Rascal's grip. "Go," she said through gritted teeth.

"I'm not leaving you," he growled back.

"I'm fine. I have help."

Rascal stubbornly shook his head.

"Rascal...don't let them get away." She could feel how torn he was. His need to protect her was greater than his drive to catch them, but both she and Rascal knew that his wolf had a much better shot at tracking down the witch and leopard than anyone else. "Trust me," she said softly.

Rascal stepped up close. "If you hurt yourself, I'll track you down in the afterlife myself."

"I'd expect nothing less," she replied.

He hesitated once more before sliding around her bubble, bursting into four legs and taking off out of the office building.

Wynona could feel him getting farther and farther away from her at a terrific speed. She had no doubt that he would take down Ms. Tailorson and Mr. Melion within a few minutes. They wouldn't get away with this, though the more Wynona thought about it, the more she was positive Ms. Tailorson was the one pulling *all* the strings. Mr. Melion's argument about not really being the one to do the killing suddenly made much more sense.

"Finish it, Wynona," Granny snapped.

Wynona nodded, putting her focus back where it belonged. She could feel her body tiring and knew she wouldn't be able to control this amount of magic much longer. The cats were screaming now, the sound enough to wake the dead as Wynona brought the shield in closer and continued to make the hole bigger.

Almost there, Violet encouraged, her grip on Wynona's neck giving away her worry.

The first cat slipped through, followed quickly by a couple more. With each cat's disappearance, the sound dropped ever so slightly and Wynona's confidence grew. She could do this. They could win.

"Looks like I showed up just in time."

Wynona jerked and her hold on the portal shook. "Dad!"

President Le Doux smiled a cold, unfriendly smile. "We knew your powers would be magnificent," he said with a sneer. Jealousy and hatred were practically dripping from every word. "But I don't think any of us imagined this." He waved at the portal. He shook his head. "You need help, Wynona. You're barely able to control it." His eyes roamed over her face and sweat-drenched clothes. "Magic should be second nature to you. Not a battle of the wills." He held out his hand. "Come home and we'll see you get the training you need."

"No," Wynona said bluntly. She didn't have the air for a long-winded speech right now, nor the brain power to listen to his. "Leave. This is a crime scene."

Another cat went into the portal.

"I have as much right to be here as you do," her father said casually, waltzing into the room as if he owned the place. "After all, Mr. Melion worked for me."

"About that." Wynona's nostrils flared. "You knew, didn't you? You knew he was involved in Zander's murder."

President Le Doux shrugged. "Maybe. Or maybe I was just helping out a man looking for work."

"You were setting yourself up to blackmail him," Wynona spat. She mentally pushed two more cats into the hole. There were only about a dozen left at this point. She needed the job finished so she could concentrate on the new threat. "You're despicable."

He moved closer, making Wynona nervous. "I'm despicable? I'm not the one sweating like a pig while trying to shoo a few cats into a hole." He brought up his hand, his silver magic swirling in a tin tornado. "I can do anything."

"But not make a portal," Wynona shot back. "You want my powers, but I won't be manipulated and I won't come help you with your schemes. I don't want power, or fame, I simply want to be left alone so I can brew tea and live my life."

He shook his head. "I can't let you do that. With great power comes great responsibility." Her father raised an imperius eyebrow. "You have too much power to be left on your own." He snapped his fingers and Celia walked in with their mother in her wake.

Celia's face was pale as she watched the portal, which was barely moving at this point as Wynona's attention was pulled away. She looked up at Wynona, fear evident in every line on her face.

"Hello, dearest daughter," Marcella sang out. "I told you this wasn't over, didn't I?"

Granny's spirit appeared at Wynona's shoulder. "Focus, dear," she said in a low tone. "One problem at a time."

"Oh, Mother," Marcella whined. "Why am I not surprised to find you here?"

Wynona looked away from her family and went back to the portal. Her family was going to be difficult enough to deal with. Trying to hold off possessed ghost cats while dealing with them? Impossible.

Just a few more, Violet said fiercely. *Get rid of the beasts and then we'll show these idiots who's boss around here.*

Wynona would have laughed at Violet's fierceness, but she didn't have the capacity for it. She twisted her fingers, keeping note that her family had moved to surround her. "Stay back," she warned, though there was little power behind her words.

"Or what?" Marcella cooed. "You're drained. Taking you home will be easier than we thought."

Wynona steadied her shaking knees.

"Focus, girl," Granny said. "Focus!"

Wynona nodded and once again renewed her effort to rid them of the cats. A sizzling sound caught her attention and Wynona jerked her head to the side.

"Stand down, Saffron." President Le Doux sneered. His hand was out, the residue of silver magic still in the air.

Granny was corporeal and had placed herself between her son-in-law and granddaughter. "I didn't spend thirty years protecting her for you to take her home and brainwash her," Granny snarled.

President Le Doux laughed. "Brainwash? We won't need to brainwash her. Once she learns how to use her magic, she'll be begging us to help rule." He leaned in. "it's in her blood. She was bred for this." He glanced at Celia. "At least one of my daughters won't be such a disappointment."

Fire flashed in Celia's eyes, but it was gone just as quickly as it appeared.

I knew it, Wynona thought. *She's being manipulated.*

Yeah, yeah, Violet said curtly. *But you have more pressing things right now. Get rid of the cats!*

Wynona pressed harder, every limb shaking as she tried to pull in the last handful. Another shot of magic startled her and the shield grew instead of shrinking. "No," Wynna said through her clenched jaw. Bringing her hands together, she used the movement to help make the magic follow. Only children needed such tricks, but right now Wynona didn't care. She'd take all the advantages she could get.

The sounds of a magical fight was growing louder and she began to worry that Granny wouldn't be able to hold her family off much longer. Three against one wasn't exactly fair.

"Give up, Wynona!" Marcella shouted. "You belong with us!"

With a shriek of anger, one of the cats burst through her bubble and began racing around the room.

"ARGH!" Wynona shouted, her own anger growing. With a slam of magic, she shoved the other three cats back inside, left the portal moving and began trying to trap the loose animal.

"What is that thing?" Celia screamed, ducking when the cat flew over her head.

"Gotcha!" Wynona cried, holding the cat midair in another purple shield bubble. She pulled, slowly drawing the struggling cat toward the portal. The cat fought, twisting and turning and making the journey much harder than it should have been. Sucking in a deep breath, Wynona held it and pushed with all her might, the cat finally slipping into the great beyond.

"Ahhh!"

Wynona's eyes shot open and she turned just in time to see Granny crumple to the ground. The smell of burning clothes and the sulfuric scent of magical electricity pierced her nose. "No!" Wynona rasped as her father stalked forward, his intent clear.

Granny had already died once, but President Le Doux was determined to exterminate the woman for good.

He raised his hand, silver sparking like lightning.

"NOOO!" It took a minute for Wynona to realize that the scream was coming from her. The magic in the room became suffocating and she could barely breathe. Her hair began to whip around her head and her vision went purple. Other screams could be heard, but Wynona's focus never left her father. "Don't. Touch. Her," Wynona said. Her voice wasn't her own, it was lower and held a bite of steel.

President Le Doux's eyes widened and for the first time since he'd arrived, his confidence wavered.

CHAPTER 30

"Wynona. She's holding you back. All I want is to bring you home," her father said in a placating tone.

"No!" she shouted, shaking the walls. Drywall began to crack, the dust swirling with the wind she had built. "You want to control me. You want to control all of Hex Haven and you're afraid that if left unchecked, I'll be a threat to your reign." She shook her head, the storm-like winds following the movement.

Her father put up his hands and stepped back, trying to protect himself.

"I don't know how to make this any more clear," Wynona continued, her jaw starting to ache from the tension. "I don't want your office. I don't want your power. I want to be left alone and if you continue to push me or hurt those I love, I *will* retaliate and you won't like what happens."

Taking a calming breath, Wynona slowed down the wind just enough for her parents and sister to move. "Leave," Wynona said calmly. "And don't come back."

In her periphery, she saw Celia race out, but Marcella didn't budge. President Le Doux studied Wynona, his gaze assessing, and Wynona knew this still wouldn't be the end of it.

Just hold your ground, Violet said. *Stay strong and eventually they'll leave you alone...for now anyway.*

One can only hope, Wynona sent back.

Choosing to ignore her father, Wynna knelt and checked over her grandmother. Granny was wheezing, holding her chest.

"How can I make it better?" Wynona asked, her brain scrambling to figure it out. How did one heal a dead person?

Granny reached up and patted her cheek. "It's alright, dear. I was fading anyway."

"What?"

Granny shook her head. "My powers were running out..." She panted. "I didn't have a good reason to be here anymore."

"No, no, no," Wynona said, her eyes filling with tears. "You're supposed to teach me. You have *every* reason to be here."

"Let her go," Marcella said in a soothing tone.

If Wynona hadn't known better, she would have thought it was a mother trying to comfort her daughter, but too many life experiences had taught her otherwise. Wynona jerked her head up. "I said, leave," she demanded. "Leave now."

Marcella looked sympathetic and dropped to her knees on Granny's other side. "It's time to let her go, Wynona. She had a good life."

Wynona could feel her magic building, the wind began whipping again and her hair blowing. But this time, she wasn't sure if she had the power to stop the explosion. It was all too much. Granny fading, the overwhelming strength of her powers, her dysfunctional family, the murderer escaping...Wynona was losing control...fast.

A hand landed on her shoulder and that was all it took to break her fragile hold.

"OUT!" she screamed. Clutching her head, Wynona leaned forward, her thoughts scattering like the wind. If her powers had been a strong wind before, they were hurricane level now. Books, papers, furniture...it all began to move and fly through the air.

"WYNONA!" Celia screamed.

Wynona opened her eyes and jerked in shock. Apparently, her sister hadn't gone very far because Celia was holding onto the doorframe, trying to keep from being pulled into the portal in the center of the room that had grown to the size of a small car. Every few seconds something disappeared inside and the portal grew hungrier.

"TURN IT OFF!" Celia screeched, kicking her legs.

"I DON'T KNOW HOW!" Wynona shouted back. She dropped to the ground and crawled to Celia, helping anchor her by covering Celia's body with her own. Wynona seemed to be the only object not being pulled toward the hole.

"You have to close it." Celia gasped.

Fight it, Wy, Rascal called in her mind, his tone frantic. *YOU are in control. Not the magic.*

Wynona shut her eyes and tried to find a way to grasp the magic running amuck.

Come on, Wynona. Press it back.

"Wynona," Celia said weakly. Her grip was slipping and Wynona gripped her sister harder.

"I'm trying," she said, grinding her teeth together. Wrangling the magic was unlike anything Wynona had ever accomplished before. She didn't have Lusgu or Daemon to save her this time. It would have to be her.

In her mind's eyes, she stood in front of the magic and began to press it back, like holding back a wild bull with her bare hands. A shift in the wind let her know something was working.

I love you.

The words had a hint of goodbye in them and weren't from Rascal or Violet. Wynona's eyes flashed open and her gaze met Granny's.

"You're the one," Granny mouthed. Her robes were whipping as her body slid across the floor.

"Granny!" Wynona reached out, but stopped when Celia screamed. Wynona's heart stopped. She couldn't save them both. She couldn't shut down the portal in time and she couldn't grab Granny without sacrificing Celia.

Granny shook her head, understanding Wynona's struggle. *I love you. Just follow the magic. I know you'll do wonderful things.*

Before Wynona could respond, Granny's form faded and Wynona watched the remains of the spirit be sucked into the portal leading straight to the afterlife.

A heart wrenching cry, from the depths of Wynona's soul, tore from her throat, the magic coming to a shuddering halt at the sound. When Wynona collapsed against the ground, the magic exploded into a burst of purple mist and the three other people in the room disappeared.

Wynona had no idea where she'd sent them and she didn't care. She lay on the floor, too spent to do anything but shake with the sobs erupting from her throat.

Violet nuzzled under her ear, but it wasn't enough.

"Wy…" Warm hands landed on her back. "Sweetheart, you're killing me," Rascal said in a soft voice. When she still didn't move, Rascal gathered her up, pressing her face into his shoulder. "I've got you," he said, rubbing her back and smoothing down her hair. "I've got you."

Wynona had no idea how long she cried against him, but when she was finally through, she could barely lift her arms up. "She's gone," Wynona whispered hoarsely.

"I know."

"It was my magic that sent her away."

"I know." He kissed the top of her head.

"It's my fault."

"Never." Rascal leaned back and cupped her face so she would be forced to look at him. "She was fading, Wy. She said so herself. Your portal might have sped things up, but she was already on her way out."

"I couldn't stop her," Wynona said, tears building again. Just how many tears could a single body produce?

"You weren't supposed to," he assured her. "She loved you. She knew she was leaving. She gave you everything you need to succeed."

Rascal left a tender kiss on her forehead. "Be grateful for the time you got and let her move on to better things," he whispered against her skin.

Wynona continued to hang limply. "I want to go home."

"Yours or mine?" he asked. "But note that I'm staying to watch over you, no matter which one you pick."

"Mine, please."

Rascal nodded, then stood them both up and swung her into his arms. Wynona laid her head against his shoulder. "Did you catch them?"

"Of course," Rascal said. "Sniffed them out on their way out of town. We'll question them tomorrow when you're feeling better."

"I doubt Chief Ligurio will want to wait that long."

"Since he's currently fighting the media on your behalf, I don't think we'll have to ask him to wait. He won't have time for anything else until then."

Wynona brought her head up with a jerk. "He's what?"

"That display of magic has the town in a riot," Rascal explained. He nodded at an officer who was by the back door. The creature opened the door and looked around before letting Rascal out. Rascal's truck was parked right outside.

"I thought you'd chase Melion on all fours," she mused.

"I did. I had Skymaw drive this around."

Rascal lifted her into the passenger seat and buckled her in. "Hang tight, I'll explain on the way home."

Wynona waited, petting Violet while Rascal got into his seat.

"The media want to know what you're capable of and if you'll be succeeding your father," Rascal stated bluntly once he pulled onto the road. "Chief Ligurio is downplaying the incident and doing his best to separate you from your family so no one gets the wrong idea."

"But why?" Wynona asked, her head lolling to the side. She yawned. "Why is he bothering?"

"He's holding up his end of the bargain," Rascal said easily. "He said he would do his best to protect you from your family if you helped, which you did. And holding back the media is part of holding back your family."

The connection was tenuous at best, but Wynona knew she wasn't thinking straight. Instead, she simply nodded and let her eyes close. She needed rest. Then she would go to Granny's grave, say goodbye for a second time, and try to figure out how to move on.

Oh...and somewhere in the middle, she would help Rascal finish wrapping up Ms. Roseburg and Zander's murder.

With that to-do list in front of her, she decided maybe she needed to sleep for a week straight. *The world might have to fix itself this time.*

CHAPTER 31

Wynona slept clear through the night and Rascal had to wake her the next day to go to the precinct. Even still, her body ached and her mind was fuzzy.

You over extended your magic, Violet said. *I'd scold you about it, but honestly, it's the only reason you and I are still here.*

"We have to get serious about this," Wynona said softly, knowing Rascal could hear as well. "No more putting it off because of a case or something else. Without Granny here, I have no one else to turn to for help."

Rascal reached across the truck and squeezed her thigh. "You're not alone," he said.

"No," Wynona agreed. "But none of you know how to deal with this any more than I do."

He nodded sadly. "I'm sorry I wasn't there."

Wynona shook her head. "I'm so grateful you weren't. It would have just been another loved one I had to watch out for." She turned to look at Rascal's profile. "I love you, but you're not a magical match for my dad."

Rascal's lips pinched and Wynona knew he understood, but the wolf didn't like it. Not. One. Bit.

The rest of the drive was quiet and Wynona was glad to see there wasn't a mob outside the station. She and Rascal walked inside hand in hand and Amaris gave her a wary wave.

"Hey," Wynona said, waving back. "Holding down the fort as usual?"

Amaris nodded, but she didn't speak and her body language was far from warm.

She's scared of you, Rascal said tightly. *I can smell her fear.*

Sadness coated Wynona like a blanket. She hadn't asked for any of this. Like any witch, she had wanted powers, but she had never asked for them to be so strong or for her family to be so rotten.

"Come on," Rascal said, tugging on her hand. *Just give her time. She'll get over it.*

Wynona let Rascal guide her down the hall, but she could feel the stares of the other officers. When they finally made it into the interrogation room, Wynona let out a sigh of relief.

"Fools, the pack of them," Chief Ligurio snapped.

Wynona gave him a grateful smile. It was small, but it was a start.

He nodded toward the seat next to him. "Let's get this over with. You look dead on your feet."

Wynona sat down gratefully, ignoring his comment about her looks. Chief Ligurio had seen her at her worst and while this wasn't pleasant, it also wasn't as bad as it had been before.

"Skymaw."

Wynona hadn't noticed Daemon standing by the door. He gave her a chin tilt before slipping out.

"We'll talk to Ms. Tailorson first," Chief said, getting right to work. "From what we're piecing together, she was the mastermind behind it all."

"The face behind the curtain," Wynona murmured.

"Exactly," Chief Ligurio agreed. "Though I can't quite figure out her abilities with Melion. Her affinity with cats is clear, but Melion isn't a house cat, nor is he a spirit. How did she manage to be in control?"

The door opened and Ms. Tailorson was brought in. The defiant look in her eye said she wouldn't give up her information easily.

"Have a seat, Ms. Tailorson," Chief Ligurio said.

Rascal's hand landed on Wynona's shoulder and she let his heat soak into her skin.

Ms. Tailorson threw herself into the chair, one eyebrow raised. "I want my lawyer."

Chief Ligurio nodded. "I'm aware and your request was sent through the proper channels. You should receive a court-appointed lawyer soon."

"Then why am I here?"

"Because I was hoping you would choose to cooperate, Ms. Tailorson," Chief Ligurio said smoothly. He folded his hands on the top of the table. "Sentencing favors."

She snorted.

"Your affinity with cats was an excellent cover," the chief continued. "Working a shelter, pretending to take care of the abandoned and forgotten."

Ms. Tailorson hissed, sounding like the animal she so cared for. "You have no idea what you're talking about," she said. "I *do* take care of them. Do you have any idea how many cats are abandoned every year? How many litters of kittens left on the side of the road?" One side of her lip curled. "Or how many felines are killed when witches don't know what they're doing?"

"So your shelter wasn't just filled with living cats," Wynona inserted. "You made homes for the ghosts as well."

Ms. Tailorson scrunched her nose. "Someone had to take them in. Might as well be me."

"When did you discover that you had the ability to control them?" Wynona pressed. Now that she was here, her curiosity was helping assuage the mourning.

Ms. Tailorson huffed. "I've always been able to do that."

"And Mr. Melion?" Chief Ligurio asked the question he had mentioned earlier. "He seems outside your normal range of abilities."

Ms. Tailorson smirked. She had no intention of sharing.

Wynona's brain began to spin. She thought of the time she'd been in Ms. Tailorson's office and the odd pausing spells. *Mr. Melion had the same quirk.* She thought of the cat, watching, waiting, the feel of the ghosts, but not being able to see them. There was a connection between the two...

"You're soulmates," Wynona gasped.

Ms. Tailorson visibly started. "How do you know that?" she wheezed.

Chief Ligurio looked at Wynona, waiting for an explanation.

"Do you remember all the pausing?" Wynona asked the vampire. "During the will reading?"

He nodded.

"They were communicating." Wynona tapped her temple.

Chief Ligurio looked back and forth between Wynona and Rascal. "Soulmates can do that?"

Wynona nodded eagerly, then winced at the pain in her head. Apparently, soul-wrenching crying left her with a terrible headache. Even her turmeric and lavender tea hadn't been enough this morning. "I think their connection is also what allowed her to control Mr. Melion." Wynona turned to see Ms. Tailorson turning red, her jaw clenched in anger. "Your affinity gave you an advantage. You could actually see through Mr. Melion's eyes, just like you did with the house cats, and your soulmate connection allowed you to control him from a distance." Wynona leaned forward. "The cats had to be spelled or controlled when you could see them. But Mr. Melion didn't have to be close to you. That's how you killed Zander while still being at home." Wynona tilted her head to the side. "Does he remember everything when you're in charge? Did he agree to your possession willingly?"

Ms. Tailorson moved to lunge across the table, but Daemon pressed her back into the chair.

"You don't know anything!" Ms. Tailorson screamed, flailing against Daemon's hold. "We needed that money. That old bat had more than enough and my cats were starving to death! All Harmony wanted was to spend time with her fishy play thing. It took years to put the plan into place!" She cackled. "And the hag never even saw it coming. Her accidental death was the perfect excuse to put our plan into action." She snorted. "Besides, if we hadn't stepped in, the money would have been left to the pool boy. THE POOL BOY!"

"Get her out of here," Chief Ligurio said in disgust.

Ms. Tailorson continued to scream, but another officer stepped in and helped Daemon carry her out. When the door finally shut, the room fell silent.

"So that *was* the real will," Rascal said with a chuckle. "Wow. I'm in the wrong business."

Wynona slapped his leg.

He grinned and reached down to take her hand. "Not that I'd ever leave you, understand."

"Of course not," Wynona said sarcastically. "What was I thinking?"

Still chuckling, he leaned down to kiss her head. "I want to be there when someone tells Monroe."

Wynona leaned her head into his side. "Yeah...at least something good will come out of it."

Chief Ligurio gathered his things. "I don't want to see you again for a very long time, Ms. Le Doux. Keep your head down and stay out of the press." He stood and began to walk away, but not before Wynona heard him whisper, "Take care of her," to Rascal.

"Always, Chief," Rascal whispered back.

He's grumpy, but I like him, Violet concluded.

"You have a thing for grumpy," Wynona murmured.

Violet chittered and began to wash her face.

"Let's go home," Rascal said. "I don't think there's any point in talking to Melion at this point."

Wynona nodded and they headed to his truck. "Before we hit the house," Wynona said, "do you mind taking me to Granny's grave?" She wanted to mark that one off her list of to-do's.

Rascal nodded. "If that's what you want."

"It is."

He helped get her settled, then drove across town. The cemetery was lushly green with a well kept lawn and stunning flowers. If it hadn't been for all the gravestone markers, it would have been the perfect place for a Sunday afternoon picnic.

They walked slowly through the grass, hands swinging between them until they reached Granny's marker. It stood taller than the rest in a fenced off area reserved for those in the Le Doux family. Her husband's stone was next to her, almost identical in looks.

"I feel like I lost her twice," Wynona whispered.

"You did," Rascal agreed. "But what a gift. Most people never get that second chance."

She leaned into his strength. There would be no miraculous comeback this time. Even Granny couldn't come back from the other side of the veil.

"Thank you," Wynona whispered to the ground. "I'll do my best to be who you wanted me to be."

Rascal turned and kissed the side of her head, but stayed silent.

They stood for a long time, Wynona letting herself soak in the peace and trying to come to terms with the loss. While she still wasn't interested in anything to do with ruling Hex Haven, she was interested in controlling her magic and becoming a help to the people. She wasn't sure what that would look like yet, but someday...she would know.

"I didn't expect to see you here."

Wynona spun and brought up her hands, purple sparking automatically.

Celia held up her magicless hands. "I'm not here to fight." Her skin was pale, her hair pulled into a messy ponytail and her face free from makeup. It was the most normal Wynona's sister had ever looked.

"What do you want, Celia?" Wynona asked tightly.

"I came to say goodbye to Granny," Celia said, her chin in the air. "She was my family too."

Wynona hesitated, trying to find the lie, but Celia gave nothing away. "Fine. We were done anyway." She started to walk away, but Celia wasn't done.

"Afterwards, I was coming to see you."

Wynona slowly spun. She could feel Rascal's tension and the wolf rising to the surface. "Why?"

Celia glanced at Rascal and swallowed hard. "I..." She paused, took several breaths and straightened her shoulders. "I'm moving in with you."

Wynona choked and Rascal snarled. "Excuse me?"

"I'm done being a puppet," Celia said, her voice shaking slightly. "I didn't have my freedom handed to me, the same way you did, but I understand why Granny did it." Her hands clenched and unclenched. "But I'm done. I want out. And you're the only path I have."

Wynona had no words. Did Celia really think anything about her life was easy? She had fought for every inch from the time she was a little girl. Even after leaving the castle, the battle had been uphill.

Still, the part of Wynona that wanted a family was whispering to help, but the rational side of her was ready to walk away and never look back.

"I know you have no reason to trust me," Celia said, her voice dropping. Tears filled her eyes. "But my life hasn't been easy either. You heard Dad." She wiped her cheeks. "I'm a disappointment. I was

never strong enough for him. And things were never the same after..."
Celia shook her head. "It doesn't matter. I won't let him control me
anymore. But I have nowhere to go." She paused. "Nowhere except
in with you."

Rascal looked at Wynona and subtly shook his head. *I don't trust
her.*

Wynona sighed. *No...but Granny did.* She thought of Granny's
last words and realized she had known this was coming. By saving
Wynona, she had also set up a way to save Celia.

"On one condition," Wynona said, trying to get her crazy heart-
beat under control. She had had a thought this morning of something that might help her in her magical journey and Celia was the
perfect way to get it.

"Name it."

"I want Granny's grimoires."

"How am I supposed to find those? Mom probably has them under lock and ward."

Wynona shrugged, feigning nonchalance. "It's the price."

Celia hesitated, but finally nodded. "Fine. Consider it done."

Wynona nodded back. "Then I'll see you soon."

What have you gotten us into? Violet asked as they walked away.

I don't know, Wynona responded honestly. *But I'm sure we'll figure it out.*

Don't Miss Wynona's Next Adventure!

**Just when she thinks she can breathe easy,
a dead body shows up a little too close to home...**

Wynona's life is finally settling down. Her family have retreated, her friends are all free of accusations, her relationship with Rascal is stronger than ever and her business is thriving. In fact, it's thriving so much that Wynona has hired a fairy to help her take care of customers.

When her new employee's boyfriend shows up dead at the tea shop, Wynona is once again forced to put on her sleuthing hat. It's a race against the clock to save her business and her waitress, when the fairy becomes the prime suspect.

Throw in magic lessons with her grandmother, a surprise from her familiar and a family member showing up at just the wrong time and Wynona knows she'll need all the skills she's developed, magic or otherwise, to help her make it through.

Grab your copy of "Chai Spice and Murder" Today!